Reborn

Anderson Special Ops, Book Five

Melody Anne

With
John Henley

Copyright © 2021 Melody Anne

All rights reserved. Except for use in any review, the reproduction or utilization of this work in whole or in part in any form by any electronic, mechanical or other means, now known or hereafter invented, including xerography, photocopying and recording, or in any information storage or retrieval system, is forbidden without the written permission of the author.

This is a work of fiction. Names, characters, places and incidents are either the product of the author's imagination or are used fictitiously and any resemblance to actual persons, living or dead, business establishments, events or locales is entirely coincidental.
Printed and published in the United States of America.
Published by Melody Anne
Editing by Karen Lawson, and Janet Hitchcock

NOTE FROM MELODY ANNE

This is the final book in the Special Ops series. We've had so much fun with these characters, which is why this won't be the last you'll see of them. As you can tell with Jasmine, there is a spin-off series coming. It won't be my normal contemporary romance - it will be more of a thriller series. I'm super excited about it, and I hope you'll take a chance and give it a try. Jasmine is going to go through much different life experiences than she's had in the Anderson world. Smoke won't let her down though.

Thanks so much to all of you who have been with me for so long for stepping outside of the contemporary world and giving this new series a try. It means the world to me. I love Joseph and I don't think I'll ever let him go, but I might torment him a little. Thanks for your support! I love you all and I'm so grateful to have this job I love. Now I'm off on a new writing adventure. Make sure you sign up for my newsletter so you can keep up with it all. My writing is always dependent on my mood, and I love to challenge myself so be prepared for some new adventures . . .

With Love
Melody Anne

NOTE FROM JOHN HENLEY

Writing a book, even as a co-author, is an incredible achievement. Without question, it has been for me. To write five books with a world-renowned author like Melody Anne has been even more incredible and amazing. It's been an honor to be asked to work with a woman who is so imaginative and willing to expand her horizons as an author and individual. There were times through these books she was challenged to allow descriptions and scenarios she'd never presented to you, her readers and fans, before — but she dedicated herself to allowing authentic stories through the eyes of military situations and I believe they've been well received. So, to Melody Anne — thank you. For the opportunity, the time, the involvement, and the year of gut busting laughs while also holding my hand through the entirety of it all. It's been more rewarding than I could have ever imagined. Your fans are correct about you — you're one of the best there is and there's no way for me to ever say thank you enough.

The character, Eyes, is loosely based on one of my best friends. A man who seems to make all of the right decisions and doesn't get fazed by chaos. We all know the type — cool, calm and collected. He'll admit that he's going a million miles a second on the inside but what he presents to the world is peace under fire. With an open ear for all, and a willingness to carry the load no matter the weight, there are few finer than a man I call a brother. Thank you, Jon, for being who you are and for allowing us to become greater by knowing you.

To my wife and children, thank you. The sacrifices each of you made while I was away for training, working overseas, and transitioning back into civilian life, are always appreciated, and never taken for granted. None of this would've been remotely feasible, or possible, without your strength and endless encouragement. Your love of family, God, and country are wonderful pillars to build the foundation of life on. Go, be great!

Last, and in no way least, thank you to the men and women serving and protecting the freedoms we enjoy. From the front-line warriors to the supply chain gurus, to the cooks in the galley, to the decision makers, and everyone in between, all of you together make the mission work, and when it works well it's a thing of beauty. From my family to you and yours, thank you for letting us stand on your shoulders. Continue to be the giants you are.

PROLOGUE

Joseph Anderson was right where he wanted to be, and with those he wanted to be with. He loved his life, loved the variety of people he was surrounded by, and loved that he could call so many *friend*. He was even happier with what he was currently holding in his hand.

"What did you guys think about that?" Joseph asked as he gently snipped off the closed end of his cigar. The small piece of rich tobacco slid into an oversized ashtray, and then Joseph used a three-flame torch lighter to heat the cigar, taking in a few long draws until the tobacco was fully lit. Thick smoke billowed from his mouth like an old coal train, the aroma sending a sweet fragrance into the air.

"Unbelievable," Sleep said, as he mirrored Joseph's actions with his own cigar.

"This is the stuff of dreams." Green sat back, letting out an enormous waft of smoke from his smiling mouth.

"Joseph, this is phenomenal. Thank you," Smoke said, his *stick* clenched in the corner of his mouth —

thinking he was doing a great job imitating the gangster men he'd seen in the old black and white movies he'd always been a fan of.

"I can't believe you had our own line of cigars made. Not only that, but at two different cigar companies," Brackish said, inspecting the label of his carefully crafted cigar. Everyone there could see his wheels turning on how he could put something like a QR code, or even better — an RF chip — into the label and gain insane amounts of data. Then he was quickly shut down as he started geeking out. "Did you know the actual name of the town is Villa de San Antonio de Pavia de Estelí. And it—"

"Thank you again, Joseph," Eyes said, unabashedly interrupting Brackish before his information went on for the next ten hours. He did give their tech god, and great friend, a smirk as he did so.

Joseph had brought the men to Nicaragua as a gift for completing their mission. They were at a secluded cabin in the forest just outside of Estelí, Nicaragua. The *private* cabin was ten thousand square feet with nine bedrooms, twelve bathrooms, and one of the most incredible infinity pools a person could find. That late afternoon the men were on the patio after spending all day at the fields, barns, and rolling facilities of *My Father Cigars* and *AJ Fernandez Cigars*.

Joseph had met with Don Pepin, the creator of *My Father Cigars*, the year after Don had started his company, previously known as Pepin Cigars, and he'd stayed in contact with the man since. On one memorable trip to Nicaragua, Don had introduced Joseph to numerous owners in and around Estelí. He'd hit it off with a young up-and-comer in the cigar world — AJ Fernandez.

Something about AJ's spirit and determination had reminded Joseph of himself when he'd been that age. After additional conversations with the young man, Joseph had decided to help mentor AJ in the business world and, if ever necessary, assist him with financial aspects. Neither Don nor AJ had ever needed the money. In their own rights, they'd become successful incredibly quick. They'd admitted to Joseph, though, that the doors he'd opened for them had helped tremendously. When Joseph had wanted to do something unique for his special ops team, he'd known right where to go and who to ask. Both of the cigar men hadn't hesitated to accommodate Joseph's request.

Joseph, Chad, Smoke, and Sleep had chosen the *My Father Cigars* blend, which closely resembled the company's *My Father Le Bijou 1922*: a deep, rich, and full-bodied cigar that was a smoker's dream. The specialty cigars were only a fraction less potent in their richness but just as enjoyable to anyone who'd smoke them.

Eyes, Brackish, and Green had gone with a cigar made by AJ Fernandez's team. Their blend closely resembled the highly acclaimed *Bellas Artes Maduro* with a flavor profile of chocolate, dark fruit, and cedar. The only difference the special ops men could note was the wrapper on their cigar was a shade lighter than the *Brazilian Mata Fina* wrapper on the original.

The special ops men were ecstatic with learning about the entire process of creating a cigar and how much both organizations, and the employees working in them, made everyone feel like family. The men agreed that a person could only fake being nice for so long, and having trained in how to read people, that fakeness would be revealed quickly. Everyone from the owner to the person collecting fallen tobacco leaves from beneath the roller's feet were treated warmly and respectfully.

The locals had a good laugh at *gringo Green* as he tried rolling his own cigar only to have it look like a beat-up snake that had swallowed a rock and then tossed it into a washing machine for ten hours. Chants for Brackish to beat the newest roller turned into giggles when the final count was Brackish: 3, a sixteen-year-old girl: 10.

The most laughs came when Chad had tried cutting the tobacco leaf. His test had been to cut twenty times, making them the same length and width. When the workers held out all twenty cuts side by side, there wasn't a quiet person in the factory. Not a single one of the twenty matched, and some of them looked more like triangles than the football shape he was supposed to be making. It was a wonderful day that allowed the men to not only have a great deal of fun and learn something new, but to thoroughly shake off at least some of the stress they'd been under for quite some time.

Joseph had received permission from both companies to use the same label for both cigars. In the center of the label, a black spear stood in the middle of an exploding green star on a broad shield. Three Corinthian helmets to the right and three to the left of the shield wrapped around the band. Above the shield, it said *Tueri in* and below the shield *Tenebris*. The rough English meaning was *Protect in the Shadows*. Under each helmet was the call sign of the team members. From left to right was Chug, Eyes, Sleep, Brackish, Green, and ended with Smoke. The men loved looking at the labels as much as the idea that cigars had been explicitly made for them.

"I have something else for each of you," Joseph practically shouted, making a couple of the men nearly jump. Joseph's voice was loud and commanding enough to wake the dead . . . in another country . . . halfway around the world.

Joseph stood from his chair, the cigar still creating copious amounts of smoke, and he disappeared through the sliding glass doors leading inside the house. One of the two men serving food and drinks to their group noted Joseph's head nod and followed Joseph inside.

"What's he up to now?" Eyes asked Chad.

"There's no telling," Chad said with a smile.

"He's always up to something, though, isn't he?" Eyes asked, knowing the answer.

"Yes, he is," Chad replied.

Before Eyes could say anything else, Joseph started back toward them. He was carrying three boxes, each approximately the size of a serving tray, wrapped in simple blue paper. The server was right on Joseph's heels and had three boxes of his own.

"You can set them on the table right here," Joseph said to his helper.

Joseph turned back to the waiting team. "This is my gift to each of you. We've gone through a lot in our relatively short time together, some soaring highs and certainly some knee-buckling lows. You've never faulted and I want each of you to know how appreciative I am for that. I also appreciate your professionalism and your willingness to serve a community none of you previously had ties to."

"Sir, I do need to say . . ." Sleep began with a serious expression that made Joseph pause. "At no point or time was Brackish ever professional. He was trying to hack into the CIA database during his off time. I also heard from someone that he doesn't like kids . . . or marriage." He paused again, but this time he smiled. "And worst of all, he *hates* kittens," Sleep finished.

Joseph had looked concerned at the beginning of Sleep's little speech. Then he was chuckling by the end of it. He should've known at least one of the men would lighten the moment. It only took another second for the rest of the group to laugh.

"You'll go first," Joseph said as he handed Sleep his gift. That might shut the man up . . . for a few seconds at least.

"Please, open it," Joseph requested.

Sleep smiled at his peers, the kind of smile a sibling gave to the other when their parents allowed them to go first.

"Oh," was all Sleep could say as he opened the box and saw the contents. He took a smaller box out and held up the main item. It was a framed box split into four equal quadrants — a photo held in place. The first photo was of him in his tactical gear during one of their missions in Seattle. The second was of him and the team all splotched up with paint from the Anderson paintball war. The third was of him and Joseph laughing at something Sleep had just said — Joseph's head was leaned back, one of his hands on Sleep's shoulder. The last was of him and Avery during their wedding. Behind the photos was a replica of the cigar label in an oil painting. The frame's effect, the images, and the artwork were enough for Sleep to lose the next joke he'd been about to spout off. He stood, took a step to Joseph, then gave the man a crippling bear hug.

The rest of the men opened their gifts, and the contents replicated Sleep's—photos of them on a mission, with the team, with their wives, and with Joseph. One photo alone would remind each of them of their time in Seattle, let alone all four images of them involved in one of the most important missions of their lives.

"Now, please, open your boxes," Joseph stated while motioning to the smaller boxes. He took a deep draw from his *Pepin Blue Label* cigar, and smiled while he let the smoke slowly release.

Three things fell out of each box: a key fob, a check, and a pair of plane tickets.

"While you men have been doing your research, I've been doing some of my own," Joseph said. He was very happy with himself.

"I discovered what your favorite car or truck was and bought it for you, complete with every bell and whistle. The check is my final payment, with a bit of a bonus, to each of you. You've more than earned it — I do *not* want to hear that it's too much. The plane tickets are for you and your wife to travel anywhere in the world. All expenses are paid, first-class. With that ticket comes the vehicle and rental you need when you arrive, as well as your food, drink, and just a sprinkle of spending cash to buy those little trinkets I know you like," Joseph said.

The men started clamoring about it being too much, even though they'd been told not to. Joseph's firm stare stopped that immediately so they shifted to where they'd take their wives, and how much better their new vehicle was than their brothers'. They started to become so loud and joyous in their banter, after giving copious amounts of thanks and praise to Joseph, that they got lost in the moment. It was a good place to be. Too often they were lost in the pain and betrayal of the underworld they were trying to break. To be lost in the here and now instead of all of the junk they'd endured in their careers was a breath of fresh air. There were true smiles of joy and anticipation on their faces.

Joseph sat down, leaned back, and looked at each of the men he'd had the pleasure of working with, feeling pride at being a part of bringing Chad and the five men together. There was no doubt in Joseph's mind that this team of men had shifted the entire culture of Seattle toward doing good instead of falling into a depth of despair and ruin.

While Joseph knew it was the men who'd done the work, it had been his vision that had brought them all together. Joseph was feeling quite superior when he laughed at himself and squashed those self-serving thoughts. Yes, he was glad he'd brought the team together, but he'd take it all back if it would've meant his Katherine wouldn't have been attacked.

He'd give up anything in his life to protect his wife and the rest of his family. This mission might be wrapping up, but there were more missions ahead. Joseph just wasn't sure what that would mean for him and his family.

CHAPTER ONE

The work the special ops team had done in bringing down two major drug cartel leaders had been garnering press over the last few weeks. Communities were starting to come out from beneath the shadows they'd been forced into. Local leaders were making sure their respective neighborhoods knew their kids could ride bikes again, moms could stroll down the sidewalks, dads could push their kids on bikes, and families were safe going to parks. They were spreading the message that the drugs and crime that had plagued their city, their neighborhoods, and their lives were no longer running the show.

As people opened their doors and windows again, still feeling slightly jumpy and looking behind them, a smart and talented reporter began showing up in different neighborhoods, interviewing business owners, church parishioners, soccer moms, and fathers teaching their kids how to build a ramp to jump their bikes. Life was getting better in every imaginable way for those living in and around Seattle — for everyone other than those degrading society with their filth in the drug world. Those people were now the ones running and hiding.

Eyes sat in the special operations conference room with five different screens turned on while watching Courtney Tucker interview random people. He was mesmerized by the way she spoke, by the way her hair fluttered in the breeze, and with how natural her smile formed while she spoke with each person, making them feel as if they were the single most important person in her universe.

Eyes wouldn't admit it but there was a ping of jealousy when she was interviewing a random man and he'd say something that could be construed as flirtatious. Courtney never skipped a beat in her discussions with the men, but Eyes wanted to reach through the screen and rip the dudes away from her.

"You know, for someone who isn't all that interested in the sexy reporter, I have to wonder why you have all of those different interviews going at the same time," Sleep said. The man, who was the closest team member to Eyes, had his back against the door frame, his arms crossed against his massive chest, and a grin that said nothing less than "you just got caught red handed."

"She's a part of the Anderson team now, so I need to know what kind of information she puts out there," Eyes quickly said while fumbling for the remote to turn off the screens.

"Oh . . . yes, *research* for the betterment of the team." Sleep laughed as he pushed himself off the doorframe and walked into the conference room, plopping down on a chair and looking at all of the screens feeding the room information. Sugar, the team's crazy little mascot, an adorable female orange kitten, jumped into his lap, and in the blink of an eye, she was purring while falling asleep.

"Yes, it *is* research," Eyes replied after a long pause while he finally managed to turn off the last of the screens.

"If that's the case, your research needs to speed up before she decides she can't wait for you to get the nerve to take her out and she finds someone else to do the job," Sleep said nonchalantly.

Eyes was absently petting the kitten while logging onto another computer. He wanted to look up a few things before they left on their mission in a few hours. The entire team would be there for a 0100 departure down at the docks Green had worked at months ago. There'd been enough intel gathered to verify that drugs were coming in via shipping containers being temporarily stored at the docks.

Eyes slid the remote across the table, trying to avoid any comments from Sleep, who stepped into the room and began logging onto his own computer.

Sleep kept looking at his team lead, waiting for him to look up and make eye contact, but it didn't happen. The amount of ribbing he'd give his brother was vast and deep, and it was an act of God for Sleep to contain his thoughts until Eyes glanced up.

"I'm not going to look at you, Sleep," Eyes finally said.

"What? Why not?" Sleep asked in a faux hurt response. He threw a hand over his heart so Eyes would understand how upset he was to hear such a thing.

"Why not, what?" Green asked as he joined them.

"Nothing," Eyes quickly replied. He knew this could get out of hand really fast.

Sleep snickered, Green shrugged his shoulders, and all three men sat in silence.

Over the next thirty minutes the rest of the team slowly filled the seats with few words. There wasn't any tension between the members of the team, but there was a quietness as they prepared for the mission that was about to begin. It was going to be dangerous and difficult.

Unlike prior missions, there was no way to control the environment as they were going to be outside. It was a Wednesday night, going into late fall, at a dock, which meant the likelihood of there being many civilians around, if any, was very slim. The one thing all of them wanted to avoid was to have their actions endanger anyone who was innocent — like a dock worker or simply a random individual walking by. There was no safety measure skipped on any mission plan.

"Good evening, gentlemen," Chad said as he walked into the conference room. His body had changed quite a bit since the first day they'd come together as a team. While he'd never have been considered overweight, he'd become a little soft in the years since he'd become a private citizen. That couldn't be said anymore. His strength and shape had come back, making even his face appear more youthful. His walk also had a bit more bounce with each step he took these days. He'd told the team his wife was quite pleased with the changes.

"Eyes, please lead us through the steps one last time," Chad requested, getting straight to business.

"Got it," Eyes said and took command of the room.

For the next forty-five minutes Eyes went over each step, each person's position and plan, and had them repeat it back to him. It was the same thing each of them had gone through many times throughout their careers, and while some might find the repetition to be overkill, when it came to decisions that might mean you or a teammate wouldn't come home, there was never enough preparation.

"Okay, let's roll out," Eyes said when he was satisfied they were ready.

Each of the men stood, left the conference room, geared up, then met at the oversized Sprinter van Brackish had turned into a rolling command center. Brackish and Chad were in the front seats, the other four sitting on the floor in the back as they left the building. Just as they passed the sensors on the driveway the massive barrier blocks shot up and trapped the van in a rectangle of cylinder blockades.

Sleep took great pleasure in sending a mocking smile at Brackish. "Did you forget something?" he asked, his voice sweet as sugar.

"Shut up," Brackish muttered as he pulled his computer pad onto his lap.

"I can't believe Brackish forgot to turn off the sensors," Green said. "I guess hell really has frozen over." The entire team was laughing now. Brackish never forgot anything so this was something they'd never let him live down.

Brackish was quiet as his fingers feverishly flew over his computer pad. It only took a few seconds for the cylinders to begin to retract.

"I swear a monkey could do your job," Sleep said between chuckles.

"Maybe so, but *this* monkey still beat you in the Olympics," Brackish quickly replied.

Sleep's mouth slammed shut. He had no comeback for that, and it sucked. It was true that the big oaf of a man had beat him. He'd kick himself for a long time for that one.

The silence of no reply made Chad look over at Brackish and the two of them gave each other a knowing nod and a quick smile. There really was nothing better than beating your friends at something they thought they were better at than you. Well, there was one thing better, and that was rubbing the win in their face over and over and over again.

"Five minutes to first drop point," Chad said after driving a while.

"Copy," Green replied. He was going to be let out at a point almost a mile away.

After Green was dropped off Eyes, Sleep, and Smoke were next to leave. They'd be making their way to the warehouse storage area from the back of the building. There were only three cameras sweeping the area and each of them had been hacked and put on a continuous loop so no one could confirm the special ops team had been there.

Brackish and Chad drove to the front of the building, parked, and strode to the two oversized forklifts they'd placed there only a few hours earlier. The two of them were wearing appropriate safety gear and would easily pass any curious glances they might receive from any possible passersby.

With the forklifts revved up and on the move, Chad and Brackish made quick work of boxing in specific avenues by moving empty Conex containers around the lot. Any traffic that made its way into the area would be strategically sent away from the warehouse that was about to become the target for some of the most determined warriors on earth.

"Phase *Traffic Jam* complete," Chad called over the comms from the driver's seat of the van. Brackish had taken up his spot in the back and began bringing computers and monitors to life as they slowly crept into a dark corner of the parking lot where no one would see the van. From there he'd release his drones. Each type had been given specific functions to perform, and all of that information was fed back to Brackish. He was in heaven doing what he did best.

"Copy, *Jam* complete," Eyes said.

"Golden Eagle in place," Green said, sounding almost bored.

"Copy, Eagle," Eyes replied.

"Prying Eyes launched," Brackish said. He didn't often get to be in the field so he was pretty dang happy, and really liked his call name for the mission.

"Copy, Prying Eyes," Eyes replied.

"Three Amigos on the move," Sleep slid into the comms. He couldn't help himself.

The first thing the *three amigos* did was make their way through the emergency exit door, which had been disabled. They then made their way to the warehouse. It was a huge storage area. It had just missed being in the top ten warehouses in the world at just under five hundred thousand square feet, able to fit approximately ten football fields inside. If it wasn't for their intel, and Brackish's drones, it would be next to impossible to find the drugs in the vast space.

Soon, they got another surprise, though. Their intel had been wrong about the amount of drugs in the facility. They'd been told a certain amount; they'd been misinformed. Instead of one row of drugs, there were dozens of rows stacked ten feet high with placards in multiple languages labeled, *Minerals*. Below the name were weights, dates, and information meant to throw off any suspicion.

"B, send the prying eyes to our location for confirmation of goods," Eyes requested.

Within a couple of seconds the faint whirl of tiny blades descended onto the special ops men and started making their way down the line of tens of thousands of barrels.

"Confirmed readout, the goods are the stuffed animals we're looking for," Brackish said after only a few seconds.

"Copy. We're going to need more buttons for the stuffed animals," Eyes replied. The men immediately got to work.

The *buttons* Eyes had mentioned were six by two-inch rods that were shot into the barrel. After the rod was deposited by a type of ram gun it created a chemical reaction with the drugs inside, at first a slow burn, and then full consumption of everything inside. It was probable a fire would set the warehouse ablaze, but the team decided the risk of a fire was worth completing the mission.

It didn't take long for the first flames to take hold, and soon the three men were working a lot faster and spacing the barrels they inserted the chemically charged rod into farther down the line from the last one. They didn't want any drugs left when this was finished. It didn't take long before they were jogging down the line of barrels with flames shooting up behind them.

"Call off the buttons, we're full of heat in here. Be ready to call the rain man," Eyes called over his comms. They'd purposely turned off the fire alarm and sprinkler systems. To have the drugs burn out completely was more important than the possibility of some non-illegal substances being destroyed. When the time was right Brackish would call the fire department — being very clear that there were drugs burning, and unless they had proper protection they shouldn't come anywhere near the fire as they could easily die from inhaling the fumes.

Soon, the previously dark warehouse was lit up brighter than the Fourth of July in the deep South, and the heat was nearly suffocating. By the time Eyes, Sleep, and Smoke made it to the end of the line of barrels, the tips of the flames were nipping at the ceiling. That was nothing compared to what happened next.

The bottom row of barrels lost their structural integrity and began crumbling beneath the weight of the barrels stacked on top of them. As one row of barrels began crashing, the domino effect began. A wave of fire rushed at the men, gaining speed and ferocity the closer it got to them.

"Go!" Eyes yelled. None of them hesitated.

Smoke reached the door first and held it open for Sleep and Eyes to rush through. All three stopped worrying about being covert, and they made a beeline for their extraction point. While they were running they could hear updates from Brackish and Chad about emergency services being called from citizens across the harbor. Since it had gone out over private lines, there was no way for Brackish to control who else might have heard the call. They needed to get out of there — and fast.

"Incoming," Brackish said.

"It's a car . . . oh . . . dammit!" Green shouted.

"What?" Eyes barked back.

"How did he get here before anyone else? It's the idiot boss's kid, Andrew. I'm going to have to stop him," Green finished before crawling down from a platform where he'd been hidden. He planted himself in the middle of the road.

When Andrew's car lights illuminated Green, it obviously shocked the kid so much he nearly drove himself into the building they were next to. Green knew he was a sight to behold with his long gun, special ops clothing, night vision set over his face, and his mask covering his mouth and nose. The kid had no idea who Green was or why he was there, making the punk unpredictable.

Green waited.

Andrew started laying on his horn, but Green still didn't move. After a few seconds of their standoff, Green was a bit shocked when Andrew had the audacity to start moving his car forward as if he'd run over Green. Green still didn't move, and the resolve was obviously too much for Andrew. He slammed on his brakes as he rolled down his window and started yelling profanities at Green, demanding he get the hell out of the road. Green slowly rose his long gun and pointed it at the passenger seat of the car. Andrew stopped his forward momentum and stopped yelling, his face instantly paling.

Green slowly walked up to the car, then knelt down, and flipped up his night vision. "Andrew, you want nothing to do with what's happening at this warehouse. Unless you're involved in the importation of drugs into the United States or want to be held culpable by happening to show up just as they're burning to the ground, I'd highly recommend you turn around and leave right now."

"Who . . . who are you?" Andrew stammered.

Green pulled down his mask and smiled. "Andrew, you don't want to be involved in this. Turn around — now!"

Green nearly smiled at the utter shock on Andrew's face when he realized it was Green. The cat was now out of the bag as it was more than obvious that Green wasn't just some warehouse worker. The kid would never guess what Green truly was, but he knew the kid would come up with all sorts of ludicrous ideas over the next several years.

Something like this stayed with a person for a long time to come.

Andrew was frozen, and Green needed him to move. He shouted this time when he spoke. "Go! Now!"

This time, Andrew did as he was told. His fingers were visibly shaking as he gripped his steering wheel, but he turned the car around and drove away on the same route he'd come.

"He's gone but we have sirens coming in numbers. I'll meet you guys at my extraction point. See you when I see you," Green said as he slowly walked back into the shadows, completely disappearing from any eyes that might swing in his direction.

"B&C, meet at zone two. Repeat, meet at zone two. We're staying here to ensure no one tries to go inside," Eyes commanded of Brackish and Chad who were in the van.

"Copy," Chad said. He started the vehicle and drove. Brackish hit a couple buttons and all of his drones made their way to their resting spots on top of the van. Once they were in place a specialized awning would cover them, making them impossible to spot.

The first fire truck arrived just as the Sprinter van took a corner, leaving no trace the team had ever been there. It took less than five minutes for fifteen more fire trucks to follow the first. Other emergency vehicles weren't far behind the engines, creating a logjam of flashing lights as they got as close as they could to the enormous blaze lighting up the entire harbor.

The press tried making their way down the road, but thankfully, they were cut off. Many of them retreated to their vans and made their way to a different road, hoping to have a better view of the destruction taking place. They wouldn't be in danger on those routes, so the team wasn't worried.

Eyes was incredibly relieved to see the firefighters heeding the warning about not getting too close to the fire, and even more relieved that none of the ambulance workers or press individuals neared the blaze. There was zero civilian interaction with the fire and Eyes wanted to keep it that way. He'd be there a while, but as long as the drugs were destroyed and the people were safe, it was all worth it.

His plan was going perfectly until he heard a woman's voice that instantly had him on edge. His head whipped around. There she was scooting down an embankment while holding a cell phone, talking to the screen while pointing her phone at the fire. He couldn't see her face, but he *knew* that voice. He'd been listening to it nearly non-stop for weeks.

It didn't take long for her to reach the pavement, far too close to the blaze — Courtney, beautiful as ever, all but glowing from the light of the flames dancing against her skin. He was about to move forward, to demand she get the hell out of there before she inhaled the deadly fumes . . . but he was too late.

A shadowy figure came out of nowhere right behind her. At first Eyes thought the shadows and flames were playing tricks on his vision. But then Courtney spun around. Some sound must've alerted her. She swung her arm in a terrible attempt at a punch. She was in trouble. The man snaked his meaty arms around her and began dragging her away, her screams muted by his thick arm.

Not caring about his cover any longer, Eyes leapt from his hiding place, and was in a full sprint within a couple of steps. He reached Courtney and her assailant just as the man swung his arm at her face. He held a huge rock.

Eyes could tell before his fist met the man's face for the first time that the man was homeless and high on something. The smell emanating off of him was enough to make one with a softer stomach lurch.

Engaging in a hand-to-hand situation with someone like him was dangerous, due to the high possibility of needles on him. He also knew the man's mind was so far gone he didn't know where he was, let alone what he was doing. Instead of seriously harming the man, Eyes flipped him over onto his stomach and brought the man's arms together where he quickly secured him with a couple of zip ties.

Once the attacker was secure, he turned his attention to Courtney who was already up and brushing herself off. Eyes had been expecting tears, shaking . . . and of course, gratitude. He'd been wrong. There wasn't a single tear in her eyes, but a level of irritation. Who in the hell was this woman? She'd just been assaulted and had nearly gotten her head smashed in with a rock and she stood there, brushing off her clothes as if this was a typical Saturday night.

Eyes was shocked even more when she held up her phone in the same position she'd had it in earlier, and then pointed it directly into Eye's face. "Did you all see that? This man came out of nowhere and literally saved my life. The man who attacked me is clearly on drugs, so I can't be angry at his actions, but the hero in front of me stopped the man from doing something he might later regret."

Eyes was speechless, possibly for the first time in his life. Courtney pointed her camera at the tied man on the ground who was twisting beneath his restraints as he shouted every curse word in the Urban Dictionary.

"This is the man who just attacked me." Her phone moved back to Eyes. "There's no doubt in my mind I'd be dead if it wasn't for you."

The only reason Eyes wasn't pushing her camera away was because his face was covered. Of course, that meant nothing with some of the systems out there that could see through materials, but it did mean that the general public would have no clue who he was.

"Thank you for saving me," Courtney said. "What's your name? I'd like the world to know there's a hero in this city." She stopped as she scanned him from head to toe. "Why are you dressed like this?" She finally noted the guns on him. "What are you doing here?" Her eyes lit with equal parts of suspicion and excitement at the idea of a bigger story than she'd anticipated. "Do you have anything to do with the fire?"

Eyes finally snapped out of his shock as he held up his hand. "Courtney, you need to get out of here. That fire is eating away at thousands of pounds of drugs and it's critical you don't get too close to the building. The fumes will kill you."

"How do you know who I am?" she asked, her eyes narrowing more. "I don't take you as an internet news broadcaster fan." She again paused. "Your voice sounds familiar."

Eyes let out a sigh. Then he reached up and took her phone, shutting it off. Courtney gasped at him in outrage.

"Hey! I'm recording," she said. "Don't think you can bully me or take me away to some secret compound in the middle of nowhere. I'm a damn good journalist and I have rights," she said, taking a step closer to him, not afraid in the least. He wondered how she'd survived as long as she had. The woman had zero sense of danger. If he was a bad guy she'd be toast.

"No more cameras," Eyes said. "I need you to trust me and get out of here."

"Trust you?" She gasped. "There's not a flying chance in Oz of me doing that. Give me back my phone."

Eyes swiftly removed her battery and stuck it in his pocket then handed her the phone.

"You can't do that!" she said, stomping her foot as she took another step at him.

"Troubles?" came a rich, deep voice filled with laughter.

"Nothing I can't handle," Eyes replied to Smoke who'd appeared out of nowhere — nothing unusual for the big man.

"Wait!" Courtney whipped around, her head going back and forth as she watched Smoke draw closer. Eyes saw recognition dawn on her face. She turned back to Eyes.

"I'd know Tyrell's voice anywhere." She again paused. "Is that you, Jon?"

"You're a better reporter than I thought," Eyes said as he removed his night vision and face mask then gave her a smile.

"What in the world is going on? *Please* give me the story," she asked but equally demanded. Smoke didn't help the matter by laughing.

"Right now, we need to get the hell out of here. It isn't safe," Eyes said firmly.

Sleep stepped from the shadows next. Courtney looked as if she'd just stumbled upon the golden egg as her head whipped around between the three large men dressed in full fatigues.

"Eyes, you take her. Smoke and I will cover the perp and hand him over to the cops. None of the firefighters are going into that blaze. They've heeded Brackish's warning. The smell's in the air now, making it more than obvious what's burning."

"Brackish just said a boat is heading in to spray the blaze, but it'll still be burning for a while," Smoke added.

"Copy," Eyes said. He turned to Courtney and held out an arm, wondering if she'd take it. She only hesitated a few seconds before she ran her hand through the opening at his elbow.

"You'd better start talking," she threatened. "I have sooooo many questions."

Eyes couldn't help himself. He laughed.

"Don't you always?" he responded. The farther they moved from the blaze, the better he felt. She'd been far too close to danger. He didn't like that one bit.

She looked up at him, then looked back toward the raging fire. He didn't need to see the blaze again; he just watched as the flames danced in her eyes. That ignition set his own body on fire. There was something happening with this woman, something that had started a long time ago and was beginning to rage now.

When Courtney had interviewed him and Sleep years ago after their near-death experience, he'd felt an ember ignite in him. Then when the woman had shown up a few months ago, it had been as if dry kindling had been tossed on that ember. Now, as she clung to his side, it felt as if gasoline had just been added to the mix.

What was he going to do about it? He smiled just as she turned and gazed into his eyes. He'd soon find out, that was for damn sure.

CHAPTER TWO

Courtney Tucker was a tiger. She knew that for sure because she'd taken the Facebook quiz that told users what type of animal they were once they finished the questions, and it had defined Courtney as a tiger.

Okay, okay, she wasn't counting on a stupid social media quiz to define who she was, she was counting on herself to know she was a warrior in the jungle of life.

Since the age of five she'd wanted to be a reporter. She'd started by interviewing her parents, and then she'd branched out to kids in her neighborhood, and then to their parents. She'd gotten one of those karaoke microphones for Christmas that year, and much to her parents amusement, she hadn't once sung into it, instead she'd placed the device directly in the face of anyone who came near her and she'd shouted questions.

Her parents had believed it would just be a phase. They'd been wrong.

Her passion for reporting had only grown from that moment forward. When she'd been eight she'd solved a crime in her neighborhood. Once a week on different nights for three months, the Kolinskis had woken up to find their garbage can had been turned upside down and placed on their lawn with four of their garden gnomes atop it.

The Kolinskis had over a hundred garden gnomes, and each night it was a different set of four placed in varying poses over the ugly green can. They reported the crime to the cops, but the authorities hadn't been too worried about what looked to be a harmless prank. They'd then asked the entire neighborhood to keep an eye out for the culprit. But without rhyme or reason to the time or day the can would be placed, the culprits hadn't been caught.

Courtney had decided she'd solve the mystery. By that time, she'd owned many investigative materials since that was all she'd ever requested for her birthday and Christmas. Her parents had told her they weren't too sure if they wanted to get her more items since she'd fingerprinted all of them, interviewed them with their hands tied to chairs, and even busted through their bedroom door, thankfully without anything happening at that moment, and told them she was on a breaking news story. She'd then proceeded to grill them about the temperature of the house and what made them choose that particular degree.

Courtney truly *was* a tiger. She didn't stop until she had her story, and if that meant she'd get her hands dirty and do those things other reporters were unwilling to do, then that's what she'd do. It had gotten her far in life. She might not be working for one of the major news outlets, but she chose that so she could be independent and not beholden to anyone telling her what she was allowed to report on.

She smiled as she thought about the Kolinskis who'd awarded her with homemade pies, a real lie detector kit, and a real White House Press badge they'd found on eBay. She still had all of those items, except for the pies of course. She'd spent two weeks camping out on her front porch at different times of the night. She'd have slept there if her parents would've allowed her to do so, but they weren't quite *that* open. She'd watched through her bedroom window until her eyes were blurry and she'd paced the sidewalk until her parents had again made her come inside.

And then, bam! She'd caught the culprit. She'd instantly become the neighborhood hero. It had happened at one in the morning. She'd woken up with her face buried in her arms as she'd leaned against her bedroom window. She'd heard a sound outside and her heart had accelerated as she raced down her staircase and quietly opened her front door.

Courtney had full-blown run from her front porch straight at the neighbor's yard, too worried about missing the action if she slowed down, to be afraid of any sort of danger she might be leaping into. She'd come to a screeching halt when she'd seen Mr. Wilson, their eighty-year-old neighbor, placing a second gnome atop the garbage can he'd already tipped over. He placed the gnome, then moved over to the garden area and looked around for several moments before he grabbed another.

"Mr. Wilson?" she'd called, but he didn't even jump. He just kept on with his task. Courtney hadn't really known what to do at that point. She'd stood there a few more seconds when she noticed her front porch light flick on and the door fly open. Her father barreled down the steps wearing only a pair of boxers, with hearts and arrows all over them, and a panicked expression.

"Dad," Courtney called. Her father halted, his head whipping in her direction. The panic turned into relief as he rushed to her and grabbed her up, squeezing her so hard she couldn't breathe for a second.

"You foolish little girl. You just about gave your old man a heart attack," her father said. "I heard the door open and close, and I knew you were looking for the neighborhood bandit. Do you even know how dangerous this is?" he asked, chastising her and still squeezing her so tight she could barely get air to reply.

"Dad, look," she gasped.

He must've finally realized how tight he was holding her, because his iron grip loosened just a tad as he shifted to look in the direction she was pointing.

"Is that Mr. Wilson?" her father asked, obviously tired since he'd been woken in the middle of the night. It was exactly the middle for him since he was up and ready to go every morning by five AM, even on Sundays. Her father loved routine. Courtney was sure that's where she'd developed the habit.

"Yes, and I called out to him, but he acted like he couldn't hear me," Courtney said.

As they watched, Mr. Wilson placed the fourth gnome on top of the garbage can, looked down at his creation, then turned and walked across the street to his house, stepping inside and disappearing.

"That was about the strangest thing I've ever seen," her father said.

"What should we do?" Courtney asked.

"Nothing tonight. We'll talk to Mr. Wilson and Mr. Kolinski in the morning," her father said.

The next day they did just that, and then found out that Mr. Wilson was in the middle stages of dementia and he was sleepwalking. He had zero recollection of his ritual. His wife had been horrified to find out that he was sneaking out of the house, fearing for his safety. She'd been hoping his medical condition wasn't as bad as she'd thought it was. She decided it was time to move to an assisted living facility where her husband could get more help than what she was able to give him.

Courtney had been hailed a hero, and she'd known she'd report on stories for the rest of her life, and not only do that, but solve crimes as well. Since that middle-of-the-night case, she'd been taking charge, kicking ass, and building a career she was incredibly proud of.

Currently, Courtney had been kidnapped by none other than Jon Eisenhart, who was about the sexiest soldier she'd ever had the pleasure of interviewing. From the moment he'd first walked up to her back in Germany she'd been in lust. She'd also known the man was a true playboy and broke a lot of hearts without bothering to take names. That didn't diminish the fact that he was good on the eyes. She didn't mind taking all the looks she could at the man.

"Jon, you might as well tell me what in the world is going on," Courtney said. He'd saved her life about thirty minutes earlier, then walked her back to her vehicle.

She'd thanked him when he'd dropped her off, then she'd watched him walk away before she'd turned from her vehicle and began heading back toward the fire. She waited then immediately backtracked trying to go back to the fire. He'd been around the corner, and he hadn't been happy, accusation flaring in his eyes and his arms crossed over his impressive chest.

He'd immediately confiscated the keys to her car and told her to get into the vehicle, saying some nonsense about women being a whole hell of a lot of trouble. She'd been firing questions at him from that moment on, and he'd been ignoring her. She just smiled. She always got her story and if Jon thought he could outlast her, he was going to be sadly disappointed.

"I'm trying to figure out where to take you so you don't get yourself killed," Jon said as he continued driving.

"I don't back down from a story, Jon. I'll stay away from the warehouse if you let me interview you," she told him. He let out a long sigh.

"No to both," he told her.

"That's unacceptable." She crossed her arms and smiled. She'd learned over the years that she could get a lot further in life with honey rather than with vinegar. Even if she wanted to roll her eyes or glare at someone, she normally forced herself to smile and help them feel at ease. That had broken more than a few reluctant people.

"Brackish, she's not backing down," Jon said, confusing Courtney for a second. Then her smile grew as she realized he was wearing an earpiece. She practically bounced in her seat, feeling as if she was on a super-secret spy movie-like mission. A little secrecy and a hell of a lot of danger was a *very* good day in Courtney's honest opinion.

Jon nodded as if the person was speaking back to him. He pulled into a driveway, then turned the vehicle around, and they started moving back in the direction they'd just come from. Were they headed back to the fire? No, he'd never do that. It killed her a bit that she had no idea where they were going or what was coming next. She'd soon find out.

"Who are you talking to?" Courtney asked. "And why? And really, Jon? Did you honestly think I'd back down? I didn't become this good at my job by cowering or accepting it when reluctant people don't want to answer *easy* questions." She was good at confusing people or throwing so much at them that it sometimes jumbled their brains enough for them to slip out some key information. She'd just push and push and push until she broke them. She had a feeling it would take a hell of a high mountain and a long drop to push Jon that far.

"No, Courtney, no one would ever accuse you of backing down from a story," Jon said with a chuckle. "And you might as well call me Eyes. You're about to hear it over and over again," he finished. He suddenly seemed more relaxed. She knew something had shifted in his brief conversation.

"I heard that name back in Germany," Courtney said. "You never did tell me why it's your call sign." She knew all about military names. She'd interviewed a lot of soldiers and a lot of them went by their military names long after their time in the service was over. They wore that name like a badge. It was a badge, in reality, one they'd truly earned.

Eyes smiled. Now that he'd given her permission to use the name, it felt natural to think of him as Eyes, especially when she thought about why he was called that. She liked anything that was out of the ordinary.

"I got the name because I have eyes in the back of my head, in my ears, even on my feet. I see *all* no matter where I'm at or what position I'm in," he told her with a wink. "I've always been able to assess a situation much faster than even the brightest soldiers, and that's because I pay attention."

"Me too. I don't think it's plausible to go into a career like mine without looking in all directions at all times," Courtney told him. "Who's Brackish?"

"He's the man who just cleared you. It looks as if you're going to get your story after all," Eyes told her.

Courtney had to force herself not to bounce up and down in her seat at Eyes's words. She knew that any story he was about to tell was going to be worth hearing, and even more importantly, worth writing about. This was the type of story she'd pursue for months with a lot of sleepless nights because it could lead to a Pulitzer.

"How did he clear me? Who is he?" she pushed. She wanted to drain every last trace of information from Eyes before she met anybody else. Sometimes when she was with multiple people she never got back to her original questions she'd come in with for the first person. That always frustrated her, but even the best of the best couldn't make time slow down or add more hours to the day. Sometimes she simply ran out of time. She didn't like to waste any of her precious hours, so multitasking became one of her many talents.

"Apparently you've been working for Joseph Anderson," Eyes said, shocking her. It was rare for anyone to do that.

"Yes, but I thought nobody was supposed to know. How did you find out?" she asked. There was no point in lying to him. It wasn't as if he could guess something like that without some valid information.

"When you meet Brackish you'll understand there isn't much we miss," Eyes said with a laugh. He turned off the road into a spot she wouldn't have noticed was a driveway. It was deceptively set back and covered. Only if you were *really* looking you could see it, otherwise it would go unnoticed.

"Are you spying on Joseph?" she gasped. That wouldn't be smart. That man had more power and influence than anybody Courtney had ever met — and she'd met some pretty influential people in her career. She might only be thirty-one, but she considered her career had started at five years old so that was a solid twenty-six years beneath her belt.

Eyes chuckled. "Yes, we spy on Joseph," he told her. "It's become a game between him and Brackish." He waved his hand in the air as if that was yesterday's news. "However, this time, Joseph gave us permission to know. He said it's time we work together. We're at the end of this operation and he wants to bring it all home with a big bang, making Independence Day look like a sparkler compared to a hydrogen bomb."

"What operation?" Courtney fired off. Now she was getting somewhere.

"I guess you're about to find out," Eyes told her.

Suddenly, there was a flashing light in front of them, and then their vehicle screeched to a halt as a siren sounded, making Courtney jump as the car was surrounded by giant metal poles shooting from the ground. She and Eyes turned to each other at the same time, both of them looking suspicious.

"Do you have a bomb on you?" Eyes gasped as his eyes traveled from her head to her toes.

Courtney shifted in her seat as she turned away from him. How in the world would he suspect she had anything on her? And what had just happened to their vehicle?

"What's going on, Eyes?" she asked instead of answering. She was really good at not answering a question by firing off one of her own.

"Seriously, Courtney, what do you have on you?" Eyes pushed. "I didn't think I needed to pat you down." She couldn't tell by his tone if he was irritated or impressed. Since she found herself quite impressive, she decided to go that route.

She reached into the fanny pack resting at her hip and pulled out a small handgun. "I go into some sketchy places sometimes and I'm always prepared," she told him with a shrug.

"With a gun?" he asked as he held out his hand, demanding she turn over the sidearm.

"I'm not letting you have this," she told him, pulling it back toward her.

He paused and nodded, and she figured this Brackish person he'd spoken to earlier was now whispering in his ear again.

"Yeah, apparently Courtney likes to keep herself well-armed," Eyes said. "I'm about to apprehend it. Yeah, it's a Sig Sauer, looks like a 365. Do you detect anything else?" Another pause. "Good. I guess it's true you never really know a person until you go through a state-of-the-art surveillance system together." He chuckled at something the man on the other end of the line said. "Ten-four."

He then turned to Courtney. "Hand over the pistol and then Brackish will release us from this cage," he said.

"Will I get it back?"

"Probably, but only after we're leaving later tonight," he promised.

"Okay, that's good enough for me," Courtney said as she handed over the device she'd never had to use before. She'd come close, and she'd been in some sticky situations, but never to the point that she felt the need to pull her gun. Tonight had happened too quickly for her to get to it.

As soon as the device was out of her possession the long metal bars began retreating back into the earth. Soon, they were moving forward again. It didn't take long for them to come around a bend where a massive building stood before them. Eyes stopped the car, and Courtney watched as two men headed their way, seeming to appear out of nowhere.

As soon as they exited the vehicle, Eyes slid the pistol into one of the many hidden pockets on his chest. She hoped Eyes kept his promise of returning it or maybe replacing it with something better.

"This is the operation center. You might want to call the other ladies on your team. It's time for all of us to talk," Eyes said.

Courtney grinned at the man who was far too good looking to be unleashed on the general public. It was a good thing she could appreciate beauty without getting all shifty and brainless like a lot of females out there. "Oh yes, it's long past time," she said, feeling better than she did on Christmas morning. She lifted her phone. The fun truly was about to begin.

CHAPTER THREE

Eyes and Courtney stepped inside the building. Eyes didn't even blink as they walked forward. She was silent as he gave her the nickel tour. He was sure the investigator in her was taking it all in and making notes. He'd already warned her she couldn't write on any of it, but that didn't mean her brain would shut down. She was a reporter after all, and this building was a treasure trove.

Her obvious astonishment prior to entering the main hub of their *secret lair* had been justified. When they'd stepped inside the conference area where all of the guys met, she was speechless. He tried to look at it through her eyes. The level of information and sophistication surrounding the walls would be impressive to even those who didn't fall under the spell of awe.

To top off all of the gadgets Brackish came up with on what seemed a daily basis, the sight of the entire team, including Chad, sitting around their table was enough to stop anyone from entering the room.

"Almost everything in here is due to the brilliant mind of Brackish," Eyes told her.

Courtney looked over to Steve, who was sitting at the end of the table typing away on a laptop. "I'm assuming you're Brackish?" she said to Steve.

"I am," Brackish replied, still furiously typing while barely looking up long enough to give her a nod before instantly going back to whatever data he was working on.

Eyes knew that in normal circumstances Courtney would have four or five questions lined up and ready to ask by the time a subject finished their first answer. However, in the overloaded room, with massive amounts of information coming at her, she couldn't seem to process a single question. She stared at the large television screens showing images streaming in from all parts of the city, as closed caption videos looped, and news channels showed clips from the fire burning at the warehouse they'd left less than an hour earlier.

"How? What? Who . . ." Courtney finally started speaking only to stop and start again without a full sentence forming.

"We'll discuss it all in the morning. I need to put my gear away and debrief the team. Let's go to the kitchen and get you some food and something to drink. Then I'll ask that you relax in a bedroom for the rest of the evening. Before you start with the hundred and one questions, I promise I'll answer any and all of them in the morning," Eyes said. Courtney started to interrupt, and he held up his hand to stop her.

"I promise to do just that." She seemed as if she wanted to argue, but it was clear she was exhausted from the exciting night. "We have plenty of toiletries here, and if you need anything specific let me know now so I can get it for you," Eyes finished. He waited as he watched her reaction. He could see when she gave up the fight.

"The only thing I need is a change of clothes. I have a bag in my car," Courtney said.

"I'll bring it to you in a bit," Eyes said. He could see that she was aware she wouldn't be allowed to wander all over the building or go in and out of the exits. She'd been in enough situations in her career to know when in a military situation, which they operated as, you had to have permission and an escort for anywhere you might need to go.

"Okay. Thank you," Courtney let out, barely audible.

Eyes and Courtney went to the kitchen, grabbed a couple of snacks, a couple of bottles of water, and a nice red wine. They quickly moved through the building to the sleeping quarters. Eyes opened the door to her room and watched as she walked inside. She didn't give him a reaction to the functional space. It wasn't decorated, but it had everything she'd need, and it was a lot more comfortable than a person might expect. He should know as he was the last man standing who still lived in the building.

"Please, stay here. I need to speak with the men and then I'll bring your bag to you," Eyes said.

"You're asking a lot of me, locking me up in this dungeon," Courtney said with a slight smile.

"I know for a fact that you've been in worse places than this," Eyes said.

Courtney looked around again, then passed by him, her hair gently brushing against his cheek. His body instantly reacted. Each time he was with this woman, his internal thermometer cranked up several degrees, overheating his entire body. It took a strong will for him not to pull her up against him and take the kiss he'd been wanting since the first moment he'd sat across from her years ago in Germany. He'd never been hung up on a woman for as long as he'd been hung up on this one. He was ready to shut the door to her bedroom and give her a new story to write that could be published as soft-porn.

Instead of doing just that, he gripped the door handle tight, told her he'd be back soon, then slowly closed the door. He stood in the quiet hallway for a minute to calm his racing heart.

The last thing he wanted to do was go back to the conference room, but there was a job to do, and work had to come first. There was plenty of time for playing when the job was done. He walked from her door and swiftly made his way back to the conference room where he knew he'd take some shit from the men.

He wasn't wrong. Sleep perked up as soon as he entered. Eyes knew what was coming before his friend began speaking.

"Tsk, tsk, Eyes. You're the first to bring a lady to the secret hideaway. You've had quite the night, though, so I guess you get a pass. You saved the damsel in distress, then brought her to the castle to stay the night. Have you done the sweeping kiss yet? Do we need to post a sentry outside of her room so you don't deflower her before the wedding night?"

"Shove it where the sun doesn't shine," Eyes retorted.

"I think that's what you'll be doing later tonight," Sleep shot back, cracking himself up, and drawing a few chuckles from the other men.

Eyes slammed his fist hard onto the table, staring firmly at Sleep. "Enough."

Sleep stared at Eyes and silence filled the room. He then raised an eyebrow. "Really, Eyes?"

"Shit, sorry," Eyes said as he scrubbed his face with his hand. They always flicked crap at each other. He wasn't sure why he was getting mad about it. Maybe because he was sleep deprived. He knew for sure he was sex deprived — and all because of one dynamite package who was only a few hundred yards away.

"Why don't we get back to work mode?" Chad suggested. The last of Eyes's attitude disappeared as he sent an appreciative nod to their leader. If it hadn't been for Chad, they wouldn't be a team. Eyes was grateful they'd all come together.

"Let's discuss the warehouse. Brackish, can you please give an update?" Eyes asked in a much easier tone.

"Yep, sure thing," Brackish said and began speaking.

For the next thirty minutes the six men discussed their operation that night, how much data they'd received, and gratefully confirmed that not a single person had been hurt from the smoke plume that had drifted high into the sky.

The entire time Brackish spoke, he also typed on his computer. It was fascinating to watch how easily the man multitasked. Just as Eyes had that thought, Brackish froze.

"What's going on?" Eyes asked. All of the men gave their full attention to Brackish.

"Hold on," the man said as he pushed more buttons.

It didn't take long for the room to fill with sound.

"Who is that?" Chad asked.

Brackish was grinning ear to ear. "I tracked down the owners of the containers," he said, referring to the hundreds and hundreds of shipping containers they'd destroyed earlier that night. "It's Vladimir Lebedev, who just so happens to be a Russian oligarch. He and his son, Gavrie, are equal partners. They live just over four miles from Joseph Anderson's property in a home they've owned since the late nineties. They're on the phone together right now." It wasn't often Brackish showed excitement, but at that moment, he practically bounced in his chair.

The father and son were speaking perfect English as Gavrie thundered into the phone, the sound surrounding the six men raptly listening.

"We've lost over ten billion dollars in products," Gavrie shouted.

"Was anything saved?" Vladimir asked, seeming more resigned than upset.

"Nothing! *Nothing* was saved," Gavrie spit out.

"Do we know who did this?" Vladimir asked, the deadly steel in his voice showing how the man had gotten into the position of power he had until Eyes and his crew had come along.

"I have no leads at the moment," Gavrie said. "But I *will* find out. If it's the Germans, they will pay."

"Whoever it is *will* pay," Vladimir said, ice running through his voice.

Their conversation was soon over and Brackish leaned back with a smile. "I have it all recorded," he told the team. "And I've already sent it over to Sherriff McCormack, who will notify the Feds immediately. Both Vladimir and Gavrie should be picked up by morning and spend the rest of their days in a nice cozy prison cell."

"Do you think the sheriff ever gets sick of being grilled on where he's getting his information?" Smoke asked as he munched on a donut. There were three boxes on the table that had been full of sweets but were now almost empty. The men had incredibly healthy appetites. Of course, they burned a crapload of calories every day and needed to replenish.

"He might get sick of high-ranking starred badges grilling him, but he won't ever cave and tell them about us," Chad said with confidence.

"Yep, his standard answer of *a package arrived on my doorstep* has got to infuriate all of the brass," Sleep said.

"The boys on top are just pissed because their egos and their itty-bitty feelings are getting crushed as the press hounds the big wigs about how a small-town sheriff continues to capture all of these big-time drug kingpins while the agencies with all of their federal funds are sitting on their thumbs and twirling around like schoolgirls on recess," Green said with a laugh.

"It pisses the big boys off even more when McCormack's interviewed and sticks to his story that he was only a messenger for the guardian angels of his city, who drop off invaluable evidence and incriminating material."

Smoke reached for the final donut. The man should weight five hundred pounds. He yawned. "I'd say it was another beautiful day of work."

"Yes, it was, Smoke," Chad said. "With that, we can adjourn." There were sighs of relief. They loved their work, but at the end of the day they were done with it.

"One more thing," Eyes said as the men began to stand. They gave him their full attention. "Please bring your wives tomorrow morning. Be here at 0700. Smoke, you don't have to bring Amira, but she's invited as well," Eyes finished.

"Mallory and I will come early and cook breakfast for everyone," Green said as the men began moving toward the exit.

"Need me to bring anything?" Smoke asked.

"Nope. It'll be a simple breakfast. I've got it covered," Green replied.

Everyone smiled, knowing that Green cooking anything was as good a culinary experience as one would ever have, even if he did call it simple. His idea of simple wasn't scrambles eggs and ham, it was a three-course gourmet breakfast that would have mouths watering and stomachs bloating.

"Okay, that's a wrap. See you guys at 0700," Eyes said. He then turned and walked from the conference room without looking back.

Eyes made his way to Courtney's vehicle, popped the trunk and instantly let out a laugh. The woman had more junk in her trunk than he could've thought possible. That line, junk in her trunk, made his mind go to other places which he tried to squash while pulling out the only zipped bag among the books, blankets, random re-usable water bottles, writing pads, magazines, and a bag of Tootsie Rolls that had lost its battle of staying intact, leaving candy scattered everywhere. He decided to throw a couple of the small fake chocolates into her bag. Women seemed happier when they were given candy and he wanted her as happy, and sweet, as possible.

He picked up his pace as he made his way back to her room. He was glad the other guys had scrambled quickly after their meeting. It was now just him and Courtney in the vast building. He smiled as he knocked on her bedroom door.

"Come in." He loved the sound of her voice even through thick wood.

Eyes opened the door to find Courtney sitting on the bed, a couple of plates laid out in front of her, almost all of the dried meats and cheese consumed. The bottles of water were still full, but the wine was at the stage where people defined your outlook on life by whether you said it was half-full or half-empty. She seemed much more relaxed than she had when he'd left her there about thirty minutes earlier.

"Oh, good, my change of clothes." Courtney smiled as she leapt from the bed and walked up to Eyes, grabbing the bag. "I feel disgusting. I had a shower, but then had to put these things back on. I should've waited." With that she went over to the bathroom and pushed on the door, but not hard enough to fully close it. She quickly ripped off her shirt, exposing just enough of her shoulder, arm, and back for Eyes to know he needed to look away. He didn't want to, but he wasn't going to cross the line of being a peeping Tom.

"Is there anything else? If not, we're all meeting in the conference room tomorrow morning at 0700," Eyes said as he moved away from the door, losing sight of the strip show he wouldn't mind watching when she was aware she was doing it in front of him.

"Just a second," Courtney called. A moment later she reappeared in a new outfit of a long sleeve shirt and sweats. It was painfully obvious to Eyes she'd removed her bra during the transition of clothes.

"Hey, Eyes, I know I can handle myself, and that I've been in some pretty rough positions, but I wanted to say thank you for what you did tonight," Courtney said. She looked young and fresh and he clenched his fingers to keep from grabbing her. She moved up to him and leaned in, giving him a heartfelt hug of gratitude.

Her scent engulfed him, the mixture of a sweet fruity lotion with the bouquet of the red wine she'd been drinking thrown in. It was more than enough to make his body react. As much as he wanted to grab her tight and satisfy both of them, he knew it wasn't the right moment. Before he could change his mind, he gave her a quick hug back, said something to the effect of it not being a problem, and then ended the hug between them.

"Unless you need anything else I'm going to call it a night," Eyes said.

"I might have a hard time sleeping, but I think I'm good," Courtney told him.

He nodded, then turned and left without saying anything more. He knew it was late, he knew he could have her, but he also knew neither of them would have much respect for the other in the morning if they rushed this. He found he didn't want to rush anything when it came to this woman.

Instead of going to bed, though, he went to the gym and tried to work out his frustration for the next hour and a half. He ran fast and hard, lifted weights, cycled at the most difficult setting, then went back and lifted more weights. By the time he finished he was certain his brain would shut down from pure exhaustion, but that wasn't the case.

After a shower, Eyes lay in bed thinking of Courtney, and that led to too much time wondering why he spent so much time thinking about her. She was a woman, one of billions in the world, and while she was *very* attractive, he'd been around many, many, *many* attractive women throughout his life. What was it about Courtney he couldn't seem to shake? He tried his breathing exercises, he tried meditating, he even tried lying on the floor. No matter what he tried he couldn't stop thinking of the woman who was only a couple of doors down from him.

By the time the 0600 alarm went off, Eyes only had forty-five minutes of sleep. He rarely allowed his emotions to control him or let his thoughts become fantastical, but all of that had been thrown out the window in the span of a few hours.

He'd literally gotten little more than a catnap because of one blonde, blue-eyed reporter, but at least he'd gotten a few minutes of shut eye. That was better than some days. He jumped from his bed and took a two-minute shower, on the coldest setting possible, then dressed.

When he stepped from his room and the smell of breakfast hit his nostrils; he felt his lips turn up. His mind had been so consumed with a certain female he'd forgotten that Green and his wife were making breakfast. At least some good was coming from this new day.

His mood vastly improved as he entered the kitchen. A podcast discussing wind variances on long range shooting was blasting over the kitchen speakers, which if nothing else, made everyone in the building know Green was there. No one else could stand his boring podcasts, but that's what made Green so great at what he did. His laser-like focus made him one of the best special ops snipers of all time — and that same focus made him one of the best chefs of all time as well. The smells that had tantalized Eyes outside of the kitchen sent his taste buds into overdrive as he was hit full force with the aromas steaming from the stove.

"Good morning, Green. It smells fantastic in here. What's cooking?" Eyes asked.

"Mornin' Eyes. It isn't that big a deal today. I don't have a lot of time and we have a large group gathering so trying to make it simple," Green replied.

One of the many things Eyes appreciated about Green was how calm he stayed under pressure. If Eyes had to make breakfast for four people, let alone ten or more, he'd have been fumbling all over the place and the food would be, at best, barely edible. Green though, went about his business with flawless precision, no look of stress or worry over his face.

"Yeah, by the smell of it I'll probably need to go to a Seven-Eleven to get a two-day-old breakfast sandwich so my taste buds will have something with flavor," Eyes joked as he poured himself a cup of hot coffee.

Something came flying through the air and Eyes barely managed to catch it before it slammed into his face. When he realized what it was the rest of his morning fog evaporated as he looked at Green and began laughing.

"I have you covered since you've made that joke before," Green said. "Enjoy your breakfast as the rest of the men eat my tasteless creation."

In Eyes's hand was a Seven-Eleven sandwich, which was cold and about as appealing as a termite.

"Okay, okay, you win. I'm in awe of your food and will never say anything bad about it again if you let me throw this away and eat at the big boys' table." Eyes didn't care if he was begging.

"That's more like it. You're forgiven," Green said, continuing to stir what appeared to be gravy. If part of the breakfast was biscuits and gravy, it wouldn't be like what you got in a diner. Oh no, it would be a masterpiece with flavors bursting on the tongue hours after the food was consumed.

The realization that Green's wife wasn't in the kitchen finally dawned on Eyes. "Where's Mallory?" he asked.

"She and Courtney went for a walk about thirty minutes ago," Green said, then gave Eyes a wicked smile. "Are they going to have anything *good* to gossip about?"

"Not from my side," Eyes said too quickly.

"Boring," Green replied. Before Eyes could respond, Green kept talking. "Since you're about as useless as a rock under a tree, set these into the oven." Green handed him two cookie sheets with a bunch of white flakes on it.

"Coconut," Green said with his back turned while working on the next part of his recipe.

"Okay then," Eyes said as he did as he was told.

"I need to get some emails finished before the group gets here. Need anything else?" Eyes asked.

"Nope, all's good in here, brother," Green replied, his focus still on the food directly in front of him.

Eyes left, then immediately went to his computer and started going through email. But it didn't take long for the team to arrive, making him shut down and pay attention to the conversation.

Chad and Brianne, who'd picked up Courtney and Mallory as the women were almost to the entrance of the driveway, were the last to arrive, and once they were in the conference room Green and Smoke, sans Amira, started serving breakfast. Everyone was silent as they dove into their meal, not coming up for air until every last bite was gone. It was by mutual agreement that the meal was among the best they'd ever had; it started off their day, and their meeting, on a very high note.

"Okay, Eyes, why don't you start us off?" Chad said as he sipped on his fourth cup of coffee.

"Copy," Eyes replied.

Eyes stood, gave a quick head nod to Brackish — indicating for him to turn on some pre-set videos. "On behalf of all of the men in the room — ladies, welcome to our operations center. All of you have agreed to take a part in opening the world's eyes to what Anna Miller did and how that relates to the crime in the city. With approval from Chad and Mr. Anderson, it was decided that each of you learn what we do here. I doubt it's much of a secret to any of you, but our team has come together to rid the city of drugs and the criminal acts they bring."

"We're glad to be here," Courtney said. It was the first words she'd spoken to him since he'd left her room the night before. He nodded at her before he continued.

"To date we've either apprehended, or given law enforcement the information to apprehend, all but one of the largest drug lords in the city. We're still awaiting confirmation on the accuracy but if it holds true, in financial terms we destroyed the largest single compilation of drugs in U.S. history last night. It's said to have had a ten-billion-dollar value. Yes, that is ten *billion* — with a *B*," Eyes said before continuing.

"On the screens you'll find a few clips of what we've been involved in, and what the communities have become since those drugs have been taken away. Previously, they were suffocating entire areas all over Seattle." There were murmurs of agreement.

"Our focus still remains on one more person so we can't give you ladies our undivided attention, but for whatever free time we do have, I give you my word the men here will assist you in whatever way we can."

Sleep, for the first time Eyes could remember, actually stopped himself from saying something in regard to how he could assist — specifically his wife. All of the special ops men saw his internal battle and smiled in unison.

"Why did Joseph decide to bring us in?" Erin asked. "I have my talents but taking down bad guys has never been on my résumé. I'm just curious."

Chad held up a hand, indicating he wanted to take this question. Eyes nodded at him.

"Joseph loves people, he loves family, and he loves friends. He also believes in everyone in his life. He clearly sees how all of your relationships have progressed, and he wants you to be a team, husbands and wives working together, as well as couples working together. I think he hopes to keep all of you around for a long time to come," Chad said.

"So, it was a pity assignment," Courtney said, not seeming at all happy with that.

Chad chuckled. "Joseph doesn't do anything out of pity. If he didn't see true talent in you ladies, he never would've made the offer." He gave Courtney his undivided attention. "And, Courtney, you're a shark. Joseph could see that immediately. He knew he had to bring you in and make you a part of the team, or you would've busted the entire operation."

Eyes nodded his agreement. Courtney smiled. She enjoyed being good at her job. Eyes felt the same way about his work. The more he was around this woman, the more he wanted to be right where he was.

A few more questions were fired off, and then the group agreed to split up and focus on where each person was needed the most. The first time in the operations center was a privilege, and the women didn't want to waste a moment of their time.

Courtney, Erin, and Eyes stayed in the conference room, and before the last person left Courtney was back in reporter mode, ripping off questions quicker than Eyes could process what was being asked. She had an uncanny ability to know how to dig into a subject so deeply that the person being interviewed didn't know which way was up or down.

Eyes held up his hand and Courtney stopped speaking . . . for a second. "I told you I'd answer all of your questions, and I will, but there needs to be just a little bit of patience while I give you answers." He then looked at Erin. "Don't forget we also have a third partner here," he said with a wink to Erin who he was a big fan of.

"I don't know if I want to interrupt. I like watching Courtney when she's on a roll," Erin said with a laugh.

Eyes gave her a mock glare. "And I was just thinking about how much I liked you," he told her. That made both Erin and Courtney laugh. "Okay, ladies give me your best," he finished.

And boy, did they. For the next hour, they grilled Eyes, demanding video, asking intelligent questions on the operation, and trying to drag out every ounce of information he had. He wouldn't be surprised if they had his birth time, weight, and size of his newborn feet by the time the day was finished. Erin might come off as somewhat shy, but when she was in the zone she was as much of a shark as Courtney.

"Okay, enough," Eyes finally said, his eyes burning, and his mind fried. He hadn't gotten nearly enough sleep to do this any longer.

"We've barely even started!" Courtney said with a huff.

"I'm going to find Brackish and see what I can drag out of him," Erin said with a wink before she exited, leaving Eyes and Courtney alone.

"Come on, Eyes, just a few more questions," Courtney said, her voice seductive, her smile innocent, and her eyes sparkling. Eyes could see how the woman always got her story. Damn, she was good. He smiled right back, coming up with an instant plan.

"I have a proposition for you," Eyes said smoothly.

"What?" Courtney asked, looking suspicious.

"If you agree to go to dinner with me, I'll give you three hours of questions with no excuses or breaks," Eyes said. He might regret the three hours part but he really wanted this woman to go on a date with him, and she hadn't been cooperative so far, even though the sexual chemistry between them was enough to light up an NFL stadium.

"I don't know why you think you're so slick. Trying to bribe me into going on a date with you isn't the most romantic gesture in the world. Also, I could always tell Joseph you aren't playing nice," Courtney replied, a mischievous smile forming on her soft pink lips.

"You're correct, you could tell him. I could also tell him I'm too busy working on my mission to help you," Eyes said. He could play chicken with the best of the best. She didn't stand a chance.

Courtney assessed him and he could see the wheels turning in her brilliant brain. He also knew the second he won. He wanted to jump into the air and have a *Rocky* moment. Victory was so sweet.

"*One* dinner. That's it. And if you try to back out of answering my questions, I'll make your life a living hell, don't think I won't," Courtney said, her eyes putting some weight behind what she said.

"Deal." Eyes stuck out his hand for a shake to finalize the verbal contract.

She took it and both of them let the hold last a little bit longer than what would otherwise be socially acceptable. Eyes knew it was only a matter of time before they were both deeply and fully satisfied. He'd have no trouble sleeping that night — not when he was getting closer to the prize he hadn't known he'd wanted until he'd crash-landed into this woman who made his heart soar.

It was time to play — and he made sure he was *always* the victor.

CHAPTER FOUR

There were times a man didn't know which way was up and which was down. There were times a man questioned who he was and what he'd done and where he was going. There were times that just didn't make sense.

This was one of those times for Joseph Anderson.

His life was a dream. Many had said he was blessed with the touch of Midas. There were others who said he'd been blessed by the gods. There were many who believed he'd made a deal with the devil.

Joseph rolled his eyes as he walked next to his nephew Damien Whitfield into the county jail. No one saw the gesture.

The reality for Joseph was that he'd made it to where he was because he'd worked hard and never took no for an answer. He'd gone after what he'd wanted from a very early age and he'd never believed he could be anything less than the best. He hadn't questioned his decisions even when he'd been hit the hardest — and that had happened more than once.

Instead of letting logjams slow him down, he'd used the opportunities to build bridges. He wasn't a man to give up, and he wasn't a man who liked to leave questions unanswered. Even with all of the confidence in the world, Joseph was still a man, and he still had highs and lows.

The lowest point in his entire life was thinking he might lose his dear wife. He loved his family, couldn't imagine life without them, but at the end of the day, it was Katherine and him in the center of his universe. He knew he wouldn't get off of his knees if he were to lose her. No matter what came, he could face it as long as he did it next to his wife.

He'd recently discovered that Katherine was in the beginning stages of dementia. His heart had cracked at the news. He'd gone through all of the expected emotions when learning the center of his universe would slowly be pulled from him — grief, anger, disbelief . . .

Once Joseph had accepted his wife would go through a new journey in life though, he'd realized it didn't matter. She'd still be by his side, and he'd be by hers. Even if he had to remind her every hour on the hour of who he was, it didn't matter — she'd still be with him. He loved her, and he didn't mind telling her the story of their love over and over again.

"ID's please."

Joseph and Damien had reached the front desk of the county jail. The man in front of them, looking weary as if he'd had a very long week, didn't alter his expression. Joseph felt for the man, knowing he had to deal with the scum of the earth on a daily basis. Joseph didn't understand how anyone could smile while working in a world of liars and cowards. That's how Joseph looked at criminals.

Sure, some of them had a legitimate excuse as to why they'd fallen into a world of crime, but Joseph believed a person's integrity was stronger than any obstacle that could be thrown their way.

"I don't see the point in going in here," Damien said as he pulled out his driver's license and placed it through the opening of the bulletproof glass.

"Because we aren't cowards," Joseph told his nephew. "We need to find out why Anna Miller has said she's your sister."

Damien sighed. "Even if she was born to the woman who raised me, we now know that wasn't my birth mother," Damien pointed out. "So, I don't see *how* she's my sister."

"That's why we're here," Joseph told him.

"I won't believe anything she says."

The guard had them sign in, and then a door opened, and they were escorted back to a small room and told to wait while they brought the prisoner in.

Though it seemed as if Damien had been a part of their family for his entire life, Joseph had learned about his nephew when Damien was already an adult. Joseph's uncle Nielson had been a terrible, terrible man. He'd carried on multiple relationships and had produced several children he'd kept from the Anderson family out of spite. He'd never cared about the women he'd been with, and he'd never cared about his children.

A few years earlier Joseph had discovered five more nephews when their mother had been on her death bed and confessed to Joseph she'd been too ashamed to come to him. Joseph didn't hold a grudge against her. She'd had a very difficult life and done the best she could. She'd raised fine sons, though, and Joseph now got to be a part of their lives. Damien was still getting to know his siblings. It would take time, but Joseph was sure they'd all be one big happy family before too long.

Today was about discovering who in the hell this Anna Miller was, and why she was claiming to be Damien's sister. If that were the case, she'd also be the sibling of his other five nephews, but she hadn't mentioned them. It was either a cruel game, or she was trying to get something from the vast fortune the Andersons possessed. It was a toss-up as to what the end game was for Anna Miller.

The door opened and Anna walked inside. Joseph nearly didn't recognize her. The former US Senator had always been so polished and poised, her hair styled to perfection, her face a perfect mask, and her clothes expensive and fitted. The woman approaching them wore a smirk on her haggard face, a rumpled orange suit, and her previously silky black hair was frizzy and ladled with grey. Jail hadn't been good to her.

"Enjoying the show?" Anna asked as she moved to the opposite side of the table from Joseph and Damien. "Jail's just been wonderful for me," she added with a smirk.

"Forget this jail, prison's where you belong," Damien said, his expression blank. Damien wasn't going to give the woman the power of letting her see he was tense and angry. It was more than clear that Anna Miller thrived on power — power over people, emotions, and the end goal of power over the entire United States. Thankfully, she'd never make it to the highest office in the land. Joseph shuddered at the thought of her being President of the United States. It could've been close had she not been caught. She was charismatic and had once had a huge following.

Her incarceration had dwindled following the criminal action but hadn't completely eliminated it. There were still some who believed in her innocence.

"I won't be here long. You see, my dear brother, I have a lot of friends, more than you can imagine. They don't want me here. I also hold a lot of secrets that nobody wants to get out," she said, leaning back, confidence shining in her eyes.

"If you hold so much power, don't you worry they'll simply off you?" Damien asked, still not showing a lick of emotion.

Anna laughed. She was so good at faking emotion, Joseph honestly couldn't say if the sound was real or not. What a depressing life to live when it was all a farce. Did Anna even know how she felt at any given moment? She was so used to putting on a show, Joseph wondered if she knew who she really was.

"We didn't come here for idle chitchat. You dropped a bomb to a reporter that you're my sister. I'd like to know how you came to that conclusion," Damien said. The words came out matter-of-factly as if he didn't care one way or the other if she answered. Joseph held back a smile. The way Damien was speaking to her was certainly getting to Anna. She didn't like it when she didn't feel in control. That was more than obvious.

Joseph decided to sit back and watch the exchange instead of piping in. Maybe he was mellowing in his older years. Normally, he'd run the entire conversation. Of course, he did have a lot on his mind these days so maybe it was time to let the kids solve their own problems. He'd have to think through how he felt about that. If he wasn't meddling he wasn't sure he'd have meaning in his life. That thought almost made him chuckle.

"I don't know if I'll give you that answer," Anna said.

Damien stood. "Okay then, I hope you have a nice day." He moved toward the door. Joseph stood as well. He wondered if Damien really cared that little. Joseph was curious, but this was about his nephew, not him. That was a difficult concept for Joseph to accept.

"Where are you going?" Anna screeched as she stood and leaned her cuffed hands on the table.

Damien only half turned, his hand hovering over the buzzer that would tell the guard he wanted to leave. "I told you I really don't care if you tell me or not. If you have something to say I'll listen. What I won't do is sit here and play games with you. I have zero feelings toward you — zip, zero, nada. I don't care if you're alive or dead. I don't care enough to read the articles about you that come out once in a blue moon as you're slowly forgotten. I agreed to come in, but that was only because other people wanted answers. I think you're a liar, and I think this is a waste of my valuable time."

Joseph realized his nephew meant what he said. He didn't care what Anna had to say. Joseph looked at Anna and realized she knew he wasn't bluffing. She deflated right before their eyes. In her few months in jail she'd shrunk. She tried to keep up her persona of a powerful woman, but each day she was incarcerated she lost a little more of herself. Joseph wondered if she regretted any of her choices. He somehow doubted it.

"Fine, no games," Anna said as she sat back down. Joseph could normally read people very well, but in this case he wasn't sure if she was still playing games or if she'd been slapped down so hard she'd been defeated — at least in this round.

Damien shrugged, turned back around, and sat down. Joseph moved back to his chair and joined his nephew. They both waited without saying another word.

"We have the same father, which I know doesn't shock you. I'm ten years younger than you, as you know." She paused and Joseph knew that both he and Damien were doing math in their heads. If she was ten years younger than Damien, their father had still been alive, but he'd been with Damien's biological mother at that time. It didn't shock either of them that Nielson had been with other women though. He'd done that his entire life.

"And how did you come to this conclusion?" Damien asked.

"Because he lived with my mother until I was ten years old. The first few years he hadn't been around much, but when I was five he moved in and didn't leave again until I was ten."

This time Joseph wasn't able to hide his shock. How did the despicable life of Nielson Anderson keep on getting worse and worse? How many times could a man fake his own death?

"Did you see him die?" Damien asked coldly.

"I was at his funeral . . ." She paused. "And it was open casket. There was no faking it that time."

Joseph was almost shocked. Even though Neilson would be about a hundred years old at this point if he were living, there was a part of Joseph that had believed the man might one day show up on his doorstep. It wouldn't have shocked Joseph one bit.

"How did he die?" Damien asked. The shock had gone away and he'd moved on. Maybe they'd all feel a bit of relief, knowing for sure that Neilson was either buried eight feet in the ground or burned up.

"My mother killed him," Anna simply said. Neither Joseph nor Damien blinked.

"Seems about right," Damien said.

Anna laughed, this time the sound coming out a little hysterical.

"My mother didn't get blamed for his death. She was far too smart for that, but she'd had enough of him. She also knew all about you, Finn, Noah, Brandon, Hudson, and Crew. She didn't care. She did check on them." She laughed again. "She even made friends with your mother who lived a couple of hours away from our home. She wanted to see who the competition was. She hadn't minded sharing him for several years. When he'd grown bored with your mother he'd left and come to us to live full time. She knew there were other women, but one day she'd had enough."

Damien didn't ask how her mother had killed him, but Anna kept talking.

"She took her time offing our dear old dad. She put just a little poison in his food every day for two months. He grew weaker and sicker but didn't figure it out. Finally, he had a heart attack in his sleep. He lay in that bed gasping for air as he clutched his chest, begging my mother to call an ambulance. She'd stood over him, brushing her hair as she told him what she'd been doing. He'd died with acceptance in his eyes as if he'd known it would eventually happen."

"Did your mother tell you about us or did you overhear something? I'm still not convinced we're related," Damien said.

"I knew about you from the time I was three. My mother made sure to shape me into the woman I am today. She told me she'd had to play a part to survive, but I wouldn't have the same life. She told me to get my revenge on the family who had so much."

"Neilson left a lot of bitter women out there," Damien said with a shrug. He'd heard this story before and he didn't even blink at Anna's words. He'd once been angry too: at the injustices his fake mother had convinced him had been done to her and Damien. He'd gotten over it all, gotten over the bitterness, the need for revenge, and the lies that had been hard to get from his head.

"Yes, I've followed you a long time," Anna said. "I liked you better when you were a man seeking revenge on the world like I always have."

This time Damien laughed. The sound wasn't full of joy, but Joseph realized his nephew really had healed from the many wounds inflicted upon him from the time he was young.

"I was angry, Anna, for a lot of years. When a lie has been set in a person's mind, it's nearly impossible to change. No matter how much truth is thrown at them, they still believe the lie. It's really odd. I don't know if I would've realized my fake mother had been lying to me if it hadn't been for the love of an incredible woman. Lucky for me, I did realize the truth, and I let it all go."

"Well, isn't that just wonderful for you," Anna said, meaning anything but the words she was saying.

"It was great for me," Damien told her. "The best part was I let go of my anger, and I now have an incredible wife and daughter, and a family who truly does love me. What is your anger getting you?"

She glared at him, no longer having fun with the game she thought she'd control. Before she could say anything more, Damien shrugged as he looked her right in the eyes. If he was playing a game of chicken, he was the clear winner.

"You *might* be my sister. I *might* have a dozen more siblings out there. If they come to me honestly and want to know me, I'm more than willing to sit down and see if we get along. But *you*, I don't like. I don't care if you are related or not. You have nothing to offer me or my family other than misery. Just because we *possibly* share some DNA doesn't make us family, and it never will. I came here because I was asked to, but I feel nothing for you, not anger, not love, and not even pity. I will walk out of this room and I won't think about you. There might be times you cross my mind, but it will be a fleeting moment and will disappear into a puff of smoke. I have no desire to take a DNA test, I have no desire to pursue this further."

With those words Damien stood up. Joseph, for once in his life, didn't know what in the hell to say or even think about his nephew's words. He stood up too, knowing this conversation was over.

"How dare you dismiss me," Anna screeched. She stood and moved around the table just as Damien rang the bell to let him out of the room. Right before Anna could grab him, he turned and wrapped a large hand around her wrist, quickly stopping her. He didn't look rattled in the least as the door opened and a sheriff stepped inside.

"We're done here," Damien said as he let go of Anna's wrist. He took another step as Anna shrieked and launched herself toward Damien again.

"I will kill you," she shouted. She started to say something more, but a gurgle came out as the officer tased her. She fell to the ground. Damien turned around, his expression blank.

"I will tell my brothers about you and let it be their choice if they want to know anything about you. I'm done, though."

With those words he walked away from Anna Miller with Joseph at his side. Neither of them spoke as they exited the jail. They moved through the parking garage and stepped into the vehicle. Damien didn't start it and Joseph waited to hear what his nephew had to say. His expression hadn't changed.

After about two minutes of silence, just when Joseph felt as if he was going to burst if he didn't say something, Damien turned to him, a relaxed smile on his face.

"That was fun," he said. A chuckle came out. Joseph was shocked at his words and didn't know what to say. Then Damien laughed harder. Joseph joined him. The two of them sat there for several minutes as they laughed. The situation was so odd that neither of them knew what else to do.

"I wonder how many more kids are going to come out of the woodwork," Joseph finally said as he wiped tears from his eyes. It felt good to laugh. It had been too long since he'd had a gut-hurting laughing session.

"I don't know and I honestly don't care. I meant what I said, blood doesn't make family, love does."

"No truer words could be spoken. Love is the bridge that brings us all together," Joseph told his nephew, prouder of him than words could say.

Joseph knew a weight had been lifted from his nephew's shoulders. In the end, it really didn't matter if Anna was his sibling or not. The bottom line was she just wasn't family.

CHAPTER FIVE

Courtney didn't understand why she was so nervous. This wasn't a real date, she told herself. She rolled her eyes as she gazed at her reflection in the mirror after having reapplied her lipstick for the third time. If it wasn't a real date, why in the heck did she care how she looked? That was the question of the hour.

She let out a sigh of disgust as she forced herself to turn around, flip off the light, and walk from the bathroom she'd already spent too much time in that evening. The only reason she wanted to hang out for a few hours with Jon Eisenhart, aka Eyes, was because she *needed* information from him. It had nothing whatsoever to do with the butterflies in her stomach.

Her doorbell rang, making Courtney stub her toe as she flipped around and hit a side table in her living room. She let out a very unladylike curse as she hobbled over to her front door. Before opening it she forced herself to take in a few deep breaths to slow her rapidly beating heart.

Her reaction to Eyes picking her up was absurd. She'd been all around the world in reporter mode and had interviewed everyone from soldiers to terrifying world leaders. She was never nervous — until today apparently.

After another few seconds, Courtney plastered a confident smile on her lips, then swung her door open. She made herself look directly into Eyes's face, not even blinking as she licked her lips, very aware of the flare in his eyes as he watched the movement.

"You're late," she said, adding just the perfect mixture of flirtiness and brattiness that she knew turned men on. She hadn't gotten as far as she had in her career without knowing how to keep a subject interested.

Eyes smiled at her, not attempting to move forward, looking as if he had all night dedicated to just her. Maybe he did. The thought of this being a real date with the two of them ending up at her place for some stress relief had her stomach tumbling again.

"I'm three minutes early," Eyes corrected her.

"That, in my book, is late," she told him while she turned and grabbed her small purse and light jacket. She was getting spoiled with the warm Seattle weather. When winter hit with a vengeance she was going to be very sad.

"I'm surprised to hear a lady say that, since it seems men have been waiting on the opposite sex since the beginning of time."

"Yes, men *should* wait on us since we're well worth it. But a lady should never have to wait for a man," she told him. She pushed him back as she stepped out her door, pulled it shut behind her, then moved down the stairs. She was acting as if she were in a hurry, but the reality was, she didn't want to be pressed up against him on her small front porch. Well, if she were being totally honest, she'd admit she *did* want to be pressed up against him, which was why she wasn't allowing that to happen.

Courtney stopped at Eyes's vehicle since it was parked behind hers. She wasn't going to fight him on whose vehicle they were taking. She smiled when he walked up and unlocked the vehicle after his hand was on the handle. She liked a man who opened the door for her. It was a sign of respect she appreciated.

"Thank you," Courtney said. She stepped up to the running board, then stumbled into the SUV as she tripped on the edge of the vehicle. She went flying forward, landing with her chest on the middle console and her ass in the air.

She heard a chuckle followed by a cough behind her as she quickly flew back up and planted her butt in the seat. She turned and glared at Eyes whose lips were twitching as he desperately tried not to let out the roar of laughter she knew he was desperately trying to hold in.

He didn't say a word as he shut her door, but her entire body tensed as she heard his muffled chuckle as he walked behind the SUV, taking his time to join her in the vehicle. She wanted to shoot laser beams at him when he finally climbed in, but she had to admit to herself she'd be laughing at him if their situations were reversed.

"That was quite the entrance," Eyes said as he started the vehicle.

"Ugh, you could at least *pretend* to be a gentleman and act as if that didn't just happen," she told him.

"What fun would that be?" he asked. He pulled onto the street and began driving. At least he'd stopped laughing.

"Well, it would be a lot more fun for me," she pointed out.

"You're telling me you wouldn't laugh if I'd been the one to splay out all over the car and show you *my* fine ass?"

Her own lips twitched at his words. "I guess you did get a bit of a show." She wasn't embarrassed he'd gotten a view of her red panties. Even though there was no way she'd have sex with him that night she loved wearing sexy underwear. It made her feel feminine and more confident knowing she had sexy lace beneath her conservative clothes. Her dress was knee length, perfectly modest for any place he might take her, but when stumbling around, making the skirt fly up, all modesty went out the window.

"Red's my favorite color," he said as he turned to briefly look at her and give her a wink. A blush stole over her cheeks. She wasn't shy, and she was a master at flirting, but somehow, she felt a little shy around this incredibly sexy man. That was new for her.

They drove through town, making meaningless small talk. She wanted to grill him, but she figured she'd get a few glasses of wine in him first. That might loosen him up and get her the information she desperately wanted.

It didn't take them long to arrive at an intimate Italian restaurant she'd never been to before. He helped her from the vehicle, and she didn't say a word as he put his hand on her back while they moved down the walk to the front door.

"Hello, Jon, it's good to see you again," the host said as they moved forward. They were quickly seated, and Courtney looked around the small dining room, only holding a dozen tables. The room was dim, the tables lit with flickering candles, and the walls were adorned with sconces that didn't add much light. The place had been built for romance.

"Could you have found a more intimate place?" Courtney asked with a chuckle. The man was pulling out all the stops.

"I don't think so," Eyes said. "The food is phenomenal though. Mama Aida makes homemade pasta, sauces, and unique dishes every morning. When she runs out, the restaurant closes. She refuses to serve anything less than the best, and believe me, it is better than the best. That's why the menu is limited."

"Good evening. I'm Giovani. Can I start you off with drinks?" their waiter asked as he approached with a pitcher and a bottle of wine.

"Yes, what's Mama Aida suggesting tonight?" Eyes smoothly asked.

"Ah, for you, sweet boy, I will make it a surprise," a large woman said as she moved from behind half doors and approached their table. She moved up to them, then bent down with worn fingers and gripped Eyes's cheeks before she leaned in and kissed each side. "I heard your voice and had to come out. I see you've wised up and have brought me a beautiful woman instead of those obnoxious men you're normally here with."

"Yes, she's much prettier than the boys," Eyes said as he reached up and gently gripped her fingers. "But you know you're always the most beautiful woman in the room."

Mama Aida chuckled as she looked at Courtney with a sparkle in her eyes. "This is a good man here. He's worth the trouble he'll surely put you through."

"Hmm, we'll have to see about that," Courtney said with a laugh. She instantly loved the woman.

"Ah, a woman with spirit. You will be good for Jon," Mama Aida said with a nod. She looked so serious, Courtney found herself squirming. She'd had a friend all through high school who was half Italian and her full Italian mother had seemed to have a sixth sense on matches. If she said a couple was meant to be, every single time they ended up married. Italian mamas seemed to possess magic. Courtney suddenly wanted to run from the restaurant before Mama Aida pronounced Eyes and her as a perfect couple.

"Don't worry, sweet girl, I won't make any predictions tonight," Mama Aida said, as if the woman was a mind reader.

"Thank you," Courtney said, not even trying to hide her relief.

Mama Aida left and the waiter waited for them to order. "We'll take whatever Mama sends out," Jon said. "That is if Courtney doesn't mind," he added, keeping him from getting into trouble.

"That sounds good to me," Courtney said.

"Wine?" Giovani asked.

"We'll take the pairings with the food," Jon said. Courtney nodded her agreement. She hadn't been a wine drinker for years, but now she'd discovered if she listened to the waiters and sommeliers who knew good pairings, she liked a variety of flavors.

Their first course was an antipasto platter with a divine red wine. Everything was going better than the way the evening started off with Courtney stubbing her toe and face planting in Eyes's vehicle. They chatted and Courtney's fingers itched to grill the man on the operation she was now involved in. She was a smart woman though, and knew he needed to loosen up a little bit more before she'd get anything.

Their second course of fresh, lightly breaded calamari arrived, and Eyes was two drinks in, so Courtney was about to start asking questions. She reached across the table to dip a piece of calamari into the warm marinara sauce when she felt heat on her arm.

Before she could figure out what was happening, Eyes was on his feet, water glass in hand. What the heck? He suddenly tossed the water at her, soaking her arm and sending droplets of water over the front of her dress and into her face.

She sat in stunned silence as she looked at the man in front of her, too shocked to say a word. The waiter came out of nowhere with a rag, another young man on his heels as they handed her a towel and quickly began cleaning their table.

"I'm so sorry," Giovani said as he cleared their table in seconds. "I forgot to put the lid on your candle. Are you okay? Do you need a doctor? Should I call 911?"

Courtney was confused as she turned her arm around and saw the scorch marks on her sleeve. "Was I on fire?" she asked.

Eyes looked as if he was in a panic as he gazed at her. "Didn't you feel the flames? Your arm was on fire," he gasped.

"I felt heat but just thought I was too close to the candle," she said. "I didn't know why you were throwing water at me."

Eyes gripped her hand and turned it over in his grasp, examining her skin. Somehow it wasn't scorched at all. The material had caught on fire and he'd doused it before it could do any damage. Giovani was standing there looking a bit pale.

"Wow, I can't believe you didn't feel that," Eyes said. He looked much better now that he knew she wasn't hurt. Well, that wasn't entirely true. Her pride had taken another hit.

"I'm fine, Giovani. I appreciate your quick thinking," she told the waiter. "I don't need 911. Maybe we can get another plate of that calamari though. It was delicious."

Giovani looked as if he wanted to argue, but he decided to just nod and rush off to the kitchen. The boy who'd cleared everything off of their table quickly reset it — no candle this time — and then disappeared. Giovani was back very quickly with new calamari.

It didn't take long for Mama Aida to come out and insist dinner was on her that night. Courtney didn't want to do that. This was a very small business and the woman worked incredibly hard. To lose a full dinner wouldn't be good for her bottom line.

"Don't worry. I'll leave a *very* good tip," Eyes said as if he could read her thoughts. She smiled at him, appreciating that he was thinking of the very kind business owner.

Courtney managed to get a few questions in for Eyes, who seemed very happy to answer them after her small disaster. That made her feel better about the loss of one of her favorite dresses. It was well worth the damage if she could get a good story.

Before she could get too far into her questions, though, a large plate of spaghetti was set in the center of the table, with small plates to the side so they could each take servings for themselves.

"There's no possible way we can eat all of this," Courtney said, surprised at the sheer amount of food.

Eyes laughed. "This is a normal serving for me," he told her. "But I'm willing to share."

She wondered if he was telling her the truth. Could he eat a serving all by himself that seemed to be made for at least four people? She was tempted not to take any and see how he did. If she wasn't so hungry, and it didn't smell so good, she might just do that.

She grabbed the spoon, about to scoop some of the steaming pasta onto her plate when Eyes took her hand, stopping her.

"What?" she asked.

"I've always wanted to do something," he said. "Would you indulge me?"

She looked at him in suspicion. If it meant she wasn't going to get to eat, then it was a hands-down no. She was getting hungrier by the second, even with the incredible appetizers they'd already shared. She hadn't had homemade pasta in a very long time.

"Have you watched *Lady and the Tramp*?" he asked.

It took a few seconds for Courtney to realize what he was talking about. When she did, she burst out in laughter. "Are you kidding me?" she asked.

He shook his head. "Come on. Be adventurous," he challenged as he held up his fork.

Courtney laughed again. "Are you going to push a meatball over to me with your nose?" she asked.

This time he laughed as he twirled his fork in the pasta and took a bite. It was so cheesy it was making her mouth water.

"That's just plain unsanitary," he said. "We only get to kiss if we happen on the same pasta noddle." With the amount of food on the plate, Courtney didn't see that happening.

She didn't argue anymore, just stuck her fork into the noodles and pulled up a perfect mouthful with a piece of tomato, a lot of cheese, and a chunk of ground veal. The flavors burst on her tongue and she was glad she was wearing a dress. If she had tight pants on, she would've definitely needed to undo them after the amount of food she was planning to consume.

They ate in silence for a few minutes, and then Eyes was reaching closer and closer to her side of the plate as he twirled pasta noodles on the tines of his fork. She was slowing down, her stomach getting fuller. She wanted to stretch out the meal, enjoying the different flavors with each bite. It was clear Mama Aida used several different ground meats in her sauce, and Courtney wasn't sure which spices she used, but it was a perfect combination.

Courtney laughed when she felt Eyes's fork clang against hers. He was trying so hard to get the same noodle. She got the giggles for some reason and right after she took a bite, he made a joke, and that was all it took for her to choke on her own bite, and then, much to her horror, she watched sauce fly from her mouth and land all over the front of Eyes's shirt.

Her laughter died as his white shirt and the crisp white tablecloth became spotted with fat dollops of red. She covered her mouth when she felt the giggles start up again. What was wrong with her tonight?

"Was that payback for the water?" Eyes finally asked as he wiped off any sauce he was able to. His words made Courtney laugh even more.

"I don't know what in the heck is wrong with me tonight. I'm not usually this klutzy or this unsophisticated," she insisted.

"Hmm, so you're telling me this is all because of me?" he questioned.

"I guess so," she said between giggles. "I did warn you it wouldn't be wise for us to go on a date."

He looked thoughtful for a moment. "Well, there's one thing for sure, though," he said.

"What's that?" she asked.

"This date will *not* be forgettable."

She laughed more. "I can guarantee you this date will never be forgotten," she told him.

They finished their pasta, had tiramisu and spiked coffee for dessert, and then before Courtney was ready, the date was over. It was time to go home. Mama Aida still refused payment for the meal, so Eyes left a monstrous tip instead, knowing Giovani would pass it out amongst the staff, including Mama Aida.

The two of them made it back to his vehicle with no more incidents, and Courtney took her time getting back into it, not willing to show him her panties at the end of their evening after they'd both consumed alcohol and were feeling a lot more relaxed. She was sure that would lead to something she didn't want it to lead to — well, she did want it to lead to that, but she wasn't going to allow that to happen. Sex fogged the brain and she needed to be clear thinking around this man.

Courtney attempted to ask a few more questions on the drive, but he was giving her shorter and shorter answers. Dang it. She hadn't gotten nearly enough answered. Was he doing that on purpose so she'd have to invite him in? If that's what he was thinking, he'd be sorely out of luck. There was no doubt in her mind that if she invited him in, they'd end up in her bed, and she in no could allow that to happen. She'd have to keep telling herself that over and over again because she hadn't wanted something that badly in a very long time. She knew, however, that she'd regret it in the morning. She was sure of it. Right now, she didn't know why she'd regret it, but she was sure she would.

They arrived at her house; he shut off the vehicle and began to get out. She stopped him.

"You don't need to walk me to the door," she told him.

He looked at her as if she was crazy, and then he climbed from the car. There was no way a man like Eyes wouldn't walk a woman to the door. Yes, he'd be hoping for a kiss, but beyond that, he was a gentleman. He might laugh a lot, and he might like hanging with the boys, but he *truly* was a gentleman. She liked that about him.

Courtney hated the end of dates. She never knew what to say. She'd gone on many first dates in the last ten years, but she rarely went on a second one. The guys never interested her enough on the first to make a second worthy. She'd actually had a lot of fun with Eyes that night and wouldn't mind a second with him. However, she didn't want to admit that to him or to herself.

"This was a very unique night," Eyes said as the two of them stopped by her front door.

"I can certainly say it was unforgettable," Courtney told him.

"I've never had another date quite like it," Eyes said. He sidled just a bit closer.

"Do we really need to do the first kiss at the end of the date?" Courtney asked, trying to put a lot of sass in her voice, but not quite pulling it off. There was too much huskiness underneath the snarky words.

Eyes laughed. "Of course we do," he said.

He began leaning in for the kiss, and Courtney decided to take the power into her own hands. If there was going to be a kiss, then she was going to be the one to do it. She wasn't letting him lead the night.

She moved in quickly just as he was descending . . . and their mouths crashed together — and not in a good way. Courtney let out a yelp as she tasted blood from her tooth digging into her lip. She jumped back and stared at him. He looked horrified as if nothing like that had ever happened to him before.

Just when Courtney was about to apologize, not really sure who'd been at fault for the crash, Eyes leaned back and laughed . . . hard. She wasn't sure if she should be horrified or join him in laugher. After a few seconds she went with the latter. They both laughed for a solid minute before their sparkling eyes met again.

"I guess every sign in the universe is telling us we shouldn't date ever again, if for nothing else, then for the safety of anyone who might come into contact with us while we're on a date," she said.

Eyes shook his head. "Nope, the universe is demanding a do-over," he told her. "I'll have to get a bit more creative in what I plan. Dinner dates are lame anyway. I know better than that."

"What makes you think I'd accept another date? I said one for an interview which you now owe me since I didn't get more than four questions answered tonight," she said.

"I'll give you a real interview with us behind glass so no one gets hurt, but *only* if you give me a proper do-over. It is the right thing to do or else my pride will be forever damaged," he insisted.

Courtney realized she wouldn't mind that at all. Neither of them had died, and it had been an adventure. Everything that could've gone wrong most certainly had, but like he'd said, if they'd had an ordinary date, she'd have forgotten it in a heartbeat.

"Fine. But make it better than this one. I can get dinner on my own every night of the week," she said with a wink. She had enjoyed the restaurant he'd taken her to, but she did like a more adventurous date if she were being honest.

He looked at her as if he was going to throw out a new challenge and Courtney decided it was time to run. She'd give him time to figure out how to impress her. She quickly went into her house and shut the door without telling him goodnight. He let her go. She heard him whistling as he walked back down her path. She listened as he shut his car door, and then peeked through the window as he pulled away.

It was true that their night had been a disaster. They hadn't even gotten that kiss. But an hour later, he was all that was on her mind. She'd been turned on by this man for a very long time, years actually, but that was without knowing him. She'd been turned on by the interview she'd had with him and his friend and how confident he was even as his body had been torn up.

With the man back to peak performance she wasn't sure how she was going to react. Even though their first date had been a disaster, it had also been sort of magical. Who wanted romance and gifts when they could have laughter and adrenaline? She was far more the adrenaline kind of woman. She wondered what that meant for the next time . . .

CHAPTER SIX

The morning of the federal trial against Anna Miller, former senator and a front runner for President of the United States of America, had arrived. She'd been loved by many without them having any idea of who she truly was.

Joseph and Damien stood together. They'd been silent for a full minute, maybe a new record for Joseph. He squirmed as he looked at his nephew.

"Are you sure about this?" Joseph asked.

"Yes," Damien replied without hesitation.

"Okay. I'm going to honor your decision, but I don't know if I'd make the same one. What Anna did to you, and to your family, is horrific — being your sister makes it worse. I . . ." Joseph was going to go down a list of reasons why family should treat each other with as much respect as possible, but he forced himself to stop. He needed to do what he said, and that meant honoring Damien's decision.

"I sent over the request to remove all aspects of the civil lawsuit against Anna to the lawyers ten minutes ago," Damien said. "I find no joy in this situation, but I know once this trial is over she'll be in prison for a large portion of her life, maybe until she dies. What's to be gained, other than ripping the financial rug out from under her? Honestly, it's taken more time and energy than anyone thought. I don't mind discussing the reasons in more detail but I'd rather not. She isn't worth my time."

"Then it won't be spoken of again, my boy," Joseph said to his nephew.

The two shook hands and turned toward the courtroom doors. As they entered the room a cacophony of sounds rushed over them. The entire space behind the barrier between the lawyers and the crowd was at full capacity. Not only were all of the seats filled with an occupant but so was every space that could be found to stand. Most in the standing-room-only section held cameras and press badges around their necks.

The judge, the honorable Macy R. Scott, had a long conversation with both the attorney general and Anna Miller's counsel, making it abundantly clear that in a case such as this the entire world needed to see how the justice system in America worked. As long as the media maintained decorum, and respected her courtroom, they'd be able to record every minute of the proceedings. She then told the legal teams it was expected that neither side would try to play this trial out in the media by giving lengthy interviews about the case or holding press conferences each day on how the ebb and flow of the trial was going.

Neither side liked the last part of the judge's mandate but agreed anyway. The judge had a strong record of being fair in the face of facts and well-played strategies within the law, but she didn't suffer a fool when it came to those who attempted to lead her, or her courtroom, by the nose by a lawyer who tried to play to the emotions of the court through the media.

More than once she'd thrown a lawyer out of her courtroom and a handful of times had found an attorney in contempt of court. None of those who were thrown out or found in contempt had complained that it was done unjustly. Judge Miller was tough but more than fair in letting everyone know where the line was, and that line was *never* allowed to be crossed. Those who did never crossed it again.

Joseph and Damien walked into the courtroom to two open seats that had been reserved for them, directly behind the attorney general. The rest of the row was taken up by men and women of the Anderson family. They all agreed to take turns attending the trial. While it was feasible for them to all show up, it would've been too much for the courtroom to handle. If they'd all wanted to come, the trial would've needed to be moved to a sports stadium.

"You know, this is the first time I've ever sat in on a trial. I wish it wasn't such a volatile situation and I wasn't involved in any way because it would be interesting to sit here and take in all sides of the story," Damien said to Joseph and Chad, who was sitting next to the patriarch of the family.

"Nah, when you have no emotions invested in the trial it's rather dry and mundane," Chad said.

"I agree. There's a big difference between being invested in the event and not caring about the outcome," Joseph added.

The crowd behind them went from a low murmur of conversations between colleagues to an instant snap of silence as the door to the side of the courtroom opened. An officer walked through with Anna Miller in tow. She wore a fine suit, but handcuffs hadn't been considered when it had been made.

It was obvious that a great deal of care had gone into beautifying the former senator, but the woman who'd previously been a true powerhouse in the Seattle area and beyond, now looked weak, meager, and a shell of her former self. Even though she'd been broken, she still held her head high. Even with a confident step in her walk, you could see the shallowness in her eyes. Jail had a tendency to do that to even the strongest of people. Before she sat with her legal team, the officer released her from the shackles.

Once Anna was seated, the hushed conversations slowly started again. All of the cameras were pointed at the back of Anna's head, each operator hoping she'd angle her face toward their lens, allowing them to get *the shot* to start off the trial, knowing it would be streamed and shared by almost every person in the country. Unfortunately for all of the media Anna didn't turn, didn't acknowledge them, didn't even give them anything to report other than she was there and was responding to her attorneys as they spoke. Even the coffee cup she drank from was focused on, but it wasn't newsworthy as there were only so many ways someone could discuss a plain white cup with a lid fastened atop.

Another five minutes passed before the jurors were brought into the courtroom. Seven women and five men made up the jury. Almost all of them looked terrified to be put in the position of having a packed courtroom looking directly at them, with cameras focused on their faces. As they sat in their respective chairs, some of the jurors looked around at the sea of faces while others barely moved their eyes from the top of their shoes.

"All rise for the honorable Macy R. Scott; this court is now in session," the bailiff bellowed.

The judge came in, asked everyone to sit, and had the bailiff swear in the jurors.

"I've spoken with members of the media already, but I need this to be heard by all in attendance, and for those who will be attending at any point during this trial," the judge said, pausing and meeting several of the audience's eyes. "I won't tolerate outbursts, conversations, or interruptions of any kind. If you have cell phones, silence them now. If your phone rings, alarms, or chimes in any way, you and your phone will be removed from my courtroom. I expect each of you are of sound mind and body — meaning you can hold your bathroom breaks until I break for recesses. Emergencies happen and I understand, but if you leave the courtroom before a recess you won't be able to return until we all return. I'm allowing media to be here, and I'll allow you to record on your phones, but your arms cannot be extended out or up in any way. Again, if you do not abide by these courtroom rules, you'll be removed. These expectations might seem harsh, but they're in place to allow the legal teams and the jury to focus on what's presented."

The judge paused again as she looked at the subdued audience. No one in that room wanted to be kicked out for the most exciting case they'd seen in a long time.

"Prosecution, you may start with your opening statement," Judge Scott stated.

"Thank you, your honor," the lawyer said.

It took the prosecuting attorney twenty-three minutes to get through his opening statement. The range of topics he was able to discuss in that timeframe, as well as the ability to create emotions attached to those topics, was incredible. The jurors eyes came to life, their backs straightened, and it was evident to all watching that the storyteller had captured each of the jurors with his cornucopia of words.

The biggest draw was how he managed to lay out how an individual who'd been on the path to becoming president of the United States had used her power to not only manipulate money and power for decades but to physically abuse someone to the point they could've died. At the very end of his monologue he simply said: ". . . and not only was all of this treacherous and horrific in so many ways, but Ms. Miller did all of this to her own brother. He had no idea they were related, but she'd known her entire life and set all of this into motion to ruin his life, and more horrifyingly to end it."

That shocking statement hadn't yet made it into the mainstream media. In fact, even Anna's own lawyers hadn't known of the bombshell the prosecutor had just dropped. The gasps from the attendees, and the reaction from the defendant's table, was usually more than enough for the judge to strike her gavel to gain control of the room, but even she was shocked by the proclamation.

Judge Scott quickly regained her composure and requested the same of the courtroom, but admitted to herself, if that information was true it was going to make things much harder on the defense team. Going after family members never bode well with jurors and at the level Anna had gone after Damien wasn't a good look for the woman currently on trial.

When Anna had blurted out her story to Courtney a few months earlier, Courtney could've gone wide with the information as soon as she'd left the front door of the jail. Courtney was smarter than that, though, and had gone straight to Joseph.

Joseph had then taken the information straight to Damien. That's how they'd ended up at the jail, meeting with Anna. Why Anna hadn't told her lawyers that Damien was her brother, or that she'd met with Joseph and Damien, was a mystery. They weren't sure what she was doing. The prosecutor delivered the news perfectly. The effect on the drooling reporters was like a bolt of lightning.

"Why would he do this to me?" Anna Miller could be heard saying to her counsel.

"Stop. Be quiet. We'll get to that," her attorney replied.

Tears started falling down Anna's face as she looked over at the prosecuting attorney and then at Damien. She just kept mouthing the word *why* while shaking her head in confusion. She brought her head around and faced the jury, so they could all see the fake pain in her face and the tears freely flowing. She wasn't done yet, though. She was good — she was *really* good. She'd perfected her acting abilities. Her time in jail hadn't dimmed that at all.

Anna Miller put both of her hands over her face and started sobbing, her shoulders rolling forward, convulsing almost uncontrollably. Whatever momentum the prosecution had created with the jurors was lost with the outburst from Anna. They hadn't counted on her acting abilities being just as powerful as her desire to destroy Damien.

"She played us, setting all of this up, knowing we'd use it," Damien whispered.

"It's the first throw of the first inning of a very long game. Let's just see how it all ends," Joseph calmly replied. His eyes were carefully examining Anna, and he wasn't going to let on about how impressed he was with the lunatic. He was confident in the prosecutor, who was a shark that would swallow Anna whole during the course of this case. Joseph had no worries at all.

The judge gave multiple warnings to Anna, then to Anna's attorneys, to stop the interruption, and to compose herself before she finally slammed her gavel down and demanded the outburst be contained.

It didn't matter to the jury that Anna seemed to recover quickly from the shock to her soul. Enough of them had softened their hearts at seeing the *poor* woman break down in an obvious state of disbelief. She'd created a sense of doubt in the jurors minds, and that was all she'd needed to do to have a chance of getting out of this mess.

Juries could free the guilty or imprison the innocent — and there was nothing the courts could do about it in an imperfect justice system.

CHAPTER SEVEN

Chad received an invitation to an event for active and former military members to gather at Naval Base Kitsap. The only requirement was that all in attendance wear their full uniform, including medals. The invitation included all five of the special ops team members.

As all of the special ops men had left their previous lives behind, packing next to nothing with them when they'd agreed to their new mission in Seattle, they'd had to send for their dress uniforms and medals, which each of them had kept safe as valuable items not to be lost.

They'd just finished dressing and walked out to the conference room when there was a gasp.

Sleep turned to find his wife, Avery, gaping at him. She slowly approached.

"You're stunning," she told him as she brushed at his chest. No one was fooled that there was a speck of lint on him. She simply wanted to touch her man.

"I don't hold a candle to you," he said before leaning down and kissing her.

"We can agree to disagree," Avery said.

"How in the world did I get so lucky as to marry you?" Sleep asked. He was still in awe of the woman who'd been foolish enough to say yes to his proposal and then to not flee when they were standing at the altar.

"It's me who got lucky." She held her finger up to his mouth and stopped his argument. "We'll just have to agree to disagree on that as well."

"Okay, enough mushiness from the two of you. My wife's insisting on photos before we depart," Chad said.

"Yes, I am. It's not too often I get to see you heathens looking this good," Bree said with a laugh.

The men and their wives posed for several photos before they departed for the Naval base. There was never a dull moment in their lives, and they arrived in the blink of an eye going way past the speed limit, and laughing the entire way there.

"We're here for the event with Captain Leach," Chad said to the sentry standing guard at the entrance of the base. After confirming their identities, the men were given directions to the club where the event was.

"Be on your best behavior, Sleep," Eyes said over his shoulder to Sleep who was in the backseat.

"Always am," Sleep replied. He then gave a nudge to Brackish and mouthed *never*. Both of them laughed.

They stepped out of the van and stood at the entrance for a moment. If there was a more impressive visual representation of military veterans, it would be hard to find. The six men caught the eyes of others walking inside. They were dressed to perfection, their uniforms perfectly fitted, their medals glinting in the afternoon sun, and their physiques outdone by only the smallest percentage of the earth's population.

They walked forward in two groups of three. Chad, Eyes, and Sleep in the front with Green, Smoke, and Brackish behind with perfect cadence. They were the ultimate representation of what the military had built and what the world thought of in terms of military power.

Chad met Captain Leach with a hug, introduced him to the special ops team, and then led the men into the massive room where many people were already engaged in conversation.

"I'm glad to meet you boys," Captain Leach told them. "I only took command of this base a few months ago."

"How's it going?" Chad asked his friend.

"I've noticed a real undercurrent of low morale."

"Is that why you're having this party?" Sleep asked.

"Yes, it's exactly why. I want to show the men and women here who they are and who they can become. That's why I wanted to bring in Chad and all of you," Leach said. "The best of the best are from the military. It's a place boys become men. I hope this event can show the men that they can give their all to the military, and then have a successful transition into civilian life when their time is over."

"It was difficult for me to transition at first," Eyes said. "The military wasn't only my job, it was where I felt I belonged in a world I hadn't fit into before."

"I feel the same," Captain Leach agreed. "I guess that's why I'm still here." He chuckled as they approached a table. "I'm asking retired military to wear this gold medallion on the upper right side of their chest so it's easy for the men to see who is current and who is former military."

"Of course," Eyes said as he stepped forward, grabbing six stars and passing them out to the rest of the men.

Smoke and Brackish stood out among the crowd of sailors and Marines in the room. Both of them were former Army, and their uniform shared little resemblance to the Navy and Marine members who filled the large room.

On a normal day, any one of the special ops men might have received the most attention, for nothing other than the special warfare pin attached to their uniforms, but it was Green's Medal of Honor that created the most buzz. There weren't many given of that most prestigious military medal. As most who received the Medal of Honor would say, they appreciated the accolade, but they didn't feel they'd done anything heroic to receive it. They'd done what anyone else would do in the same circumstance. It made those who received them try to avoid much of the attention the medal brought.

"You know, if you hadn't fallen on your face for Mallory, you'd be my wingman tonight," Eyes said to Green.

"Yeah right, bro. I saw you checking your phone non-stop on the way here. You don't need a wingman, you need a pastor and a chapel," Green replied.

Eyes ignored the reply while scowling as he moved toward the table they'd been assigned.

"You boys have fun tonight. I have to kick off this event," Captain Leach said with a laugh as he walked away. He took the podium, and the room went quiet.

"I want to thank all of you for being here tonight. I have so much respect for those men and women who have paved the way for the rest of us, for those who have sacrificed their time, their bodies, and their minds to protect and serve their fellow citizens. This is done with little acknowledgement, and little pay, but that doesn't matter to most, because it's a calling that must be met."

There were words of agreement shouted out at his words. The captain continued laying out the evening and listing the speakers who'd entertain them during dinner. Most of the men and women in that room enjoyed hearing stories of military in action. Some of them seemed far-fetched, but those who'd served knew just how easy it was for the world to flip upside down in situations of war.

"If you all notice there are two open seats at each table. That's so our current personnel who live on the base can move around and get to talk one-on-one with those who've retired." He paused and looked over to their table and winked at Smoke and Brackish. "I apologize in advance but some of you will have to sit with two former Army soldiers. They're both bigger than I am so I won't make too many jokes, but since they were in the Army, they probably wouldn't understand them anyway. Tyrell and Steve — Chad told me to say that, so if you feel like punching someone go after him."

The room laughed at the time-honored tradition of making fun of other branches of the military. Most of the room stopped when Smoke and Brackish stood and started looking around at those laughing, making a snapping sound as their fists slammed into their open palms. Each person who dared to make eye contact with one of them didn't have the intestinal fortitude to hold the gaze for long.

"Do you two feel good about yourselves, scaring all of the little kids?" Eyes asked, unable to contain his smile.

"Yep," both men said as they sat back down.

As the hours passed, the room became more relaxed. They ate and visited as people shifted in and out of seats. The men were ready to do some of their own shifting as the night progressed, none of them able to sit for too long.

Eyes sat with three young active Navy sailors and one mid-career Marine. The former military members at the table included two twenty-plus-year retired men and a female who'd been an officer. None of them, other than him, held the special warfare pin above their heart.

"I'm Jon Eisenhart. You guys can call me Eyes. I served as a SEAL for a year or thirteen before medically retiring. I'm now in the private sector, leading a specialized security company out of San Francisco. In my free time I enjoy running and gambling on underworld bead stacking competitions," Eyes started after the last person sat.

"The *what* stacking?" one of the young sailors asked.

"Bead stacking competitions. Big money, highly competitive, and quite hush hush but I figure since I'm among friends — who now know I'm a former SEAL — they won't be telling anyone outside of this table. Right?" Eyes asked as he narrowed his eyes. It was all for show.

All three of the young sailors immediately looked away from Eyes as he slowly scanned their faces. Not one of them wanted to challenge a man who'd served as a SEAL, especially knowing that those who'd received the trident pin were incredibly scary —

based on nothing more than what they'd heard about SEALs, almost *all* through rumors.

"You're going to make them piss their pants by the time dinner's over," laughed one of the retired men.

"You guys, he's busting your balls," said the other retired sailor. "No offense," he added looking over at the two women sitting with them.

"Really? I wouldn't be an officer if I was offended that easily, you snowflake," replied Officer Preen as she rolled her eyes. The other sailor nodded her agreement.

Eyes continued on before a reply could be made. Some of the men in the military still had a hard time with ladies serving alongside them. Not all, but some. "Am I really joking?" Eyes asked, again looking at the youngest at the table with a death stare he'd perfected. When the kid really did look as if he was going to piss his pants, Eyes began laughing. "You'll eventually learn that most of us are all talk . . . that is, until action's needed."

Instant relief washed over the young men's faces. But Eyes was pleased to still see respect in their expressions. There was just a tinge of fear there too, but they were fresh off the farm, so he wasn't surprised. A few years of battle would cure that insecurity real fast.

"Marine . . . what do you do here?" Eyes asked.

"I'm stationed here with the Marine Corps Security Force Battalion. I oversee security for the submarines. Been here for two and a half years," the Marine shared.

The table took turns explaining what they did on base or with their lives now that they were out of the military. The three sailors were each attached to submarines, the two retired men were active volunteers within their respective communities, and the former officer worked as the head of engineering for a department with Boeing.

Time flew as people continued moving from table to table and they got to know one another through reminiscing about the good and bad times they'd had in their years of service. Before too long, the event was over. Captain Leach gave a closing statement, thanked everyone for their attendance, then threw out an invite for those who could make it to a night of bowling.

"If you're all of age and want to hear more *colorful stories* let's head to the bowling alley," Eyes said to his current tablemates. "The first round's on me."

Several eager young men and women stood, seeming quite infatuated with Eyes. He couldn't help being as cool as he was. He met up with his team, then gathered more of a crowd as he walked outside, Captain Leach among them.

"I'm off to regale these kids with stories of yesteryear," Eyes said in a terrible British accent.

"No one wants to hear about you learning to read at the age of twenty-eight, you knuckle dragger," Sleep quickly replied.

"True, but they'll want to hear about how you shot me more times than you can count, and I walked away from it with just a little scratch," Eyes said, his well-known goofy smile coming across his face.

All of the men were laughing as they walked through the door of the bowling alley. There was a crowd who'd beat them there. The *youngsters* wanted to spend more time with the only men at the event who, if only by their special operations pins, struck fear into others. Those pins, and what they meant, always brought a lot of attention.

"Okay, I'll share more with you all as I know my life story is better than Disneyland, but I'm also going to kick all of your asses at bowling, so let's shoe up," Eyes said. He had his own pair of shoes but was stuck with the rentals since he hadn't known he'd be bowling that night.

They geared up, then finished a round while he kept the men and women in stitches with his storytelling. Sleep played off of him perfectly, just as the two of them had done for their entire careers. They finally sat at the table to have a third, or maybe tenth, round of drinks when their evening was rudely interrupted.

A young sailor came up to their table, pushing his way through a couple of dozen people, and then slamming into Eyes, making the kids around him gasp. Who in the hell had the nerve to do that to a former SEAL? Eyes briefly glanced up at the young man but gave him no additional thought.

"Hey . . . guys . . . hey," the young man said.

"Stop interrupting, dude. Mr. Brackish was telling us about a time he was swimming in a lake . . . naked, and the cops were chasing him," someone said.

The interloper put his hand on Eyes's shoulder, spilling some of the contents in his cup onto the seat, splashing Eyes, while steadying himself as his equilibrium started to falter from too many drinks. Each man on the special ops team saw the event unfolding one of two ways for the young man.

Either Eyes was going to take the kid's hand, twist and yank down quickly, putting the young sailor's face onto the table with a flash of movement that put the young man into some weird yoga-esque position, or Eyes would simply remove the hand from his shoulder and ignore the individual's bad public behavior.

Luckily for the young sailor, Eyes decided against option A.

"Oh . . . you're the *old* SEAL. Is BUDS really that hard? I heard the only reason people quit is because they're injured to the point of not being able to physically continue," the sailor said, leaning into Eyes, looking closely at his trident pin.

The entire group went utterly silent.

"What's your name, sailor?" Eyes calmly asked.

"Monterubio," the young man replied with a bit of a slur.

"Well, Monterubio, I'm going to give you *one* opportunity to take your hand off of me. If you don't, you'll learn first-hand what being injured is all about. After your hand is removed you'll leave this table. You're disrespecting the men sitting here, as well as myself, and I won't tolerate it," Eyes said.

"Oh . . . hey . . . uh . . . I'm so . . . I'm sorry," Monterubio said, finally realizing danger even in his drunken state. He quickly spun around and stumbled away.

The tension around the table eased considerably, but the men sitting around it watched the actions of the young sailor carefully. Intoxication makes people do stupid things. Doing stupid things next to men of war is bad for the body and soul.

Brackish finished his story, almost everyone howling with laughter at the thought of this oversized man being hauled into a third world country's jail, naked and slime covered.

"I was wondering, what is that ribbon? The blue one there with the white line in the middle?" Monterubio asked as he snuck back closer to their table. He was a glutton for punishment.

"Are you an absolute idiot?" a sailor gasped.

"Damn it, shut up," another barked.

"You're seriously embarrassing yourself, bro," a petty officer said.

"What? Sorry for asking!" Monterubio said both embarrassed and a bit angry. Not a good combo at all.

"It's the Navy Cross," Eyes said. It was obvious to his team the tipping point was starting to fall in the wrong way for this sailor who continued to be in Eyes's face.

"Oh, the Navy Cross. What did you have to do to get that? Did you actually kill someone? It must've been so cool," Monterubio said with a laugh.

Sleep shot up from the table in a flash and had the chest of the discourteous sailor's uniform clinched in his fist. Before anyone could react, Sleep pushed Monterubio away from the table and was ready to slam the sailor to the ground.

"Don't you *ever* ask that question again. You're lucky we're in uniform because if you weren't, I swear on my life, you'd be eating out of a straw for months. Don't say another word. Leave right now because if you don't, it'll take an entire battalion to get me off of you," Sleep finished through clenched teeth.

Monterubio became stone sober in the blink of an eye. Looking over the shoulder of Sleep to all of the special ops men now standing in the ready-to-kill position, made the disrespectful sailor about pee his pants.

"Let him down, Sleep," Eyes calmly said to his best friend.

"Do I have to?" Sleep asked.

"Yes," Eyes replied.

Sleep did as requested, giving Monterubio a quick jolt to the sailor's torso as a parting gift. It knocked the wind out of him.

"Monterubio. Come and sit," Eyes said as he pointed to the seat next to him. The calmness in his voice frightened everyone. The kid looked as if he wanted to run, but he did as Eyes commanded.

"I was twenty-five years old, on my second tour with my team, and we were sent into an especially terrible place in the northeast corridor of Africa. No, I won't tell you the exact location, but it rhymes with Djicooti," Eyes said. The joke had the intended effect as a few chuckles rolled around the men and women.

"Our mission was to obtain an individual wanted for doing very bad things to a lot of people. Let's just call him Bob. Bob had people who worked for him who hated Americans just as much as we hated what Bob and his friends were doing to thousands of innocent people. What I learned from a very early age is that if someone wants something more than you, they'll find a way to get it. Long story short, our government decided they wanted Bob and his friends to never hurt innocent people again," Eyes said, not taking his eyes from Monterubio. Everyone leaned in closer so they could hear every single word.

"My team arrived at our location, and we were ready to begin the climax of the operation when everything went down the drain. The vehicle we were in started taking fire and was quickly disabled. My team made a quick exit strategy and we started to enact that plan when the first part of the shitstorm started raining hell down on us. Somehow, the exact time and location of our arrival was known." He paused for a long moment.

"There's no explanation for how precise that attack was and at that moment it didn't matter at all. The small-arms rounds were followed by two rocket-propelled grenades that hit our vehicle. One of the men on my team didn't get out in time and he died instantly. I was on the opposite side of the vehicle, jumped in, and pulled his body out." There was another pause to give respect to the soldier who'd died.

"From that point our team was split between those who exited the vehicle from the left and those who exited from the right. The teammate I pulled out was bleeding all over my shoulder. Fully geared up and lifeless, he was extraordinarily heavy. It didn't matter though because I wouldn't leave him. The things they'd do to his body while filming was something I'd never allow to happen," Eyes said.

The air around the table became thick, people having a hard time taking a deep breath while they raptly listened.

"The team members who got out on the opposite side of me got sucked into a pinch point. They were fired on by people above them as well as from different angles down the roadway. They were trapped. The fire on the vehicle made it impossible for them to go anywhere. I could hear them yelling for assistance and while we were trying to get to them we were taking on fire ourselves. I sat the driver down, making sure his body was secure, and then began engaging in subduing those who were trying to take us out. Me, and the two men with me, tried exploiting the angle we had on those shooting at our trapped team members. It was obvious we weren't going to get much accomplished with plan A, so we had to quickly develop a plan B," Eyes said, the fire of the story starting to show its flames in his expression.

Eyes started speaking with more emotion, inching closer to Monterubio. "It was then that I decided to take action. I told my team my plan and each of them argued, but I knew it was the only way we were going to get the men on the other side of the vehicle out of that situation. So, I slid my long gun over my shoulders, handed it and my extra ammo over, turned toward the burning vehicle, and started sprinting for it. It was the scariest thing I'd ever done. All of the underwater training, almost drowning on more than a couple of occasions, combat training, days of no sleep — none of it compared to the fear, and heat, I felt when I jumped into the back of that vehicle. The smell of the burning metal and plastic was almost as intense as the heat surrounding me. I only opened my eyes one time once I was inside the vehicle, and that was to find the door handle on the opposite side of the vehicle I'd exited from."

"Wow," someone said.

Eyes didn't acknowledge the single word and continued. "Thankfully, even after being blown up, the door wasn't completely broken. Once I opened the door I jumped out the other side and rushed to the men. When I arrived two of the four had been shot. Thankfully neither of the wounds were fatal. But one of them could no longer stay in the fight. I made him leave his weapon with the men who were still firing and dragged him through the open door of the burning vehicle to the other side. Once I secured him I went through the vehicle again and took control of the weapon that had been left behind. As soon as I started engaging with those firing on us I told the other men to start making their way out of that spot and through the vehicle. As the last man and I were ready to make the line out of there, another rocket-propelled grenade ripped through the vehicle — completely closing us off from our team."

"Oh shit," someone said.

Eyes leaned in very close to his new *friend*. "I refused to allow myself or the teammate to become a lost name in a no-named town doing a no-named operation. There was a moment of complete clarity, or complete blackout. Either way I saw nothing but the way to get out of there. Bullets were ripping into every single surface around us and the likelihood of getting out of there was next to nothing. So, I grabbed my flash grenades and launched them as high into the night sky as I could. As soon as they exploded in a blinding bright white ball my teammate and I took off running as fast as we could. That created enough of a diversion for us to get into a new spot, and from there we started taking out the insurgents. We were almost out of ammo when the Blackhawks arrived. By that point I had eighteen confirmed kills and saved the lives of those men stuck on the other side of the vehicle. I only thought of my team and what I could do to make sure they got home. Unfortunately, not everyone comes home every time we go out on a mission." He stared at the sailor who was no longer spouting off nonsense.

"Monterubio, understand this carefully," Eyes told the young man. "This ribbon was awarded to me not for the human life I took or for the risks I overcame. I wear this ribbon for those I was able to bring back home — both alive and dead. One of my friends didn't make it home. I'll forever honor who he was and what he did for me and this country. He died for all of us and was more than willing to do it. Can you say the same? Would you *do* the same? Are you willing to be blown up by a rocket-propelled grenade for the men and women standing around us right now?"

The kid didn't answer, shame written all over his face.

"The fact that you're sitting where you are, and I'm sitting where I am, is all the answer I need," Eyes said coolly. "The next time you feel the need to drink too much and start acting disrespectful to those who have gone before you, walk out the door instead of over to the table. If you don't follow this advice the next guy you bump into could be Sleep, and as you've already come to know, he has a more, let's say, *provocative,* sense of instant justice. It could easily end up being very unlucky for you if that were to happen."

The sailor barely nodded his head in acknowledgement of Eyes's words. He then slid from the table and walked away; his head hung down. It was a lesson he'd remember for the rest of this life.

"Now let's forget the interruption and have one more round before my teammates and I hit the road," Eyes said.

Just as quickly as the man had been subdued, the special ops men's instant readiness dissipated. The problem had been solved. There was no need to dwell on it. Tomorrow would be a new day. Tonight, they were going to finish off this gig with a bang.

CHAPTER EIGHT

Eyes pulled up to Courtney's house and turned off his vehicle. Their first date had been a disaster of apocalyptic proportions. This second date was thought out, and he was going to make sure it went well. He couldn't get this woman out of his mind, and he was getting a hell of a lot of shit about it from his teammates. He couldn't look at his phone in their presence anymore without them making kissing sounds and asking how Courtney was doing.

If he were being honest, he'd admit he might deserve all of the ribbing, considering how much crap he'd flicked at the men over the past year on them falling down the rabbit hole of love. He'd been against romance and long-term relationships, let alone marriage, for so long that he wasn't sure what he thought about it anymore. His head was a mess, and his heart thundered anytime he was around that woman. What in the hell was she doing to him? Had this been what the other men had gone through? Was he in the foxhole with all guns trained on him?

Eyes ran his fingers through his hair as he let out a long sigh. He didn't have answers for any of his feelings, but he knew beyond a shadow of a doubt he wasn't going anywhere until he figured this thing out with the brave, stubborn, and somewhat crazy woman who was always infiltrating his thoughts — even when he slept.

Before Eyes stepped from his vehicle, he saw Courtney's door fling open. She did a little hop down her steps and he barely had time to jump out of the SUV and jog around to her door before she arrived and reached for the handle.

"Good evening," he told her as he pulled open the door. "You look beautiful as always." Damn, she took his breath away. He'd told her their date would be more casual and to dress comfortably.

She wore a pair of jeans with sparkles on her luscious ass that had his fingers tingling with the need to see how well his hand could cup his favorite curvy part of her body. He tore his gaze from her butt as she turned, giving him a view of the apple red sweater that hugged his second favorite part of her, showing just a bit of cleavage that had his mouth watering. Bright red lipstick adorned her kissable mouth, and it appeared mascara was her only other makeup. She didn't need much. She effortlessly looked both seductive and innocent in the same glance.

"Thank you. You look quite handsome yourself," she told him as she licked those shining lips, making his groin tighten.

Their first kiss had been a disaster. Eyes knew he wouldn't make it through the night if he didn't remedy that tragic moment. He grabbed her hips and pushed her back against the vehicle. Her eyes widened as her mouth parted. He gave her a few seconds to protest if this wasn't what she wanted. Her hands came up and gripped his large biceps.

Eyes leaned down, taking his time so they didn't bounce off of one other this time, and finally their lips connected. Instead of bruising her this time, they melted together as if they'd been meant to be. Her taste sent a surge through his body as he swept his tongue over her lower lip, then dipped inside her mouth. Heaven, this was pure heaven.

He pushed against her as his fingers tightened on her hips. She groaned against his mouth as her tongue began dancing with his. He continued the kiss for a few more seconds then pulled back with reluctance. She slowly opened her eyes as she gazed at him, a slight pout now resting on her lips.

"Okay, we need to start off every date just like that," he told her.

Eyes was pleased when Courtney laughed at his words. "If we did, we might never get out of the house," she said with a bit of huskiness to her voice. Eyes was about to throw her over his shoulder and march back up to her door when she pushed against his chest. "No you don't, big boy. We had a terrible first date. I want a better one so I can get my interview."

With that she scooted to the side, then leapt up into his SUV, and firmly closed her door, leaving him standing there with a painful erection and a smile. She entertained him while still turning him on. No one had ever done that before.

After Eyes managed to calm down his body, he walked around to the driver's side of the vehicle and climbed inside. Her scent instantly surrounded him, and he knew this was going to be a long night, filled with both joy and a lot of pain. If he didn't bed this woman soon, he might be able to claim a disability for a permanent erection. Was it after four hours he was supposed to call his doctor? He smiled again. He had a better solution, and it was to sink deep inside this feisty woman.

"Are you going to tell me where we're going?" Courtney asked. She seemed unaffected by their kiss or being so close to him in the vehicle, a bit of a hit to Eyes's ego. This was the biggest SUV they had at their headquarters, but he might as well have been in a VW Bug as closed in as he felt.

Eyes loved sex. Any red-blooded person in the world did, but he could normally keep himself under control. Of course, his excuse was it had been a while since he'd gotten to enjoy the fruits of a great orgasm. He felt slightly comforted that it wasn't this woman making him a mess, it was just a serious lack of doing the bedroom tango.

"We're going to the movies," he told her. They stopped at a light and he looked at her. There was a scowl on her cute forehead.

"Are you trying that hard to get out of the interview?" she asked, accusation dripping in her tone. "Because you know very well we can't talk during a movie."

"We'll get food afterward and then I'll talk," he promised. He was planning on talking. He just wanted the opportunity to spend more time with her without feeling he was begging. Had that been what he'd been reduced to? A zit-filled teenage boy begging for a date? He didn't want to have that thought or visual image in his head.

"Fine, we'll go to the movies. But I'm ordering a large popcorn, large soda, and as much candy as I want," she said with an evil smile. "And *you* have to pay for it all."

Eyes burst out laughing. She looked like such a petulant child in that moment . . . and he found her absolutely breathtaking.

"Deal," he said. He could see she was slightly disappointed there was zero argument from him. Of course, she wasn't aware of the amount of money he possessed. She probably thought it would hurt his wallet a little to have a hundred-dollar snack bill at the theater. He wasn't going to tell her how wrong she was. He felt there needed to be mystery between a new couple.

That last thought had Eyes going silent as it processed in his brain while he drove to the theater that wasn't much farther away. They weren't a new couple. They weren't anything. Yes, he wanted to date her, at least a couple of dates. But he only wanted to do that because of the sexual chemistry between them. He wanted to bed her, that was for sure. He surely would lose interest after that. He always had in the past.

They found a parking place and stopped the vehicle. He wasn't sure he'd lose interest. He was absolutely positive she wouldn't be a one-and-done. Just knowing that about Courtney should make him run from her as fast as he possibly could.

"What are we watching?" Courtney asked as they approached the outside posters advertising what was playing.

"I know what I planned to watch, but I guess we should discuss it," he said. There was a great thriller, but unfortunately there were a couple of cartoons and even worse, some chick flicks. There was no way he'd go to a chick flick.

"Oh, this one," Courtney said, as she pointed and jumped up and down, a big smile on her face. He was afraid to see what she was pointing at. When he looked, he grinned, knowing now that he'd hit the lottery.

"You want to watch *Profile*? I was terrified I'd have to duel you to get out of a chick flick," he said.

"Are you kidding me?" she gasped as she rolled her eyes. "Of course I love a good chick flick — and *this* is the ultimate one." She was eagerly moving forward. There were no more complaints about going to the movie.

"How in the world is this a chick flick?" he asked. He shouldn't be arguing with her as she might change her mind, but he *needed* to know.

"First off, I *am* a reporter," she said, looking at him again as if he was a little slow. He hadn't thought about that aspect of the film.

"I guess that would appeal to you, but why is it a chick flick?" he pushed. They got to the cashier window and paused their conversation as he bought two tickets. He loved this theater because the seats were large and had footstools. He'd fallen asleep at a few boring movies he'd been dragged to, not complaining at all since he was comfortable.

"It tells the story of a British journalist who investigates ISIS recruiting young girls. She almost falls in love with the terrorist. And to make it more of a chick flick, she has a boyfriend the entire time. There's love, lust, greed, war, explosions, and lies. How *isn't* it a chick flick?" she asked as they got in line for goodies.

"Well, chick flicks usually have a boy and girl going on some cheesy adventure, not knowing they're in love until the very end where they confess their undying love and devotion. I don't see that happening in this film," he said.

They made it to the front of the line and had to pause their conversation again. Eyes was shocked when she ordered the largest popcorn and soda, a container of hot cheese to dip her popcorn in, a package of Twizzlers, Milk Duds, and M&M's.

"Will you actually eat all of this?" he asked before making his order.

"I'll share the popcorn if you agree now to go get the refill," she told him. "But the candy is all mine. You have to get your own." The young clerk looked at her in awe as she said that. This woman's body was incredible. Eyes wasn't sure how she ate that many empty calories in one setting and kept as beautiful a body as she did.

"The movie might be too good to leave. I better get my own," he said. She nodded as if he had a point. Not to be outdone, Eyes ordered a large popcorn and several boxes of candy for himself. He had a feeling his stomach was going to hurt like hell later that night. He liked his junk food, but this was pushing even his iron gut.

They were about twenty minutes early for the show, so they had plenty of time to keep talking.

"I read the early reviews of this and it said the film is done through screen-capture," Eyes told her as they sat.

"What does that mean?"

"It's filmed as if we're seeing it through the computer screen. They said that makes it feel more intimate as if we're there, talking to her or the terrorist," he told her.

"Oh yeah, I did hear that," Courtney told him. "It's truly insane how much you can learn in this new world of Zoom and doing so much through computers. We can see what's in people's houses, find clues about who they are, and get information on them that they have no idea they're sharing. I'm not at all a fan of Facetime, Zoom, or any other video messaging. I prefer to keep the cameras out of it. You never know what you're sharing without knowing you're sharing."

He laughed at her last sentence. "So, was that a double entendre?"

"Oh, whatever. I mean we don't know how much information we give without saying a word," she pointed out.

"I know. I don't get on a video message unless I'm away from my home or have a screen behind me blocking out anything that might be in my place," he said.

"But they can still break into your computer and get information on you," she pointed out.

Eyes laughed again. "Not with Brackish putting security on all of my devices. The damn NSA couldn't break into my electronics," he bragged.

"I'm going to have to speak with Brackish," she said.

"He's always willing to help a beautiful lady."

Before she could reply the previews for upcoming films began and they both sat back, eating their treats while watching the coming attractions. The movie just began when Eyes felt something hit the back of his head. He was starting to turn to see what had happened after he felt something pelt him again. Then Courtney jumped as she flipped her head around.

They both gazed behind them but saw nobody acting suspicious.

"Is someone throwing things at us?" Courtney whispered.

"Shhh," someone called from at least a row away.

"I'm not speaking loud," Courtney whispered again.

"Shut up," another person said.

Courtney turned and glared behind her. No one confessed to who'd snapped at them. Eyes wanted to throttle someone, but these were civilians. It wasn't as if he could go row by row and pound the crap out of each person in there.

"It has to be a kid," Courtney said, this time her lips on his ear, her voice so low he barely heard her. There was no way someone else could hear what she was saying.

"Do I need to call the manager?" someone asked. Eyes was furious.

Their second date had begun so damn well, and now it was going downhill fast.

He started to stand and Courtney put out her hand to stop him. "Please don't," she said.

"There's no way I'm allowing some jacktard to disrespect you," he told her.

"Eyes, it's just kids having some fun. If you ignore them they'll grow bored," she assured him.

Eyes wasn't sure how he managed to maintain his cool, but, for this woman, he didn't pummel the idiot or idiots who were walking a fine line of staying in one piece. He stayed seated even though he wanted to go all Rambo and take everyone in the theater out.

As good as the movie was, it was overshadowed by his frustration at not being able to take care of a problem. He was sure it was some young punk who'd been trying to impress his friends. The damn kid would sneak out and be long gone before Eyes could teach him a lesson he'd never forget. The end credits started and Courtney turned and looked at him.

"That was so amazing," she said. "It felt so much more intimate with the way they filmed it. With the close-ups of Amy and Bilel, their emotions were clear. I almost felt sorry for him a few times. However, I was really scared for Amy."

"I loved the suspense through the entire film," Eyes said. "I would've loved it more if the idiot at the beginning of the film hadn't ticked me off." He was trying to shake off his bad mood. Their date wasn't over yet.

"I forgot all about it after the film started," Courtney said with a wave of her hand. "The scariest thing about the entire film is how easily a young girl could fall for this scheme. This woman was smart, talented, and successful and she was nearly pulled in. I don't know if a teenager could resist."

"It happens too often all around the world," Eyes said with a shake of his head. "The lives of predators have gotten a lot easier since the internet was invented. They can cyberstalk their victims and no one knows it's happening."

They left the theater and were in the parking lot when all of a sudden they were pelted with popcorn. What in the living hell? Eyes whipped around, no longer caring if it was a kid. He was going to teach the young punk what a real hit felt like. This had now gone too far.

Before he could move Courtney started laughing. He looked at her in surprise. How could she not be irritated as hell? He was ready to start World War III.

"Well, hello boys. It seems we were at the same show," she said. Eyes looked up, then wanted to commit murder even more.

Sleep and Smoke were standing there, each with a bucket of popcorn and a satisfied smile on their lips.

"Good film, wasn't it?" Smoke asked with a laugh.

"It would've been a hell of a lot better had we not been assaulted at the beginning of it," Eyes said. He considered punching Smoke, knowing he'd get hit back and it would feel like a sledgehammer going through a window. It would still be worth it.

"We didn't know you were coming here, but boy were we glad to see you," Sleep said.

He and Courtney reached the boys, and then Eyes whipped out both hands and hit the bottom of their buckets which only had a little popcorn left. It was enough to fly over them. *Now*, Eyes felt better.

Sleep and Smoke laughed. "Yep, we probably deserved that," Smoke said. "Especially since I quickly slipped by Courtney and put a mic on her so we could then shoosh you when you talked."

"That was *you*?" Courtney gasped. "You're such a pig. I was so embarrassed."

"Yep, that was me. You didn't even know it was there," Smoke said, quite pleased with himself. He reached out and took the tiny mic from the collar of her sweater.

"Okay, I'm a *little* impressed. Plus, the chances of me seeing anyone in that theater again are slim to none," she pointed out.

"We thought for sure Eyes was going to jump up and go crazy on the poor people behind you guys. We were a bit disappointed at his restraint," Smoke said with another laugh.

"That was me. I had to beg him to stay seated," Courtney said.

"And she almost lost. If one more piece of popcorn had come our way the entire theater was going to pay," Eyes growled.

"Dually noted," Smoke said, looking far too pleased with his actions of the night.

"Where are your wives? They never would've let you get away with this," Eyes said.

"They had a girls-night thing so we decided to watch a film," Sleep said. "Lucky for us."

"Yeah, I feel *real* lucky," Eyes said while rolling his eyes.

"Do you guys want to grab some grub? We're heading over to the Outback," Sleep said.

Courtney began to nod when Eyes quickly stopped her. "No, we have other plans. We're gonna leave now," he said, grabbing Courtney's hand and pulling her away to the sound of Sleep's and Smoke's laughter. There was no way Eyes was letting the rest of their night get interrupted. He was going to end this date on a *very* high note . . . or so he hoped.

Without more than a couple of seconds warning, a vehicle turned right in front of them. Courtney was looking down and so was the driver. Eyes grabbed Courtney and turned, but it was too late. The car smacked right into them, with Eyes taking the brunt of the hit. They were sent flying backward and he landed on his back with Courtney cradled in his arms.

There was a squeal of brakes as the car stopped. Eyes heard the door open and someone jump out. "Are you okay? Oh, my gosh, I'm so sorry. I only looked down for a second," a panicked woman cried as she ran to them.

Before Eyes could respond Smoke and Sleep were right there, keeping the woman back. She might look innocent, but they knew a lot of bad guys used decoys. They didn't assume the best in people — ever.

"Are you okay? Is anything broken on either of you?" Smoke calmly asked as Sleep took the woman back to her car.

"My pride is broken for not catching that. Does that count?" Eyes asked.

"Eyes, you took that hit for me. You already have a bad hip and leg. That was foolish," Courtney said as her hands moved down his body. Eyes met Smoke's eyes, giving him a message to go away. Smoke laughed.

"Clearly, you're fine," Smoke said. "We'll get the woman on the road."

Smoke moved over to the driver and assured her they were a little bruised but were fine. She could leave now. She argued for a second, but when both Sleep and Smoke gave her a stare, she decided leaving was the best option. She got into her car and left the mall parking area. She must've decided to get the hell out of there before they changed their minds and called the cops.

"Courtney, if you keep rubbing me like this, I'm going to get real embarrassed in front of my friends," Eyes said as Courtney's hands came dangerously close to his groin, which normally he'd very much appreciate.

"I'm sorry," she said, her cheeks heating. "I'm just worried about you."

He smiled at her. Sure, he was hurting. It wasn't only his pride that had been hit. His leg was going to be sore for at least a week, maybe longer. But it was all worth it to get Courtney's full attention.

"I might need some tender loving care over the next few days. I might have a concussion," he said with a wiggle of his brows.

Courtney laughed as she pulled away from him and got to her feet, then held out her hand. He took it and rose to his feet, not letting her help him, but wanting her hand in his.

"I'm supposed to be the one to help you up," he told her.

"Sometimes the girl can be the hero too," she said.

He laughed as he wrapped her in his arms. Their date was now officially over as he needed to get her home so she could check for bruising . . . Then again, maybe she'd need some help checking those hard-to-reach places. Maybe it wasn't such a disaster after all.

CHAPTER NINE

Eyes was on his belly, his rifle secure and in position. His eye focused through the scope, his fingertip on the trigger, and the target five-hundred yards away was steady. He took in a breath, then let it out and pulled the trigger . . . and didn't come anywhere near the target let alone hit the bullseye.

"Miss. What in the hell is up with you?" Green asked while keeping his focus through the spotting scope. "You aren't me, but in all of our time together you've been very consistent at five-hundred yards." He paused and looked at Eyes's target. "This, however, is terrible. To miss completely — something's definitely wrong. Let me get on there a second."

Eyes let out a frustrated breath as he rolled onto his back and gazed up at the cloudy sky. For once he was happy to have no sun as he was in a dark mood anyway.

Green took a couple of seconds to ensure the rifle was lined up correctly, fired, and hit dead center. He said over his shoulder, "It isn't the rifle, brother. So, what is it?"

"I don't know. I'm off," Eyes said. It was rare for any of the men to admit they weren't at peak performance. Even if the other team members could see they weren't themselves, they'd still act as if it was their best day ever. For Eyes to say he wasn't performing at his best, stopped the reply Green had been about to say.

"Talk to me," Green demanded.

"Women!" Eyes said, letting out another long-suffering sigh.

Green laughed. "Yep, they're the reason the world goes round," Green told him as he sat up from the rifle.

"And they're the reason men suffer," Eyes grumbled.

"Yep, more than one war has risen because of the opposite sex," Green said.

"It's frustrating the amount of power a woman can have over our lives. She can make us fight, put us in a great mood or a terrible one. She can make us lose focus. She can completely upend our world . . ." He paused. "And the worst part is that there's absolutely nothing we can do about it."

Green laughed hard at those words. "Well, we can stop fighting it," he suggested.

"Stop fighting what?" Eyes snapped.

Green looked at Eyes thoughtfully. "Every situation is different, but we can stop fighting what we're feeling and just go with it."

Eyes thought about that for a minute. "I'm not fighting what I'm feeling for Courtney. I don't know exactly what it is, but at least I'm not running from it like she is."

"We all have a different timeline," Green said. "I didn't know what in the hell was going on with me when I met Mallory, but all logic went out the window. I finally had to go with the flow."

It was rare for Eyes to let down his guard and talk seriously to any of the men. Sarcasm had been his protection for a very long time. But it felt good to talk to a friend, to try to figure out what in the hell was happening with him. After all, all of his team had gone through a hell of a lot women trouble over the past year. Maybe it was his turn.

"That worked out for you, but it doesn't always conclude with a happy ending," Eyes said.

"What would your happy ending be?" Green asked.

"When in the hell did you become a therapist?" Eyes asked with a roll of his eyes. He couldn't completely erase the need to be cool and collected.

Green laughed, not at all offended. "Probably about the time a sexy undercover FBI agent snuck beneath my skin and changed everything I'd ever believed about how life was supposed to go."

"I don't want to change. I love my life, love that I've had no restrictions. I don't know what I'm going to do when this gig is up, but I don't want to have to consider someone else's feelings when making those choices. I like women, but I like bachelorhood. The only sure thing right now is that I'm confused as hell."

"Then you won't have a shot with her. Relationships are about compromise. The thing is, we don't care in the end because we love the person we're with enough that their happiness is more important than our own."

"I see how happy you and the other guys are, but I still don't get it," Eyes said.

"Well, let's see if you can hit the wide side of a barn, and if firing the gun doesn't make you feel better, then maybe you should just go speak to the woman. I know a lot of women will find a weakness and poke right into it until you're bleeding, so be strong and confident and see if that changes her attitude," Green suggested. "Maybe she's enjoyed being single as much as you have, and maybe she's fighting it just as much. It might do you both a hell of a lot of good to let down your defenses. Then you might actually get somewhere."

"Are you trying to get my ass kicked?" Eyes asked.

Green laughed hard. "That would be a bonus for sure," he said.

"What's the hold up?" Smoke asked as he jogged up to them and dropped down. He looked at the sky, trying to find what they were seeing. "Did a UFO fly by?"

"Eyes is love struck," Green said.

Smoke laughed along with Green. "Been there, done that," he said. "But this is guy time. Let's blow some shit up and forget about women for a while."

Sleep approached. "I have that on video. I'm sending it to Amira right now."

"If you attempt that, I'll have you tied into a pretzel so fast you'll never use your fingers again," Smoke said, lying back with his hands beneath his head, staring at the same brooding clouds as Eyes. The funny thing was the man could be up so quickly the rest of them wouldn't stand a chance if he really did want to take their phone away and tie them into a pretzel. It was strange how such a large man could

124

move quicker than the brain could process the movement.

"Are you ladies done sharing your feelings? We have a course to finish," Brackish said as he joined them.

"Yeah, I'm more than done. I don't need advice from Neanderthals," Eyes said. He sat up. He needed to pull himself together.

"Okay, we're going through the moving target range. Get your head in the game," Chad said, the last of their team to join the knitting circle.

"Let's do it," Eyes said.

He rose to his feet and followed Chad to the warehouse that was all set to go with a maze they had to get through, lights, smoke, and moving targets. They got a point for every bad guy they killed, and docked for every victim, animal, or inanimate furniture they hit. There were also hidden mines and bombs they couldn't set off. This was the kind of game Eyes normally loved. Today his head just wasn't in it.

"Let's go," Chad said, then stepped through the doors.

The men geared up for the scenario. This was set up as a nighttime rescue operation in hostile territory that held multiple families within the compound. Chad would be watching their movements via CCTV screens, and give a final point tally. The operation would be considered a failure if the men set off any of the paint bombs hidden throughout the warehouse.

"Eyes, I know you're a bit off today. Do you want someone else running point?" Green asked as he fastened the strap of his helmet to his chin.

"No. Same formation as always. Me, Sleep, Smoke. Then you and Brackish. Stop busting my balls, it's over with. We now have a mission to focus on," Eyes replied with a hint of irritation.

One thing that was great about this warehouse was how easy it was to move module walls around to make different sized rooms, different hallways, and new situations with each operation.

They could be working with natural light, office light, random small LED lights, or in pitch black. There were almost an infinite number of layouts that could be created so it was perfect in helping the special ops team keep their tactical minds engaged and sharp. This scenario was one in which they didn't know the layout and would have to be cognizant of non-combatant individuals. It meant that someone with a keen eye, a sense of the situation, and clarity of mind would need to be the point guy. Green knew they were doomed before walking through the front door.

When they moved into the first room it was a purposeful transition to complete darkness, making them slide down their night vision goggles. The room came to life in green hues and the images shocked the team. Chad had brought in a bunch of mannequins and dressed them up like the creepy ass clown from the movie *IT*.

"Oh, hell no!" Smoke said and shot every single one of the dummies in the face within seconds. They were using paint tipped bullets in this exercise so the explosion on each of the faces just gave them a creepier look. Smoke fired off three more shots at each head just to get the faces covered and the creepiness factor down a bit.

Chad's laugh came over the intercom and all Smoke could do was raise his hand in the air, flipping off the cameras he knew were focused on them.

"Whoa. Wait! Did you check the door?" Sleep asked Eyes as he started to pull the first door in the compound open.

"All good," Eyes grumbled at him, but he knew he'd just screwed up the very first thing he'd touched. He told himself to get in the game and focus. He wasn't actively thinking about Courtney, but his focus was utterly shot.

Slowly the men filtered into the room, each man fanning out into their tactical positions, ensuring the area was secure. The men were as quiet as mice. The microphones placed in each room were connected to sensors, and if the decibels reached a certain limit there'd be a reaction. Sometimes it was a cat scurrying across the room, sometimes it was a person waking up, and sometimes it was enough to trip the alarms and the men, and their presence would be known to the *enemy* inside the compound. If that happened the special ops men were in serious trouble.

In this room, not a single reaction happened. The men went unnoticed.

"Smoke, Green, take the left room. Brackish, watch our six. Sleep and I will take the right room," Eyes said in a whisper.

The five men slowly crept down the dark hallway toward the two rooms that needed to be cleared. They all knew there'd be additional rooms as the warehouse was massive and they'd only covered about four hundred feet of it. How the split from those rooms happened was an unknown.

"Thank God, I'm with you. Eyes is a mess today," Green said to Smoke as soon as he knew they were far enough away from Eyes to hear them.

"Who knew our fearless leader was a thirteen-year-old boy who just got his first kiss and now doesn't know what to do with himself," Smoke said through a chuckle. He and Green had conveniently forgotten they'd been acting the same way in the not-so-distant past.

"Just make sure the camera is off and you don't get caught yanking it on a Zoom call when Courtney turns you down again," Smoke said, loving to mess with his team leader.

Eyes shot daggers at the man. "I'm not a reporter from the New Yorker," he replied. "Now get serious." There were a couple of chuckles before they all grew serious again.

Eyes looked at Sleep, gave a silent three count and then ripped the door open. The two of them were met with an oversized room that was completely empty with a door on the opposite wall.

Sleep, ever diligent with his responsibilities, continued walking around the room, looking for anything that might be a trap. Eyes let go of the door, and instead of staying open like all of the others had in the exercise, it slid shut. A deep clunking sound was heard from the door, and as Eyes inspected it he realized there was no interior handle. He attempted to reach Brackish via their comms, but nothing came back — not even static. Eyes and Sleep had been completely cut off from the rest of their team.

Eyes gave three light taps on the door, and three taps came back. It was enough for Eyes to know Brackish understood the situation. The team of five was now two teams of two and three and they'd need to find their way back to each other.

"What the hell? There's water coming in," Sleep whispered as water began rising from the floor.

Within seconds the water was at their ankles. Both men started rushing for the opposite door where they'd entered, but found it flush with the wall, unopenable. Most people would shut down and lose their ability to think through the chaos of the situation, but these men were far from average people.

"Get your laser up, start scanning the walls," Eyes commanded as he brought his long gun up, equipped with a laser, and started shining the wall opposite of him.

Sleep quickly slid over and started scanning his red beam all over the wall across from him. The water was now up to their thighs. The two men worked in unison, moving and scanning the walls with the small line of light tracing all sections.

"Got it!" Eyes called, keeping his laser pointed at the spot as Sleep pushed hard to get to the opposite side of the room to the location that Eyes had lit up. The water was at his chest by the time he was halfway across the room, the pressure from it slowing him down. He finally made his way to the red dot on the wall and smiled when he felt the material. It was glass.

"We've got it, Chug," Sleep yelled out in the dark room. It was the call they were to make indicating they'd found either an escape, a bomb, or whatever surprise Chad had in store for them. That way they didn't have to destroy or dismantle the item. Chad would simply stop the exercise from the control room.

This was the first time they'd ever been placed in a water tank, but Eyes knew that if there was glass, or any other type of reflective material, his laser would react differently to it than the module walls and that would be their way out. If they were in the real world, they'd have simply shot through the glass, shattering it, and then gotten the hell out of the room.

"Nice one, Eyes," Sleep said as the water drained and the door they entered through suddenly popped open.

"Team, Check," Eyes said over his comms, checking to see if they were operable now that the door was open again.

"Copy," came back an instant reply.

"We made it out of the room and are coming up behind you," Eyes said to the three men who'd moved on from them.

"Copy, we'll stand down," Smoke's voice came over.

It only took a couple of minutes for Eyes and Sleep to make contact with the other team members. When they caught up, it was clear they were trying not to laugh at their team leader making such a rookie mistake.

"Nice time to go for a swim while we're all over here working on the mission," Smoke said, some of his laughter slipping out.

"Yeah, yeah, yeah — get it out now so we can finish this thing and get the hell out of here," Eyes replied while walking up to the next door they needed to get through.

The next door they opened was the first big test with *people* firing at them. As soon as the door was ajar, shots rang out, paint splatter covering the walls and door.

"I'm going to kick this door open. I want Brackish firing right side, Green low middle, and Smoke high middle. Five shot sequence and then I'm going to send two grenades in. We'll repeat with Sleep throwing two grenades in. Copy? On three," Eyes called over the sound of the fake shots being sent their way.

The men did the sequence exactly as Eyes laid out, and after Sleep threw his grenades the shooting stopped. Eyes did a silent ten count and then indicated to the team they were going into the room. In overwhelming speed, the five men ripped into the room, at the ready to fire upon *anything* that might be operational. Everything in that room had been shut down.

"It seems Chad decided we did good enough for this room. Let's push forward," Eyes said.

The next area created hell for Eyes, as if he needed more thrown at him when he wasn't at one hundred percent.

As the team walked down the hall, they heard something in one of the rooms. With a quick glance Eyes could see the props for the room. A mannequin was in a recliner, watching television. Next to him was an AK47 and on the side table was a pistol. A familiar voice caught his attention. Coming from the TV was a news report given by Courtney Tucker.

Eyes dropped his guard and stared at the TV, trying to see what it was she was discussing and when he saw that it was the clip from years past when she'd interviewed him in Germany his brain went blank. His lack of movement caused Sleep to give him a quick nudge, a quiet request for information.

"Clear the room," Eyes absently said and started to walk in without any additional discussion.

The movements were well choreographed — the same formation they'd done what felt like a million times. However, one of them kept looking over at the TV while walking through the room. His team captured the mannequin watching the news report, but Eyes didn't pay attention to the capture. He stood in front of the screen, watching a young version of himself, and how he'd been such a fool to not notice the genuine smile Courtney had been giving him or the flirty little laughs she'd made when he answered her questions. Well, he'd noticed, but he'd been so stuck in his own head, he hadn't been in a place to do anything about it at that time.

"Clear," Sleep said, indicating they could move on to the next phase of the operation.

Eyes snapped himself out of the daydream he was in and walked to the next door. Without saying anything, or talking to his team, he started to pull it open. He was only going through the motions while his mind was somewhere else.

"Eyes!" Sleep yelled, but it was too late.

An explosion of massive bright lights started popping off at random interludes and a cacophony of sounds encapsuled the men. Shots rang out from all directions and, for all intents and purposes, this was the end of the game for the five men.

"Out!" Eyes yelled as he ran for the hallway they'd just come from. Instead of turning down the hall they'd already been in, he went right and started going to the next room. He looked back to make sure his team was behind him, waited for them to get into position, and then busted through the next door.

Eyes found a door on the other side of the room, ran to it, and ripped it open. When he did a series of bombs went off in the room Eyes had just left. The first series was paint that all but covered the four men behind Eyes, and then less than a second from that was an avalanche of glitter that stuck to the paint and everywhere else on their bodies. Eyes didn't have more than a drop on him.

"Damn it, Eyes. What in the flying monkey's ass was that?" Smoke yelled as they stepped from the building.

Chad was laughing so hard he couldn't speak as he approached the men who were all glaring at Eyes. Their team leader had been reckless and out of control the entire mission. None of them minded screwing up in a mission, hell it was how they learned to become better, but this wasn't just bad, it was embarrassing, and worse, they were covered in paint *and* glitter. No way would their wives believe they weren't at some crazy strip club all afternoon.

"There will be payback for this," Smoke said, trying to brush the glitter and paint away. It was useless.

"Sorry," Eyes said, knowing he'd screwed up badly.

"Don't even bother. Get your damn head in the game or step back for the next training session," Sleep said as he ran his hand through his hair, making the glitter and paint mix, looking as if My Little Pony had just farted all over him.

Eyes just walked away. He needed to get it together — and there was only one way he knew how to do that. It was time he upped his game where Courtney was concerned. It was time to step up or get the hell out of the way of the oncoming freight train.

CHAPTER TEN

Joseph was sitting in his office. It had been a long but satisfactory day. Things were happening in a very good way. He wasn't foolish enough to believe it was an easy road they were going down with Anna Miller, but he was sure in the end justice would be served. He poured himself a nice shot of Scotch, then cut off the end of a cigar and warmed it to perfection.

Before he could take his first satisfying puff, his phone rang. Joseph thought about letting it go to voicemail, but his wife wasn't home. She'd insisted on going to her doctor appointment by herself, telling him he hovered too much and made the staff at the hospital nervous. He only did that to make sure nobody screwed up. She was his world, and he needed to make sure she was treated like the queen she was.

"Anderson," Joseph said in a gruff voice.

"Mr. Anderson, we have a little issue," the woman on the other end of the line said, her voice timid.

"Who is this?" Joseph demanded, instantly sitting up, all thoughts of his liquor and cigar forgotten.

"This is Katie at the memory center in Dr. Ito-Rice's clinic."

Joseph felt sweat break out on his brow as his heart rate accelerated.

"What's the problem?" he asked, trying to convince himself not to panic.

"We've . . . um . . . well . . ."

"Spit it out for hell's sake," Joseph snapped. He didn't want to be a monster, but his wife was at that clinic and he wanted to know what was going on right now.

"We can't find your wife," the girl said in a small voice.

Joseph roared, pulling the phone from his ear. He had a million questions, but he knew there was no point shouting them at this girl. She didn't have the answers and there was no way Joseph could sit there and wait to hear from someone else.

"Jeffery!" Joseph thundered as he tossed the receiver to his phone, not caring where it landed. He rushed from his office. He knew he was too upset to drive anywhere.

"Yes?" Jeffery said as he came rushing around a corner, knowing something was wrong. Joseph was always boisterous, but he must've looked like a crazy man at that moment.

"Get me to the clinic right now. They've lost Katherine and I'm far too upset to drive," he said as he rushed down the hall toward the garage. He had no doubt Jeffery would follow.

"I'm so sorry, sir. I'm sure she's safe, but let's get you there to ease your fears," his loyal employee said.

Joseph jumped into the passenger seat of the vehicle, not even noticing he'd forgotten his cell phone and wallet. When he looked down, he realized he didn't even have shoes on. He didn't care. All that mattered was he had to find his wife.

Jeffery spun out the driveway and took the quickest route to the hospital. It still took them thirty-three minutes. Joseph was a hot mess by the time Jeffery pulled up to the clinic. He was swinging open the car door before Jeffery came to a full stop. The man didn't say a word as Joseph flung himself out and rushed through the medical center doors. He didn't bother with hitting the elevator button; he just rushed to the stairs and took them two at a time.

By the time Joseph pushed through the doors on the clinic's floor, he was well out of breath, his hair was wild from running his fingers through it on the drive, and he was sure his eyes were on fire. A woman was in his path and let out a squeak as she jumped back. He didn't have the breath to apologize. He'd have to later once he knew his wife was safe.

"Joseph, I've been trying to call you," Amira said as she rushed past her harried-looking nurse who'd scooted back as soon as Joseph approached the counter.

"Where is my wife?" Joseph thundered. The woman behind the counter jumped and looked down.

"She's back, Joseph. She's back," Amira said, reaching out and touching his arm. "She's safe. Let me get you to her so you'll calm down, and then I'll explain," Amira said.

Joseph felt tears of relief sting his eyes and he looked away as he composed himself. Amira didn't say anything else. She just took Joseph's arm and led him down a hallway. She normally met with her patients in the room she'd created with items from her patient's homes and private areas, so they felt comfortable.

There was a door at the end of the hall that Amira opened. Joseph stepped in with her, and much to his shock a tear escaped, rolling down his cheek as he looked at his beautiful wife who was wearing a smile on her pink lips while she sat across from Brooke Anderson, the wife of his nephew Finn, and the head provider for the Veteran's Center.

"Joseph," Katherine said as she turned and looked at him. "What are you doing here, darling?"

"I wanted to see you," Joseph said, trying to control the emotion in his voice.

"Silly man, I just saw you a few minutes ago," Katherine said with a chuckle. Joseph felt another pang at his wife's loss of her sense of time. Each day he lost a little bit more of her, but he could make it through anything as long as he had even a small piece of her.

"I know, darling, but you also know I can't stand even a minute apart," Joseph said. It was almost true. He didn't need time alone. He didn't need space apart to appreciate his wife. He could be happy being at her side every single minute of every single day. She was his one obsession, and he knew that feeling would never go away. Katherine had taught him boundaries, but he'd now teach her patience, he'd show her it hadn't only been words he'd been saying to her for their entire lives together, it was a conviction of his heart.

"Oh, Joseph, it's good to have some time with other people," Katherine told him with a giggle.

"Well then, I'll let you and Brooke visit while I go and find a coffee. Then I want to take you out for a romantic dinner and give you a foot rub while you watch 90 Day Fiancé," he said, finding himself choking up again.

She chuckled as if she were a blushing bride, who she'd be forever as long as he was concerned. He stepped from the room and Amira shut the door behind them as they both walked down the hallway.

"Let's go outside and get some air," Amira said.

Joseph stopped. He was torn on whether he wanted to be that far away from his wife.

"She'll be fine, Joseph. Brooke won't let her out of her sight. You know she or I won't let this happen again."

"What happened?" Joseph asked.

Amira sighed as they reached the stairwell. They began their decent much slower than how Joseph had come up them.

"Katherine was in the bathroom and the nurse with her had a patient's daughter approach and ask her a question. She turned away for only a minute, but that's right when Katherine came out of the bathroom. She was gone so quickly the nurse didn't have a chance. She somehow found the elevator and ended up on the second floor. It took us forty minutes to find her. My nurse called you after seven minutes. We decided to be safe rather than sorry."

"I'm glad you did," Joseph said. "That makes me sure that I can trust you."

"Of course you can, Joseph. Not only do I have great respect for you, but your wife's very special to me. I care about your entire family."

They made it outside and moved to the path for the walk around the hospital grounds that had been so well maintained it felt as if you were in a park. For those patient's family members who needed a space to pray, grieve, or clear their heads, it was the perfect setting. The cool grass gently falling under each step Joseph took washed away much of his pent-up stress away. He was still barefoot and had completely forgotten until his adrenaline had dimmed down.

"How much longer do I have with my wife still knowing who I am?" Joseph asked. He stopped in front of a small pond, not able to look Amira in the eyes. He was too close to losing it.

"Unfortunately, I don't have a definitive answer for you, Joseph. There's no set time. Every patient is different." Amira paused and Joseph wasn't able to say a word. "I do want to warn you, though, that Katherine's progressing rather quickly. I don't know if it's because of the surgery she had this year, or if something else exasperated it, but it does concern me. I don't want to say this to you, but I want you prepared. These will be hard times for both you and Katherine, and the entire family."

Joseph hung his head as he stared at the ground. He had to clear his throat before he was able to speak again.

"How long can she survive with this horrific disease?" he asked. This was the one thing he'd never asked. He didn't want to be told he could lose his wife in months, or even years. He wanted at least twenty more years with the woman he loved. He wanted to beat the odds and live with her until they were two-hundred years old.

Amira placed her hand on his arm again and squeezed. "Unfortunately, I can't really answer that either. She's healthy, Joseph, minus the Alzheimer's. She could live another twenty years. But she could be taken home sooner as well. Just keep bringing her to me, keep reminding her of who she is, and keep family around her. The more her mind's stimulated, the better chance you have of keeping her mind with you a little longer.

"I don't know how I'll make it through this," Joseph said, this time not trying to stop a couple of more tears from escaping.

"You'll make it through this because you're the strongest man I've ever met. Don't tell Smoke I said that," she told him with a chuckle.

"I've always felt strong, but right now I don't feel that way at all," he admitted. He honestly couldn't remember ever saying that, much less thinking it.

"It's okay for us to have human emotions, it's okay for us to admit we are sometimes weak. I don't worry that you feel weak; I'd worry if you thought you could get through this without help. You *will* need to lean on all of the people who love you more than they love themselves. You need to admit when you need a friend. You need to tell them when you need a hug. You need a shoulder to cry on. If you admit that to yourself and you utilize those who love you, then you'll make it through this because I've never seen a love story as beautiful as yours and Katherine's. I will be with you the entire time. I'll never deceive you, and I'll never give up," Amira promised.

One more tear fell from Joseph's eye, and he swiped it away and squared his shoulders. He *would* make it through this because there was no other option.

"Thank you, Amira," he said. He normally referred to her as doctor because she'd earned the respect of being called by her title. But in this moment, she was truly his friend, and it was more respectful to call her by her first name. "I do love my wife. I love her enough to be her anchor in any storm. Thank you for reminding me of that."

"I will do it each and every week if that's what you need," Amira told him.

"I might," he admitted. "Right now I need to see my wife."

"Then let's get you back to your love," she said.

Joseph smiled as he looked to the sky and thanked God for all of the time he'd already had with Katherine. He then prayed God would give him a lot more time. He felt peace in his heart. God hadn't failed him yet, and Joseph knew He never would, even if He put some bumps in the road that had to be leapt over.

CHAPTER ELEVEN

Jasmine Anderson had just finished her second day of freshman orientation at the University of Washington, and she was on cloud nine. She'd been accepted to almost every college she'd applied to, but she'd known if the Huskies accepted her, that was where she was going to get her undergrad degree.

Jasmine was destined to work within the FBI and she knew she'd get degrees in both Psychology and Sociology before moving on to get her master's. That wasn't enough. She'd finish off with a doctorate. She wasn't sure where she'd do her higher degrees, but she'd be ready to leave Washington by then. Right now, though, she was free from being smothered by her overprotective family. She was meeting new people, and she was happy, very, very happy.

"Hey Jasmine," a girl's voice called out.

Jasmine turned to see two girls quickly walking up to her. Both of them had friendly smiles and she recalled meeting them the day before in a breakout group. If she remembered correctly their names were Colleen and Lyla.

"Hey, what's going on?" Jasmine asked.

"We saw you walking alone and thought you'd like company. We're running up the road to get some Korean barbeque for an early dinner. Do you want to join us?" Colleen asked.

"Yeah, come with us. We can get to know each other more," Lyla encouraged.

Jasmine didn't have to think about the offer. Not only did she love meeting new people, but she wanted friends in college that had nothing to do with her family and didn't know she was one of *those* Andersons. There were a few kids from her high school attending U-Dub, and she'd begged them not to reveal her secret. They'd promised to act as if she was a typical blue-collar girl like the rest of them. She felt as if she could fly with her new freedom.

"I'd love to go. Korean BBQ is one of my favs. It's been too long since the last time I had some. My car's parked in the south lot. Do you want a ride? I'll need directions," Jasmine said.

"You can ride with us," Lyla said.

"Perfect," Jasmine replied. She knew her father would have a fit about her riding with strangers without a full background check ran, but she was officially a college student now, and he'd have to get used to her being just like anyone else. She wanted freedom, and she wanted to experience a normal college life without bells and whistles . . . and without protection all of the dang time.

"I need to call my dad really quick. Since I'm not *officially* in college yet, I still have to check in with him or my mom," Jasmine said as she pulled out her phone and found the contact number for her dad. She still respected her parents. She just wasn't going to tell them absolutely *everything*.

The three girls walked toward Colleen's car while Jasmine told her dad she wouldn't be home because she was having an early dinner with two girls she'd just met. Her father, ever the protective one, wanted to know the girls' names and where she was going. She omitted that she was riding with them. Then he told her to have a wonderful time and not be out too late. She could've been a jerk about it as she was eighteen, but she truly did respect her parents and knew they only wanted to keep her safe. That's why they'd kept her face out of the media as much as humanly possible. There had been a few scares in her family over the years. Of course there were when the kind of money was involved that was in her family.

"Sorry about that," Jasmine said.

"No worries. I had to do the same thing, just happened before we caught up with you," Lyla replied.

"This is my car," Colleen indicated a blue Toyota Camry as she pulled out the key fob and unlocked the doors.

Jasmine waited a half second for Lyla and Colleen to open their doors and get in before mirroring the same on her side. Since she'd begun her mentor/mentee relationship with Smoke and Mallory, any time she got into a car with passengers she'd scan her surroundings, ensuring no one was approaching a door they could jump into, or grabbing anyone riding with her. The likelihood of that happening was low, but it was always better to be cognizant of the surroundings than to be surprised.

"It smells so nice in here. What's the scent?" Jasmine asked.

"It's *shimmer* by Febreze," Colleen said in a mock haughty voice.

"Oh, *shimmer* you say. How regal!" Lyla replied back in the same voice.

The three young ladies started laughing as Colleen pulled onto the road toward their destination. They chatted about school and what classes they were taking for the few minutes it took to get up University Way.

"The restaurant's here on the right," Lyla said.

"Where do I park?" Colleen asked.

"Go up to the light and hang a right, and then at the alley take another right. There's a small parking lot behind the restaurant," Jasmine said as she looked at the map on her phone.

They found the small parking lot, parked the car, and made their way to the restaurant. They tried to find a way in from the back side of the eatery, but the kitchen staff wouldn't let them walk through. It wasn't a long walk around the strip mall and while the weather was starting to cool in the Northwest it was still warm enough for the girls to get by with long-sleeved shirts.

"Have you been here before?" Jasmine asked.

"No. We were talking about what to eat tonight as they finished orientation and Lyla had the perfect idea for Korean BBQ. This is the closest one we could find," Colleen replied.

"Yep. If it turns out to be terrible it's *not* my fault," Lyla said with a smile as they reached the entrance to the restaurant.

"Oh, I'm *definitely* blaming you," Jasmine said as they opened the door, a simple bell chiming as an indicator that patrons had entered.

The girls quickly got a table, but it was obvious the place would soon be full.

"We got here just in time," Jasmine said with a laugh. She'd been so spoiled her entire life she didn't know what it was like to wait for anything. She was excited to start college and be like any other normal, poor student. She refused to use her trust fund. She wanted to live on a budget and feel as if she was in the real world.

"Yeah, this junior who was helping us earlier said get here soon cause it's a hot spot for the campus," Colleen said.

"How long have the two of you known each other?" Jasmine asked.

"We've been besties since the sixth grade," Lyla answered.

"That's amazing. Where did you grow up?"

"We grew up in Yakima, which really blows compared to Seattle. We've made a vow of never going back unless it's for a visit," Colleen said.

"Yeah, it's gone downhill," Lyla said. "But like everywhere, there are some really amazing places there. They have a botanical garden that's absolutely beautiful. I think, though, when I'm finished with school I'm going to live on the coast. I'm ninety percent sure I'm going to get my degree in marine biology."

"That's amazing," Jasmine said. "You could travel the world with a job like that."

"I was thinking the exact same thing. I want to travel and see what's out there. We didn't have much money while I was growing up, so we didn't vacation much. I've never been farther than Idaho, so I want to go all over the world. I want to be single and have fun until I'm at least twenty-eight. That's ten solid years of freedom." Lyla finished.

"Lyla and I have a vow that we won't get married a day before we turn twenty-eight. We've seen too many family members, and classmates, get pregnant young, or married young, and then hate their lives. When I'm married I want to be an amazing wife and mother. So, I need to be selfish for a while first," Colleen said with a smile.

"I never thought of it that way before, but I think that's smart," Jasmine said. "I'm going to join you in your vow. No marriage until at least twenty-eight." She started laughing.

"What's so funny?" Colleen asked.

"We'll have to make sure my grandfather doesn't hear that. If he finds out I'm not going to give him a great grandchild for another ten years it might cause a stroke."

Both girls joined in laughter with her.

"My mom feels the same. She always says she wants me to live, but then in the same breath she tells me she can't wait to be a grandmother," Lyla said.

"Yeah, my gramps isn't like anyone you've met before. He thinks it's a sin for his friends and family to not give him more grandchildren and nieces and nephews," Jasmine said.

"I can't wait to meet him. He sounds like an amazing man," Colleen said.

"He truly is," Jasmine told them. It gave her a little pang in her heart to not have these girls whom she had a feeling were going to become great friends, meet the most important man in her life. She idolized her gramps. He was her favorite person on the planet. Of course, she loved her parents, but she and her gramps had something special that Jasmine was well aware not many people had. Once she was secure in her friendship with these young women, Jasmine would take them to meet her grandpa — just maybe not at the mansion.

The girls finished their meal while learning more about one another and were walking out when Colleen asked if they could run across the street to Target. Jasmine and Lyla readily agreed. Jasmine sent her dad a text of where she was going just so the National Guard wouldn't be sent out if she was a little late getting home. She internally laughed at that, but if her gramps thought she was missing for even five minutes, it wasn't too far off that the Guard, the Navy, the Marines, and the entire Seattle PD would be sent out to search for her. There was comfort and annoyance in her family's protectiveness over her.

Jasmine loved shopping — and she loved it even more on a budget. That might sound strange to many who'd love to buy anything they wanted whenever they wanted. But learning to live on her own was a huge treat for her. She got to pick out every single item that came into her room. She got to choose her clothes, how to wear her hair, and how to live. It was heaven. She hadn't grown up in a controlling house, she'd just grown up in an environment where safety had needed to come first. And, unfortunately, if she'd acted like a typical bratty teen it would've been all over the papers. Now, if she wore a pair of sweats and her hair in a ponytail, she'd look like every other college kid. It was freedom to the max.

They went through the clothing department, helping each other pick out some clearance items, then to household goods where they bought the minimal of what they'd need for their dorm rooms. Jasmine didn't enjoy spending her allotted budget on soap and sponges. But she wasn't quitting on day one of making her decision. The pretty earrings that were full price were out of her budget. It made her laugh to realize she couldn't afford a thirty-dollar pair of earrings when she literally had ten-thousand-dollar earrings sitting in her jewelry box at home. Those had been a present from her grandfather on her sixteenth birthday. They were stunning and she only wore them on the most special of occasions.

By the time the girls left Target, it was dark and getting damp and chilly outside. They knew it was time to head home. "We have a couple of weeks left and then we can stay out for as long as we want," Jasmine said as they jumped in the car.

"I love that your parents still have rules for you until you head to college," Lyla said. "It makes me feel like less of a freak. Colleen and I are staying in a weekly hotel with our parents during orientation, but they're still here. I can't wait to get into my dorm room and be on my own."

"Yeah, my dad has definitely lightened up, but he's always worried, and he wants me to set an example for my unruly teenage brothers, who are just itching to see the world. I don't mind respecting his rules because he gave me a good home for my entire life and he loves me unconditionally," Jasmine said.

"Some of the kids here have been assholes about it," Colleen said. "They've been disgusted that we check in with our parents. Some of them have been doing whatever they want since they were fifteen."

"I thought that would be heaven when I talked to kids in high school who had similar experiences at home, but then I realized they weren't as happy as they thought. A lot of those kids got into drugs, and some even dropped out. There's security in knowing your place in life and where you belong. Yes, I want freedom, but I love that my parents have always made sure I've been responsible enough to earn it," Jasmine said.

"I haven't thought about it that way, but I love that. We should make a poster. Where are you living?" Colleen asked.

"I have a room in a house one block from campus," Jasmine said. She'd allowed her grandfather to secure that for her. She hadn't wanted him stressed. She had a feeling he'd bought the house, but she'd rather not know the truth. If it did belong to her gramps, she'd feel as if she had less freedom.

"Oh, that's so much better than the dorm," Lyla said, her bottom lip pouting.

"There's one more room left with two beds in it," Jasmine said, feeling suddenly excited.

"I can't afford a house. They cost more than the dorms," Lyla said.

"No, it doesn't. This place was a real deal," Jasmine insisted. It was another reason she had a feeling her gramps had gotten it even though she'd gone through a property management company that her gramps had insisted she go through.

"How much?" Colleen asked.

Jasmine pulled out the card for the company and handed it to Colleen. "Tell them I sent you. It's a huge room, and there's a fully fenced backyard with a barbeque area, horseshoe pit, and volleyball net. There are only four other roommates in the entire house. It has a huge living room, kitchen, and study area. I was shocked at the price. My gramps is good at finding deals."

"I'm going to call tonight," Colleen said, jumping up and down. "I don't know if they'll answer, but I don't want to lose out. I can save a lot of money if the price is better than the dorms. That means more late-night Denny's runs while studying."

All three girls laughed at that. Midnight Denny's was supposed to be the ultimate for college students. Jasmine was in no way admitting she'd never eaten there. She was sure she'd love the food.

They'd stood there too long so they speed-walked to their car. Each of them would get a lecture if they didn't return home soon. They started driving back to campus as soon as they jumped inside. Luckily they weren't far away.

"You can drop me off here at the sidewalk," Jasmine said.

"You sure?" Colleen asked.

"Yeah, my car's right there and it's a pain to turn around in this parking lot," Jasmine insisted.

"Thanks for coming with us. It was fun. I'll give you a call and we'll talk soon," Lyla called out her window.

Colleen leaned over and echoed the same sentiment and then they pulled away. Jasmine watched the back of the Camry drive down the road and smiled at how easily this new friendship was forming.

After the taillights were gone, Jasmine began moving to her car when she saw two men walking toward her. It wasn't that they were intimidating looking, or that they'd given any signal they meant to harm her, but it was the fact that she'd let her guard down enough to not notice them until they'd gotten so close. She quickly put her hand inside her purse, ensuring the pepper spray cartridge was in its familiar location while she grabbed her keys and placed them between her fingers.

When Jasmine reached her car door she realized she'd been holding her breath. The men passed right on by her without even glancing her way as they talked sports. She watched their backs and finally realized her lungs were burning as she took in a deep breath.

After she shook her head, disappointment in herself for getting so worked up over what was nothing, she wondered if the training she'd been going through the last few months was actually making her overly paranoid. Instantly panicking at seeing two men on the street made her think that maybe she was starting to get in a little too deep with her training.

"What's your issue, Jazz?" she quietly asked as she unlocked her car door and opened it.

As Jasmine began stepping inside the vehicle she was violently pulled back. She couldn't feel the earth beneath her, completely weightless for what felt like an eternity. Then her back violently landed on the ground, knocking the breath from her. She tried to get her feet underneath her but couldn't as the attacker drag her toward the back of her car.

"Nooo . . ." Jasmine hissed as loud as she could, but her shirt was pinching her throat, closing off her ability to speak.

"You're mine, beautiful," the attacker whispered in her ear, his vulgar hot breath hovering over her skin.

Jasmine finally regained her footing, and as she did, she pushed backward hard. She knew she could knock the attacker off balance enough to turn her body and confront the man who was trying to harm her. It didn't happen quite the way she wanted, though. Instead of having both hands on her shoulders, her attacker moved one hand up to her hair, grabbed it tight, twisted her body hard, and threw her to the ground again, this time face first. The weight of his body was instantly on her back, pushing the air from her. The pavement and loose pieces of gravel scratched her face.

Jasmine knew she was in trouble. She knew if she panicked, she'd likely get raped, and possibly killed. The man was speaking vulgar words to her, making bile rise in her throat. She had to fight to calm herself.

She closed her eyes and stilled, and then Smoke's voice entered her mind. The man's lewd comments, the aches and pains from his rough treatment of her, and the fear that had been consuming her all disappeared. There was nothing else in this moment but Smoke's low, calm voice as she thought of their training sessions.

When the world's crashing down on you, you must keep your mind clear. No matter what the situation, no matter how terrifying. If you keep your mind calm you'll set yourself up for success.

That's easy for you. You're an uber military superstar badass, Jasmine had replied.

Smoke would stop the training and remind her that everyone finds their courage, and their ability to get through those situations, from training over and over again. The training, and responses to the training, would become more and more severe as their knowledge of themselves grew.

It was *that* training she was thinking of when the man flipped Jasmine from her stomach to her back and slapped her in the face, grabbed the hair at her forehead and pushed the back of her head against the pavement. Outside of the sting on her cheek and the pressure between the back of her head and the asphalt, she calmed herself and took in the situation.

The man looked fiercely into her face, sliding his hands to her neck and starting to squeeze. Jasmine saw the moves play out in slow motion and she performed them to perfection. She brought her hands together, in the middle of her chest, and quickly slid them up with as much force as she could in between his arms. The movement stole the grip off her neck and left the attacker off balance.

Before the man could regain his composure Jasmine wrapped her left arm around his outstretched right arm, bringing it down tight against her ribs. At the same time, she took her left leg, placed it over the back of his right leg, and slid it up so his butt was resting on her knee. All of this happened as fast as he'd ripped her away from her car.

Then in a fraction of a second, she gave a hip thrust, throwing the man's balance forward. As he started to fall Jasmine put her free hand against his jaw and twisted hard. The two of them fell over, and for a moment she was on top. It was enough for him to start to scramble, his arms and legs flailing.

She knew if she tried to get up at that point he'd easily drag her back down, so she had to incapacitate him. She took advantage of the position they were in. In rapid succession she hammered her knee into his groin. It was quick and hard enough to take his mind off of the desire to harm her and turn his attention to protecting himself from the onslaught.

As his grip became non-existent Jasmine scrambled to her feet, quickly turning around to run. Standing in her way was a large, dark figure. Her heart was thundering. She'd been lucky to get away from the first man, but there was no way she was going to get through this giant of a man.

"FIRE! FIRE! FIRE!" Jasmine screamed. Her grandfather had preached to her over and over again to not yell for help. If she were to get into a situation she needed to yell *fire*. If strangers heard the word

fire, they'd come running to help. If they heard the word, help, they'd be too afraid to get involved.

Her grandfather had also told her if she was ever alone and someone tried to break into her house, she needed to call the fire department. They'd be there within five-minutes where the cops might be too far away. He said he'd pay whatever fine needed to be paid just as long as she was safe. He'd told her to start a damn fire if need be, that her life was far more important than anything material in the whole wide world.

She went from a physical mindset to a strategic mindset as she faced a new giant in front of her. If she couldn't beat him, hopefully she could get enough attention to scare away the beast. Until someone did show up and, hopefully, help her, she was going to give every ounce of energy into keeping herself upright and out of this man's hands.

Jasmine planted her feet, balled up her fists and was ready to fight. The man who'd attacked her started retching as he rolled onto his hands and knees. Through his fits of trying to catch his breath he was trying to say something that was undiscernible.

Then he finally choked, "What the hell was that?"

"You'll be fine," the new man said.

Jasmine narrowed her eyes at the big man. "What did you say?"

"I told him he'd be fine," the man said. His voice smooth, even, and deep.

Jasmine narrowed her gaze in suspicion. No way! She might be wrong so she was still on total alert, but if she was right someone was going to die. Her new shirt she'd paid for with her *very* small budget had been ruined.

The man took a step forward and Jasmine steadied her feet, trying to keep her body loose enough to move but tight enough to weather any type of blow the person might throw. The new attacker took another step forward and Jasmine lunged, attempting to surprise him, giving her at least a small chance of getting free. The quick jab to his midsection was like hitting a brick wall and before she could make her next move a hand snatched her wrist like a vice.

"Enough," he said.

He wasn't disguising his voice anymore and Jasmine wanted to hurt him . . . and knew there was no chance of that happening. She took a half step back, looked through the shadow of the night, straining to see the face of the man who could lift her off the ground with one hand with two broken fingers on it . . . it was Smoke.

"What in the hell?" Jasmine spat, filled with indignation.

"Okay, okay, okay," Smoke said, holding up his hands as he tried to calm her. Good luck with that!

"What the hell, Smoke?" Jasmine said again, pulling away from him.

Smoke released her wrist, and a big smile crossed his lips as he did. Jasmine took another retreating step. She was seriously pissed off.

"Jazzy, calm down," Smoke said, but he didn't seem repentant at all with the grin he was wearing.

"Smoke, what's going on?" Jasmine demanded again.

"I told you when we started this to always be ready. Your training is never going to stop as long as we're working together. This man's an associate of mine — well, he might quit after the ass-kicking you handed him tonight." He paused, seeming quite pleased by that. "While it felt like he was going to hurt you, he was in control the entire time. Well, until you kneed him in the nuts," Smoke said with a smirk.

"What?" Jasmine asked. She was still trying to calm her nerves and not understanding what Smoke was saying.

"Take a breath, Jazzy. You're safe. You handled that situation perfectly. Absolutely perfectly. However, you should've brought that lead arm up to stop the slap because it could've easily been a fist. We'll work on that this week," Smoke said.

"This was a test? I could have . . . But he," Jasmine stammered as she turned back toward the man who was now standing but still trying to regain his composure.

"Yes, a test. I told you the world will roll you at any time or any place. It doesn't care if you're a man, woman, young, old, black, white, or any other thing. The violence of life can rip you from your comfort zone in the blink of an eye. It isn't that you need to be looking over your shoulder every second of every day but, like you did tonight, you need to understand how to keep yourself calm enough to get yourself out of the situation as fast as possible," Smoke said, a proud look on his face.

"You did good, kid," the man who'd attacked her said as he gingerly walked past her, stopping next to Smoke, shaking his hand briefly, and then continuing on into the darkness with a noticeable limp in his gait.

There was a pause, the only sound around them coming from a car slowly driving past, and then Jasmine started to laugh. It started as a slow chuckle but within moments it was almost enough for her to keel over in an attempt to catch her breath.

"That was awesome!" Jasmine said once she brought herself back from the laughing fit.

"Yeah, it was." Smoke smiled at her.

"Everything slowed down, just like you said it would. Did you see the mount defense move? I rolled him over like a baby!" She'd gone from furious to elated in a single heartbeat. She was so much more capable than she'd realized. It was a euphoric feeling.

"Just like we've been training for," Smoke said.

"Oh man! That was perfect. You're right, I should've defended that slap. Such a newb move. But that was so cool. When I locked his arm in I knew I had him. Once I had that it was simple to thrust and spin him over. So friggin' cool."

Her energy was starting to reach maximum level and Smoke could see that if he didn't stop her, she might start jumping up and down.

"Okay, enough of the chatter. Let's get out of here. Your mom and dad know you're with me, so we're going to get some ice cream and talk about what's next for your training," Smoke told her.

"Ugh, fine! But you're driving because I need to call Mallory and tell her everything!" Jasmine said as she tossed her keys at Smoke.

Jasmine pulled out her phone as she walked to the passenger side of her car. The last thing Smoke heard before he started the car was Jasmine say, "Mallory, hey, yeah, I'm good. Guess what just happened!"

Smoke smiled. He was hella proud of this spitfire of a young woman.

CHAPTER TWELVE

Eyes was done messing around. He was finished, fini, finito . . . done! He'd had one absolutely disastrous date, and then a second not so perfect date, but somewhat improved. It still hadn't ended where he'd wanted it to end. So he'd done some research into what Courtney truly liked, and he was quite pleased with his new plans. He was most certainly giving himself a pat on the back.

"I see you've ordered a Hummer limousine," Brackish said as he leaned on the door to Eyes's room. Yep, he was still staying at the operation center. He hadn't yet felt a need to move out. It had everything he needed and more. But now that he was dating and trying to get Courtney into his bed, it might be a good idea to get a place. Maybe he could find one in her neighborhood.

He cringed. On second thought, that might be a bit too stalkerish. But he could get one within a few miles of her home. It wasn't like he couldn't afford anything he wanted. But he wasn't planning on being in Seattle too much longer. Was he changing his mind?

"Do you have fun stalking all of us?" Eyes asked as he slipped on tennis shoes.

"Yes, I do, very much." He paused and raised a brow at Eyes's clothes. "Aren't you a bit underdressed for a limo ride?"

"Nope. Just because I hired a fancy vehicle doesn't mean we're going to a fancy place," he told his friend.

"True, the Family Fun Center isn't exactly my idea of a romantic limo-worthy date," Brackish said.

"Really, Brackish, quit breaking into my computer searches," Eyes said with a low growl.

"Nah, not when it's so damn easy to do," Brackish told him. "I get bored far too easily so spying on all of you gives me brief moments of entertainment."

He didn't give Eyes time to fire back before he turned and left the room. Eyes was ready to head to town. Of course, the limo couldn't come out to their command center, so he was meeting it a couple of miles away from Courtney's house. Then they'd drive to meet her.

He didn't bother telling the rest of the team he was heading out, just slipped through the door and jumped into his vehicle. He hadn't seen Courtney for a few days and he was sick of texting back and forth. He'd thought for sure their last date would end with an invite into her house . . . he'd been wrong.

He arrived at the pick-up location for the limo and climbed into the front seat with the driver who seemed nervous to have his passenger right next to him.

"Don't worry, I won't be bugging you all night. We're picking up my date, and then I want to be back there with her," Eyes told the man, who laughed.

"It might be fun to have you up here with me even if I looked freaked out at you climbing in the front seat," the man said. "I'm not used to passengers next to me. By the way, I'm Joe."

"It's great to meet you, Joe," Eyes told him.

The man looked down at his notes then raised his brows as he looked at Eyes. "We're going to the Family Fun Center?" he asked as if he had to have the address wrong.

Eyes laughed. "If you knew how bad my last couple of dates have been you'd understand *why* we're going to the fun center. This woman isn't your typical date. She's intelligent, talented, and a ton of fun. She's also an utter klutz, and I've seemed to have lost all of my mojo since meeting her. I figure nothing can go wrong at a place created for kids."

Joe laughed. "Sure. What could possibly go wrong at a place with bumper cars, heavy balls, and swings going sixty plus miles per hour?"

Eyes paused for a second and then laughed hard. "Well, if we make it through this night, maybe we're meant to be," he said.

"My friend, I'd have to agree with you on that," Joe said. He pulled out into traffic and the two of them chatted as they made their way across town to Courtney's house.

"I'll get the door. You wait here," Eyes insisted. Joe nodded. He stepped from the limo just as Courtney walked out her door. Her eyes widened at the sight of the huge limo parked at the curb.

"What's this?" she asked with a big smile as she walked toward him.

"I figured I needed to impress you," he told her. "Am I doing all right?"

She came right up to him and threw her arms around his neck, pressing her body against his as she gave him a long hug and giggled.

"I've never ridden in a limo, so yes, I'm very impressed," she said. She pulled back, then pushed away from him as she looked at the limo. "Let's go," she insisted when he just stood there staring at her as if he was a kid picking up his stunning prom date.

Eyes chuckled as he moved to the backdoor and flung it open. "After you, my lady," he told her.

She eagerly climbed inside, then let out a gasp as she looked at the colorful lights adoring the roof of the limo. "This is great," she said, looking all around. "Do I get a drink?"

"What would you like? I have it stocked with wine, beer, a few liquors, and champagne."

"I want a mimosa," she said. "There's something very fun about drinking champagne in a limo."

Joe opened the back window. "Do you have any stops you want to make before your final destination?" he asked.

"Nope," Eyes said. "Thanks, Joe."

"No problem, Mr. Eisenhart. We should be there in about forty minutes. There's a buzzer on the right side of the vehicle by the door if you need me. Otherwise, I'll leave you two be." With that, the window closed, and they were all alone as the vehicle began moving. Eyes didn't miss the waggle of Joe's brow. As much as Eyes would love some hanky-panky as he knew many people had done in many limos, he didn't want his first time with Courtney to be in the back of a vehicle.

Eyes handed over the mimosa to Courtney, then grabbed an IPA for himself. He sat back as she chatted about a story she was working on about homelessness in their city. Eyes listened to her rant and rave as the two of them had a couple of drinks and relaxed for their evening to come. He didn't know what the solution was to the ever-growing homeless population. He thought the cities could come up with something better than having them on every street corner though.

Eyes knew he'd made the right choice when they stepped out of the limo at the fun center and Courtney turned toward him with a sparkle in her eyes and a huge smile on her lips.

"You've done good," she said. "I've wanted to come here since I arrived in Seattle but have never made the time. No other date has been this smart."

She moved forward and he had to jog ahead of her to get the door before she opened it herself. He didn't like her mentioning other dates, something new for him. He'd never had a problem with females having a life before him. It was ridiculous to think she hadn't been with lots of men. She was stunning, smart, talented, and drew people in. He didn't understand why she wasn't married yet. Those men had to be idiots to have allowed her to get away. Then again, wasn't that what he had planned? He hadn't ever thought in terms of forever — at least never before meeting this woman.

"What's first?" Courtney asked. She looked all over at the kids running around, the parents with smiles on their faces, and the teenagers acting as if they weren't having the time of their lives because they were too cool for such a kid place.

"The Screamin' Swing," Eyes told her.

"I have no idea what that is, but it sounds amazing," she said. He took her hand as he led her toward their first adventure. When she allowed him to do it, he felt like a king. This woman had gotten to him more than he realized — and he didn't care anymore.

They arrived at the swing and were soon strapped in. Even though Eyes had jumped from helicopters and done the most fear-inducing activities all over the world in his military days, he still found this ride to be a hell of a thrill.

Courtney screamed as the swing launched them into the air at sixty-five miles an hour. The ride had been named accurately. He found himself laughing as the negative 4 G's took their breath away. When it ended Courtney insisted on going again. They did the ride four times in a row before she allowed them to move on.

"I want to come here every single day and do that ride," she said. Her cheeks were flushed, her bottom lip slightly swollen from biting it, and her eyes glowed with happiness.

"I'll take you on any ride you want at any time," Eyes said. She paused then laughed as she threw her arms around his neck again.

"I'll just bet you will," she said with a giggle and a wink.

"And no one has been injured yet on this date," he said in a husky whisper.

"The date's just begun," she said. Her laughter was dying though as she looked into his eyes. He didn't hesitate any longer as he took her lips and kissed her the way he'd been wanting to for days. She sighed against his mouth as she leaned into him, trying to get closer.

"Get a room, you old farts," a teen called out. Eyes was tempted to show the teen how young at heart he was.

Courtney pulled away from him and looked at the teen who was fist bumping his companion thinking he was so cool.

"Don't be jealous of things you can't get," she said with a bright smile. She then flipped her hair back, grabbed Eyes's hand and walked away, making sure to give her fine, *fine* ass a little shake to make the kid eat his words. Eyes might be falling in love with the woman.

"You just keep getting hotter," Eyes told her.

She laughed again. "I think we're as old as we allow ourselves to be. I refuse to get any older than twenty-five."

"I can't date a minor," he said.

"That's a perfectly acceptable dating age," she told him.

"Yeah, for a twenty-five-year-old. I wouldn't want a woman barely out of teenage years. We'd have nothing in common. I want a woman," he assured her.

"Well, I'm certainly *all* woman," she told him. She then slapped his ass and moved ahead when she realized they were heading toward the go-karts. He was ready to throw her over his shoulder and show her he was *all* man.

They rode the go-karts with only minor scrapes as she crashed into the wall on a few of the hairpin turns. He didn't normally let people win, but there was no way he was passing her on the course when the woman was a disaster in waiting. He was amazed she didn't flip the car. They only did the course twice, and the second time he got the jump on her quickly and didn't let her pass. He felt he was protecting everyone else on the course with them.

"You're such a cheater," she told him as they exited.

"I do whatever it takes to win," he said with a laugh.

"So do I," she assured him as she walked ahead of him again.

They moved into the arcade area and he trounced her in several games of basketball, and then she kicked his butt in a zombie shooting match. He was glad the guys weren't there because he'd never live down having the journalist destroy him at a shooting game. He didn't have to worry though, because he was sure she'd remind him often of her victory. She refused to play a second round with him after that, saying it was a one-and-done so she could relive the feeling of beating him over and over again.

"What's next?" she asked. Two hours had already passed, and she wasn't even close to finished. He really had chosen a great date. He was quite pleased with himself.

"We have a date for some laser tag," he said. "This time you won't beat me." If she did he prayed Brackish wouldn't look into their computers and see the score. He'd never live that down.

"I've never done that before either. You're giving me a lot of firsts tonight," she said as she clapped.

"I can give you more," he said. He pulled her close and gave her a quick kiss. He didn't want to get too distracted before they played. "Like multiple orgasms."

She smiled, always being quick with a comeback. "How do you know I haven't had that already?"

He was speechless this time as she walked away. He tried telling himself she was trying to psych him out before the game. Even knowing that, her distraction had worked. He couldn't stand the thought of another man making her scream.

They suited up, then headed inside where the teams were split up. Luckily, they were on the same team so they wouldn't be fighting against each other. The start signal began and they ran into the arena.

Eyes instantly went into special operator mode and was using all of the angles and lines that he'd been taught through his many years of repetitive training. When he saw Courtney's vest light up, indicating she'd been shot, and her laughing hysterically and then running to a corner, he knew he needed to let go and simply have fun.

"Eyes, come on!" Courtney yelled as she ran through a hall that had been filled with fog and lit up by randomized strobe lights popping off at intervals that were too difficult for the brain to understand. He could only see her silhouette, and then saw the red light, indicating she'd been shot again. Her laughter was contagious.

For five minutes the two of them ran through the maze with loud music blaring from overworked speakers and kids yelling and screaming with pure joy while they zapped family members, friends, and strangers. When that round expired and the teams went back to their respective corners, Eyes was shocked to see his team had been decimated, and even worse, he'd come in last place with only *four* kills.

"The next round starts in thirty seconds," the young employee responsible for this section called out.

"Hey everyone," Eyes said to those in the small room awaiting the clock to hit zero and allow them back into the arena. "Let's kick their butts. Listen carefully. Work in teams of four. Go in a single line so when the first person gets hit they can run to the back of the line and be safe from the onslaught. If we score twice as many points as them I'll give everyone a twenty-five-dollar card to the arcade."

The kids started jumping up and down like they were going to pee their pants, and quickly partnered up into groups of four.

"Remember, stay together and work as a team," Eyes reminded them as the clock showed five seconds remaining before the doors opened and laser tag hellfire was going to be unleashed on the despicable *blue* team.

"GO!" yelled the kid attending them, and everyone took off in what seemed like a hundred different directions.

The red team, searching for serious points, started out strong, but it seemed odd that they weren't racking up as many points as Eyes thought they would. It wasn't easy to get eight-year-old boys to stay focused so maybe his briefing on staying together fell on deaf ears.

"I got him!" Courtney yelled. As she began pumping her fist in excitement her vest started glowing, showing she'd also been taken out.

"And they got you," Eyes replied with a smile.

He could've sworn Courtney said, "You're the only who's got me," as she started crawling away from him, searching for her next victim . . . but maybe that's what he *wanted* to hear her say. The music made it next to impossible to know what anyone said unless they were yelling words directly in your ear.

The round ended and Eyes was actually shocked to see his red team had done worse that round than the previous. The lowest scoring player on the blue team had a higher score than the best player on his team, which happened to be Eyes that round. He took no pride in being the best of a terrible team.

"Okay everyone, listen up. We're down two games but this round we have triple point scores, so we have a chance to make it back and take the victory. Remember, we have to work together. Don't move until everyone in the group is ready. Surround the enemy, and don't let them get away. Everyone pick up points as fast as you can," Eyes directed.

"You're an absolute nerd. You realize that, right? We're playing laser tag and outside of that dad over there, we're older than all of these kids by at least twenty years," Courtney said as she leaned into him, her eyes sparkling with mirth.

"That's it!" Eyes exclaimed.

"What?" Courtney asked.

"I never got close enough, but I saw that the other side had at least six adults, maybe even seven. Our team's too short to hit the spots on the enemies vests," Eyes said, shocked he hadn't realized the folly of his instructions sooner.

"If you're shorter than this kid," Eyes started as he grabbed a kid who was about the average height in the room, ". . . as soon as the doors open, run as fast as you can upstairs. Yes, all of you that are his height or shorter. We need to get to the high ground and shoot on top of them. I promise you, it'll work but you have to stay up there. Don't let them run you off. The rest of you kids need to be a major distraction. You're going to get shot a lot but we want to win as a team, right? So you have to hoot and holler and yell as much and as loud as you can. Of course, you can shoot them, but stay in their faces. We don't want them realizing they're being fired on by the little guys up high."

"Five seconds," the kid overwatching the room yelled.

"I don't know if this is going to work but I can tell those kids think you're a hero already. And I tend to agree with them," Courtney said as she leaned in and gave him a kiss on the cheek.

The timing was perfect. As soon as she pulled away, leaving him speechless, the doors opened, and she went running from the room with the rest of the team.

If Eyes was expecting Courtney to play by his rules and be serious, she'd definitely let him down. She was a kid in a candy store and ran around cracking up at being shot or while shooting someone.

"I've been shot," Courtney said as she made a grandiose gesture with her hand coming up to her forehead. "I . . . I . . . I never got to tell you everything I wanted to say," she finished as she fell into Eyes's arms.

"Well, I guess I'll just use you as a human shield then since you're of no use to my team," Eyes said. As easy as he'd pick up a sack of oranges he lifted Courtney and threw her over his shoulder. She started giggling and slapping his butt while telling him to let her down, but he kept on running around the maze.

"I guess I might as well be of *some* help," Courtney yelled as she started shooting at members of the evil empire known as the blue team.

The intercom came over the loudspeakers letting all of the players know there was thirty seconds remaining. Yelling and screaming could be heard bouncing through the entire area as the energy level in the kids jumped up. Eyes scanned the scoreboard and saw that his team was tied with the blue team.

"Courtney, we can win! Follow me," Eyes said as he gently brought her back down to her feet.

The two of them ran around a corner. Eyes was firing as fast as his little plastic gun would go, and

Courtney fired right over the top of his shoulder. They caught three blue team members in a corner and started rapid firing on them. Each of their vests would glow red, indicating it was hit, inactivate for two seconds, and then come back online. The problem for the three kids was there was nowhere for them to go, and each time their vests reactivated it instantly popped red again.

"Hahahaha . . . die, you scum!" Courtney bellowed in a maniacal scream at three kids who couldn't have been older than twelve. Eyes couldn't keep himself from laughing at how silly she was acting.

The music abruptly ended, the lights came back on, and the PA system told everyone to come back to their rooms for a final tally.

It was a sick joke the laser tag operators did. Each game, with about fifteen seconds left, turned off the scoreboard so there was no way of knowing what happened with the points in that timeframe.

Sometimes the scores were so lopsided it didn't matter, but this time it mattered a lot. Each of the red team members came in all but crawling out of their skin wanting to know who'd won, but more than that, the kids were high fiving each other for staying alive for so long and knowing they had a bunch more hits than in the previous games.

Eyes was smiling as Courtney went around to the kids, giving them fists bumps and relaying how great they did. He was so busy watching her he didn't notice when the scoreboard came to life in their room. The glow from the screen on her face gave her an almost angelic glow and Eyes would never admit to anyone he couldn't catch his breath due to how stunningly beautiful she was.

He was in his own world, not noticing the cheering, jumps of joy, kids running up to him and trying to pull him toward the screen to show him they'd won that round and scored enough points to win overall.

The dad who was the only other adult on the team came over, laughing, and said Eyes had just become the greatest human to ever walk on earth in the eyes of his son and daughter, who were both grinning from ear to ear as their names were near the very top of the point total for that round.

"You have no idea how awesome you are, my laser tag warrior," Courtney whispered to Eyes in a sexy voice as she gently kissed his ear.

"Do that again and I promise you this warrior will carry you out of this place and there will be no more family fun center for you tonight," Eyes said to his beautiful date.

The two of them laughed and were walking close together as they left the laser tag room. They turned the corner to buy arcade cards for the kids and then ran into a group of men. When Eyes focused on the faces in front of him he just about started throwing punches.

"Were you guys in there just now? Son of a bitch! What are you doing here?" He stopped, his eyes narrowed. "Dammit, Brackish!"

Sleep, Green, Smoke, and Brackish were all standing there, Cheshire smiles as long as a summer day splayed across their faces.

Courtney started howling with laughter, which instantly made Eyes lose any tension he might've been feeling, and within a couple of seconds the entire group was laughing.

The men didn't intrude on the rest of the night, but they did *randomly* bump into Eyes and Courtney to make sure Eyes was behaving himself or asking Courtney if she needed any of them to take her home because Eyes couldn't be trusted.

"Tonight, I'm the one who might not be trustworthy," she said with a wink, knocking Eyes's feet right out from under him.

"Check please," he said to the air, making Courtney laugh. They immediately walked out of the fun center after that.

The limo reached Courtney's house and stopped. Eyes looked at her, wanting an invite inside, but not pushing it. He'd had a perfect date with the woman, and he wanted them both to walk away happy, not pressured.

"Come inside, Eyes," she said. He didn't argue. He pushed the button for the driver.

"We're all done for tonight. Thank you, Joe. Your tip's on the seat," Eyes said, throwing a few hundred dollar bills down as he exited behind Courtney.

They moved up her walk, and he noticed her trembling fingers as she put her key in the lock. He had to keep his fingers in a fist to keep from grabbing her.

"Do you want a drink?" she asked.

"I'll have whatever you're having," he said. He moved into the living room and sat on the couch on one side. That way she had a choice to sit on the other side or right next to him.

She went into the kitchen then came back with two glasses of wine. She handed him one, then downed half of her glass in one drink. "I should've brought the bottle in," she said as she looked at the couch as if trying to decide where to sit. He took a sip of his wine — it was good — then set the glass down.

"Come here, Courtney," he said. His voice and eyes told her exactly what would happen if she did just that.

She didn't hesitate. She set her glass next to his and sat right next to him. Eyes picked her up and set her in his lap. He'd waited far too long for this to happen.

Eyes closed the small distance between them and brushed his lips against hers. He meant it to be brief, but soon they were unable to keep away from each other. Courtney was making it clear she didn't want him to leave. Eyes had the same idea.

"Take me to bed, Eyes," she whispered when their lips broke apart. Again, he didn't hesitate. He stood up and set her on her shaking legs, he then took her hand and led her down the hallway where he discovered her bedroom door on the first try. They slowly backed toward her inviting bed.

He knew they were moving a bit too quickly, but it felt as if it had been an eternity since he'd last felt her touch. He couldn't stop what was happening, and even if he could, he wouldn't want to. He needed her in a way that went beyond simple urges.

He backed her up until her legs hit the edge of her bed, and then he pressed against her, the evidence of his arousal pushing against her stomach. She was slow as she reached for him, unsure of herself for the first time since he'd met her. He let her grow more comfortable as he tried to control his breathing.

She moved her hands from his well-defined shoulders, slowly bringing them down his chest, unbuttoning his shirt along the way. He shuddered as she felt the contours of his solid chest. While she was working on removing his clothes, he began to slowly strip her. Goosebumps broke out on her skin as the cool air whispered along each inch he exposed. Excitement surged through him.

"I need you," he growled before nipping her earlobe. She shuddered as his warm breath tickled her. She was so damn responsive. Their entire night had been about magic and this was the perfect ending.

They were both finally stripped of their clothes, and he gently lifted her in his arms, laid her on the bed, and quickly joined her. He ran his hands over her body. His fingers skimmed her satin skin, sending ripples of delight through her. She became bolder as she ran her fingers across his heated body. He couldn't hold back his moans of pleasure at her delicate touch.

She reached his hip and circled around to touch his arousal, then she gasped. He was so ready for her, and he was large and hard. She looked at him with slight fear in her expression.

"I won't hurt you, I promise," he told her, sensing her fear. She relaxed at his words and his gentle touch.

He kissed her deeply, exploring the contours of her mouth, touching every satiny surface. Finally, he moved his head down her slim throat and nipped at her beating pulse. She brought her hands up, running her fingers through his hair, holding him against her enticing body.

He moved over her breasts, swiping his tongue across her peaked nipples and then blowing warm air across the tender buds. The sensation caused her back to arch off the bed and a groan to escape her throat. He felt wetness building at her core as he dipped a finger inside of her. He was losing his mind with the need to take her. She must've felt the same because she arched her hips against him, trying to stop the playing. It was clear she was no longer nervous.

"Patience," was all he said as he continued down her body.

He finally reached her thighs and gently spread them apart, exposing her to his touch. She was on display for him, and he enjoyed what he saw.

"You're breathtaking," he whispered before he brought his head down and nipped the sensitive skin on her stomach.

He moved his lips down, his tongue slick against her hot flesh. When he inserted two fingers into her tight passage she started trembling and gripped him tight. He moved faster, pressing his hands and mouth forward in a rhythm that quickly had her exploding.

Her eyes rounded in shock as wave after wave of intense pleasure washed through her. He slowed his movements and made sure she enjoyed every single moment of the intense orgasm. When the final shudder left her body, he traveled upward again.

When he reached her still incredibly sensitive breasts and gently nipped one of the hardened nipples, she gasped as her eyes flew open. That gentle bite started to wake her body once again. He lavished her breasts before moving upward so he could once again take her mouth with his. He was no longer slow and gentle. He was fast and demanding and she was answering his call. The more feverish he became, the more she demanded he join them together.

He reached down and lifted her leg around his hip, pressing his arousal against her entrance, just the tip of him resting there, waiting to join them together. She jerked her hips, obviously no longer afraid of his size.

He continued to caress her mouth with his, while his hand rubbed along her hip and the smooth curve of her butt. Everywhere he touched sent shivers through them both. She jerked her hips again, showing him exactly what she wanted. Finally, he lowered himself inch by inch.

His thick shaft effortlessly parted her slick entrance, and he thrust deep inside of her. There was pure pleasure as she gripped him tight. He barely fit, but at the same time it was as if they were built for one another. He sunk deep within her and paused, both of them relishing the feel of being so close together.

He looked deep in her eyes; the moment was so beautiful he lost all power of words. He slowly started moving in and out of her tight entrance, causing ripples of desire to course through them both. The moment shattered as pleasure completely consumed them.

He locked his lips back on hers as he reached around, gripping her hips tightly in his hands, and he started thrusting in her body harder and harder. An explosion of pleasure ripped through her as she tightened around him, making it nearly impossible to move as their movements became frantic. She thrust her hips up, meeting him stroke for stroke. He threw his head back with a guttural groan as he released his pleasure deep into her core.

He collapsed on top of her and neither of them could breathe for several moments. With his last bit of energy, he shifted their bodies, so he was lying on his back with her snuggled tightly against his side.

"Thank you," he whispered as he gently caressed her back. There was no response as she drifted to sleep. He soon followed her.

CHAPTER THIRTEEN

The trial against Anna Miller began its fourth day and the courtroom was as packed as it had been since the opening minutes earlier in the week. The amount of information coming out about what was involved with the woman who was previously running for the highest office in the nation was overwhelming for the jurors and some of the witnesses. For others, they didn't actually care about the information being shared — they were simply excited to watch the biggest circus they'd ever seen — and the price of admission was free.

For those serving as jurors it was a call to duty. Eyes and Sleep were seated next to each other, three rows back from the former senator with Sleep next to the aisle. They were both dressed in slacks and button-down long-sleeved shirts. Nothing about their appearance would make anyone in the room think they were some of the greatest warriors of their time.

"Those reports Steve put together were given to our boss and he sent them to the execs across town," Eyes said to Sleep.

"Yeah, we had a great quarter. I'm glad he knows how to run those numbers and put them onto spreadsheets," Sleep replied.

A woman sitting next to Eyes didn't mean to snicker at their conversation, but she couldn't help herself. The joke was on her though. She thought she was laughing at two guys who didn't know how to work simple computer software while they were talking about all of the deep dive information Brackish had gathered and passed on to the district attorney. The world people think they see is quite often an illusion, especially when around the special ops men.

"I wish we could get Green in here. Anna would crap her pants at seeing him. I'd sit him right behind her," Sleep said, smiling at the thought of who'd be more uncomfortable — Green or Anna. It would have to be Anna as Green had thick skin and enjoyed making bad guys sweat.

"I'd put him in a tux, holding a single rose. Make her think he wants her back. That would screw with her big time," Eyes replied with a laugh.

The woman next to Eyes was trying to understand what they were talking about but gave up and went back to reading news reports online about money laundering and numerous offshore bank accounts the former senator was in possession of.

As had happened each day of the trial, the process became familiar to those who'd been there more than once: Anna Miller arrived, then the jury, then the judge, and then the proceedings began. It was the same every day and, while the news cameras hoped to capture a different reaction from the defendant or the jurors, nothing ever changed between them.

"Please sit," Judge Scott stated after the bailiff introduced her.

"Before we begin I've received a very troubling note, and while I don't prefer to have this done in an open forum it's the only way for me to know for sure if the information is correct. A few minutes ago, I was given a note indicating one of the jurors has a recording device on them and has been making audio and video recordings throughout the trial," the judge said.

The gasps throughout the courtroom were instantaneous. Camera operators shifted their lenses from the judge to the faces of the jurors, and then to the audience, some of whom had opened their forbidden phones and began instantly typing information and sending it to their friends, family, or social media pages. This was *huge* news.

"Well, this just got exciting," Sleep whispered to Eyes.

"I think I found him. Top row, third one from the right, wearing the open jacket over the black polo," Eyes whispered back.

"What makes you think that?" Sleep replied.

"He's staring too long at the judge. He's trying too hard to look relaxed. Look at the rest of the jurors. They keep glancing around and then looking back at the judge. He's the only one with a lock on her. He *has* to be the one," Eyes said, fully confident in his deduction.

The judge exclaimed that she was going to have each member of the jury leave the room, one at a time, and be examined for any type of recording devices. There'd be a female officer to check the females and a male officer for the males. As she announced this information four new officers entered the courtroom — two males and two females.

"Officers, please take the jurors with you as discussed," the judge said. "I apologize for the unconventional procedure, but we won't begin until the searches are complete. For those jurors not involved in this — I apologize for the intrusion and putting you in this position."

The actual process of getting the jurors checked went fairly quickly and they were halfway through when the commotion started. The juror Eyes had thought was the one with the recording device sprang from his seat, jumped over the juror box, and ran behind the district attorney, sprinting up the aisle toward the doors where the public entered and exited.

Sleep slowly stood, and with perfect timing, grabbed the man's jacket, shifted his weight only a few degrees off its axis, and then let go of the escaping juror. It was far too quick for anyone to see that it was a perfectly coordinated judo move. The juror had flailed for a couple of more steps and then ended up face first on the hardwood floor of the courtroom. Quickly the bailiff and other members of security were on top of him and led him through the doors he'd been heading for. Now, though, he was handcuffed and held by three law enforcement officials.

"Okay, everyone out. We're taking a recess while we get things under control. A public announcement will be made if I allow members of the public back into the courtroom. Jury members, please sequester yourselves in your rooms. Officers, please take Ms. Miller to holding," Judge Scott said with an even tone.

"Act like you're hurt," Eyes quickly said to Sleep.

Sleep sat back in his chair and leaned his head against the rest. As the courtroom filed out in lines of two, the inaction of Sleep and Eyes gained the attention of the bailiff. He came over and told the two men they also needed to leave but after realizing Sleep was the man who'd tripped up the juror, his attitude instantly mellowed. The man in charge of security for the courtroom turned back and discussed the situation with the judge.

"Are you a part of the media, sir?" Judge Scott asked.

"No, your honor. Mr. Eisenhart and I are military veterans and now own a company focusing on security for executives," Sleep replied.

"Are you okay? Do we need to call for emergency services?" the judge inquired.

"No, your honor. I just got twisted up some, tweaked my back a little. If you don't mind giving me a couple of minutes to rest my back, I'll be on my way," Sleep said respectfully.

"I'm fine with that. If neither of you take out your cell phones and can sit quietly while I talk with the counsel, you can stay as long as needed. When you feel like you can make your exit under your own accord please excuse yourselves without making any noise," Judge Scott stated.

"Yes, your honor," both Sleep and Eyes replied.

"Nicely done," Eyes whispered to Sleep.

The next ten minutes were fraught with tense words about the entire trial needing to be suspended and opposing arguments that it shouldn't be suspended as a replacement juror could be brought in. There was much discussion of how the spectacle of it all was an embarrassment to the court.

After hearing from both parties, the judge decided the trial would continue, understanding it would be done under protest from the defense, but gave everyone a one-hour recess and notified the bailiff that while she was upset with what had happened, it wasn't due to those attending from the public and they shouldn't have to miss the rest of the trial. Once the recess was complete they'd be allowed to return. From there she and the counsel for both sides left the courtroom. Once all were gone, Eyes and Sleep got up and strolled out. Sleep didn't have a limp or any indication of being in pain — which he never had to begin with.

"Interesting development over here," Eyes said over the phone to Brackish.

"I'm already on it. The juror's name is Joshua Ellishaw. He doesn't have much to him. It's been four years since he's held a job — at least one that paid above board. He currently lives in a two-bedroom apartment with, what looks like, two other individuals. I'm ripping through his information now and while I need a little more time to get it all, I'm willing to bet he was paid to do this as he doesn't look as if he has the aptitude to figure out how to get this set up, let alone relayed to an outside source. Don't know who, or what, that source is yet. Could be media, or the defense team, or some outside source — hell, it's too difficult to know at this point," Brackish replied.

"Text me when you know. This is a high-profile case, and a lot of people want information, but I want to make sure nothing else is forming," Eyes said to his tech genius.

"Copy," Brackish replied.

After Eyes had hung up with Brackish he got ahold of Chad and said he didn't feel good about the situation, that something was *off*. The men had been working together for long enough for Chad to drop everything, grab Smoke, and make their way to the courthouse.

People filed back into the courtroom after the recess and most found their seats from the morning were occupied by others. There were grumblings and whispers, but this was an open room, first come first served. The notable differences in the sea of faces was that Chad and Smoke had arrived. Chad made his way to the front row, all the way to the outside, closest to the jurors. Smoke sat in the front row, behind the defense table, the farthest seat from the jurors. Eyes also sat in the front row behind Anna's team, on the aisle. Sleep sat in the same seat he'd had at the beginning of the day.

"Ladies and Gentlemen, this morning we had a very unfortunate incident in which a juror was found with a recording device. It's never going to be acceptable for anyone to do what that juror did. He's been taken into custody and will have charges brought against him. I appreciate all of you for maintaining discretion during the interruption," Judge Scott said.

The judge then went on to discuss how the rest of the day and the trial was going to go, and how an alternate juror had been brought into the fold. Tension floating through the air could be felt but wasn't broken with a single sound.

For the next two hours the district attorney supplied evidence, brought in witnesses, and was well into a groove when chaos overtook the courtroom for the second time that day.

"Judge — get out! Now!" the bailiff yelled as he ran to the door and opened it for her.

Judge Scott did exactly as she was told, not asking questions. As she did the bailiff was yelling for everyone to get out of the courtroom immediately.

People scrambled from the courtroom, and the four special ops guys kept their attention forward, staying calm and scanning the area where the bailiff saw something that had started the panic.

"There! Stenographer seat," Eyes yelled.

A small box was smoking. The room was out of control with everyone trying to get through the doors. Each of the special ops members were about to take action to get the situation calmed when something none of the men expected happened.

Three men pushed their way past the crowd, jumped over the railing, and grabbed Anna Miller. One of the men stepped up to one of the officers and punched him without saying a word. The same man turned his attention to the other officer and the two started struggling with each other. Anna's lawyers tried to pull Anna away from their grip, but they were easily disposed of. At that point the intruders plans went to hell.

"That's enough boys," Eyes calmly said.

One of the men who had ahold of Anna let her go and took a large stride toward Eyes. That was his first mistake. The attacker took a long, wide swing at Eyes but didn't come close to making contact.

"You don't want to do that," Sleep's voice came in from behind Eyes.

The man trying to attack Eyes looked at Sleep, scoffed, and took another swing at Eyes — and missed again.

"I told him to stop, but these guys obviously aren't too bright," Eyes said over his shoulder.

The man came at Eyes again. This time Eyes acted as a matador, sidestepping the man, sending him straight at Sleep. If anyone was paying attention, the smile that lit up Sleep's eyes would've been an indicator of true danger. This was exactly the type of world Sleep loved, especially when he had free rein to enact violence on bad guys. The crack of Sleep's fist into the jaw of the man was loud enough to make an audible snap throughout the entire courtroom.

"Not bad," Eyes said to Sleep as he looked at the now sleeping man.

"I was kind of hoping for a little more than one shot," Sleep replied.

"That's what she said." Eyes laughed as he turned back to the other man still engaged with Anna Miller.

The man who'd been fighting with the officers was currently flailing around like a fish out of water. Smoke had walked up behind him and, like a bolt of lightning, slipped his arm under his chin, squeezed hard, and pulled him away from the officer. With his feet barely touching the ground, the man did everything he could to get out of the death-grip he was in, but his attempt made him look as if he was a cartoon ice skater.

"Look at the situation," Eyes told the last man standing. "You're done. Let Anna go."

"Shit!" the man cried out in frustration.

He tossed Anna Miller away and put his hands over his head. The officer Smoke had saved from being assaulted came up and cuffed the man. From there he cuffed the unconscious man Sleep had taken care of.

After interrogating the man briefly, they learned the men had placed the box behind the stenographer, but it wasn't a bomb, simply a diversion. The smoke and sparks were for effect. They'd been trying to abduct the former senator for a multi-million-dollar ransom payment they were guaranteed if they could get her out. The attempt probably would've worked — at least had a much higher probability of working

— if the special ops members hadn't been in attendance.

After things settled, Eyes, Sleep, Smoke, and Chad came together for a bit of a debrief.

"What made you think something was going to happen?" Chad asked Eyes.

"When we learned of the juror who got caught with the device was a nobody, it meant someone with some kind of money had gotten ahold of him. Anyone with enough money to try that is willing to do more. They hired these guys, but, as we all know, they weren't professionals. We should recommend to the DA that this trial goes into lockdown and not let anyone near this case from this point on," Eyes said.

"I agree, and I'll talk to Joseph and recommend the same. The last thing any of us needs is for this to blow up into something truly dangerous," Chad replied.

It only took a few phone calls, and just about as many minutes to get through all of the channels needed. Judge Scott agreed the trial was no longer going to be in open court and no outside entities would be allowed inside.

"You know, we should look into Anna for this. She might not have much access to the outside world but that doesn't mean she doesn't have *any*. I've had enough commotion for the day and I'm starving; let's get lunch," Eyes said as they walked from the courthouse.

"That little squabble made you hungry?" Smoke taunted. "It didn't even raise my pulse."

"Some of us don't eat twenty-four/seven," Eyes said.

"When you're built like a tank, you eat like one," Smoke said as he pulled a bag of Skittles from his pocket and dumped a handful into his mouth.

"I never complain about a meal. Let's head to my wife's place," Brackish said as he rubbed his belly.

"Good thinking. We're done for the rest of the day," Chad said. "And I can use a milkshake."

"How do you think this will play out in the end?" Sleep asked as they climbed into their SUV.

Chad looked thoughtful. "I wish I had the answer to that. I don't know."

The men sat back as they thought about all of the scenarios of where this could go. They knew in the end they'd be victorious. They just weren't sure of the detours they were going to be forced to take on the rest of the journey.

CHAPTER FOURTEEN

"Come in, come in," Joseph called to the women approaching the door of his home office.

A big smile shaped his lips as his arm arced over his head, waving for the women to follow him as he made his way to his den. It had been a couple of months since they'd initiated the media blitz against Anna Miller. Even though Damien had called off his lawsuits against the woman who'd attacked him, which meant the attorney aspect of the plan was now off the table, there was still plenty for them to do.

"Sit, sit," Joseph said as they entered the room that was a haven to him. A fire was blazing and the room was both efficient and inviting. It was a perfect place to feel comfortable in bringing ideas to the table.

He was excited to have the young women in his war room. More deals than he could recall had happened in there. He was sure another happy conclusion would be reached in his favorite place in his home. This was definitely where pet projects were created, non-profit organizations were started, and where parents dreams of sending their kids to higher education came to life via scholarships.

"It doesn't matter how many times I step into this house, I'm still in awe," Mallory told him.

"I wonder how many deals have come to pass in here," Avery said.

"I was wondering the same thing," Erin piped in.

Joseph laughed. "Yes, a myriad of deals has come to pass in here," he admitted.

"That's why you've earned such a positive reputation in the business world," Courtney said. She clearly admired the man.

"Your giving heart has also endeared you to many in Seattle and far beyond," Erin said.

Joseph certainly wasn't a humble man, but he found himself fidgeting a bit in his seat. He was used to praise, but he admired these strong women and appreciated their compliments.

"Being a billionaire comes with a lot of perks, and one of the greatest is that I'm able to help people in any way I choose," Joseph said.

"The great thing about you is that you choose to help people. You don't give a one-time gift; you give for a lifetime by leading the way for people to have a better life. If everyone thought the way you do, we'd be a much more successful society," Avery said.

"I don't know about that, but I do wish the world operated a bit differently," Joseph said.

"Well, each of us appreciates the opportunities you've brought into our lives," Erin said.

"And I love the work you do," Joseph said.
They'd certainly be rewarded for their hard work, but he wasn't going to bring that up right then. He moved

the meeting forward. "Do you want the good news or the bad news first?"

"Rip off the Band-Aid," Mallory said.

"Agreed. Just get the bad news out of the way," Erin agreed.

"Well, here it is. Since Damien stopped his lawsuit against Anna we won't have that money from the lawsuit to put toward the non-profit," Joseph said.

"Okay. That isn't wonderful news, but in the scheme of life it could be worse," Avery said after a few seconds of silence. "What's the good news?"

"The good news is I've had some of my more philanthropic friends insist on helping a new start-up they believe in so much. The name of the non-profit is the *BKPT Women's Institute*. The acronym is each of your last names, in alphabetical order — Black, Klum, Pivens, and Tucker," Joseph said.

There was a pause before the women were beaming.

"That's great!"

"Amazing!"

"Thank you!"

"How great to be a part of an organization that's all about helping strong women who simply need someone to believe in them. With a population of almost three and a half million people in the city and its surrounding suburbs, there will be plenty of people in need of help," Mallory said.

While Mallory, Erin, Avery, and Courtney weren't going to be involved in the day-to-day operations of the company they'd have more than enough input on how to assist individuals who attended the Institute.

"This is such a wonderful gift, and an amazing resource for so many. I know my mom could've used something like this when I was young," Avery said.

There was no sadness in her comment, but relief that a single mother would be able to get help when there seemed to be nowhere else to turn.

"That's the point in this. With all of the drugs that have been running rampant for so long, and all of the families who've been decimated due to those drugs, it's important to help rebuild the communities the best we can. I'm going to set up a similar nonprofit for men as well. I'll ask the special ops guys to be a part of that organization. It's just as important, necessary, and needed to get men help who have been decimated by that world," Joseph remarked solemnly.

"That's a great point, sir," Mallory said. "There are plenty of studies showing how important it is for concerted efforts to build up all aspects of society. The easiest to leave behind and in destitute situations are men. The FBI has looked into this issue more times than I realized, and this is wonderful insight on your part, Mr. Anderson."

Since Joseph was on a roll with their conversation, he ignored the fact that the women still couldn't seem to call him Joseph.

"Now, for the reason you're here. I want to go over what we've accomplished in the past month. I've seen some of the spots on TV and heard a couple of the radio broadcasts that were released." He paused as he looked each woman in the eye. "What else have you accomplished?" Joseph asked.

"If you don't mind, I'll go first," Courtney said. There were no objections.

If Courtney were to be honest about the situation, she'd admit she'd been surprised at how easy it had been to work with this diverse group of women. There'd been a few times in her past that she'd worked in tandem, or within a group, on a story, and it almost always turned into some kind of competition instead of a collaboration. There had been none of that negativism within this group. While there was a vested interest in their respective parts being highlighted, they were more interested in doing a great job and utilizing each woman's strength.

"As you saw from our report, prior to the trial starting we began a four-phase information spread. Television, radio, newspaper, and social media. The market went crazy over it and we saw the normal segments in each platform respond positively. Unlike most media, we weren't trying to spin the news being shared in any specific way but rather dropping puzzle pieces that were factual. That first series was a lot of fun as we saw the fruits of our labor create a lot of growth and attention," Courtney said.

"Oh, I know. I had a poker night with some of my old colleagues, and they were talking about it and mentioned how even their children and grandchildren were talking about this fight on crime in Seattle. It's without a doubt the most interesting thing going on right now," Joseph interrupted, and then quickly held up his hand, indicating he'd stop talking so Courtney could continue.

"It's one of the few times, at least that I've seen in my career, that it transcends generations, and that all aspects of society can agree with their respective disdain for the actions of certain individuals. Anna Miller's a monster, and it's good the world is discovering that," Courtney said. The other women wholeheartedly agreed.

"None of the knowledge we've gathered on her part of the underground world prepared us for what happened after the opening statements at her court hearing, and how Anna proclaimed she didn't know why they were saying she and Damien were related.

After that there were servers crashing on sites. It was, and is, madness in terms of the amount of traffic coming in. The website that Erin was able to create, along with a couple of social media pages, have had visitors come in from every corner of the world," Courtney said.

"That site is fantastic, Erin. You did a great job of getting those images up and integrating them in a timeline with how the events have unfolded," Mallory told her.

"Thank you, it's been fun getting the creative juices flowing again," Erin admitted.

"We've been surprised by the amount of engagement from the under-twenty-five group. Market research shows that this group rarely follows any sustained interest in things like this, but that hasn't been the case here. It's my personal belief that having Damien's daughter involved in some of the interviews and the visuals of how a young woman's life can be impacted so deeply has touched a nerve around the country," Courtney continued.

"It doesn't hurt that she's a cutie and has a sharp tongue and quick wit. I like her," Avery added with a smile.

"Remind you of someone you know, Avery?" Joseph asked with a chuckle.

"Maybe. Sorry Court, please continue," Avery relinquished the attention.

"So, we're continuing the multi-pronged approach and look forward to wrapping this up and finding closure for Damien and his family. The communities that have been affected by it will also be relieved. It's been interesting to see how people started taking note of the rapid drop in drugs and everything the drugs touch. Not only was Anna captured, but many of the drug lords have been too.

The general consensus is people now believe Anna was a much bigger problem in the community than any of us realized," Courtney finished.

"Nice update Courtney, but I think you're forgetting to add what you've been up to in all of this. The investigation you've done in all things connected to Anna has been nothing short of remarkable. I promised you I wouldn't involve myself in pushing those in positions to make decisions on awarding certain individuals Pulitzer's, and I haven't, but I'm having a hard time letting the process go through its normal slow steps. I don't say this lightly, but what you've done on this case is nothing less than remarkable," Joseph said.

"Thank you, but I've had more help and access to resources than most in my field. Heck, there've been times I've been worried Erin was going to punch me because I was spending so much time with her beefcake husband," Courtney said with a chuckle.

"Please, he knows it would be him who got punched if he'd tried anything — by both you *and* me," Erin said with laughter. Courtney and Erin had become incredibly close since meeting. Their life experiences were polar opposites, and they didn't have a lot of shared interests, but when they played or worked together they always ended up laughing until their stomachs hurt.

"I love how even though your husband might be one of the scariest men I've ever met, you have total confidence you can take him," Joseph said with a laugh.

Erin waved her hand in the air. "Brackish is a big teddy bear," she told them, making all of the women laugh.

"He infiltrated my security system without even blinking," Joseph reminded them. He then looked at the cell phone on the coffee table. "I wouldn't be surprised a bit to find out he's listening to us right now. That man can break into any system in the world." He laughed again but he did look at the cell phone one more time, making each of the women laugh too. "Enough of the men, though," he continued. "I was discussing Courtney and how her work should be highlighted." An evil smile popped onto his lips. "Not only have you had time to write Pulitzer prize winning work . . . but you've been getting in some pretty great dates too."

"I guess romance has struck us all," Courtney said. The night before the four women, along with Amira, had gotten together for a ladies night, and the topic of Courtney and Eyes had certainly come up. There'd been plenty of jokes about how terrible the first couple of dates had been, but it had been very clear that Courtney was gaga over Eyes.

"It certainly has, but I'm not unhappy about it," Erin said.

"Yeah, I'm falling hard," was all Courtney could add as her cheeks turned a couple of shades of pink.

Joseph sat there with a smile, knowing another wedding was well within reach. He couldn't wait. Maybe he should've been a wedding planner. He shook his head at the thought he'd never utter aloud.

"We'll talk more about love and romance later," he said after a minute, then focused so they could complete their meeting. "What else is on the docket for the media?" Joseph asked the group.

Mallory replied. "I can confirm that the district attorney requested information on the case the FBI has been building. Much of it was turned over to him, and while I didn't watch yesterday's portion of the trial and, obviously, didn't watch today's, my understanding is the information gathered is going to be presented to the court. I was told early on that it was unlikely I'd have to stand in as a witness, which was odd considering how much time I spent with her. I do think my relationship with Hendrick and everything that went along with that made my testimony potentially detrimental instead of helpful, though."

"If this had been my case I would've put you on the stand," Avery said. "If for nothing else than to cause a psychological rift for Anna. Seeing you up there would've messed with her head and possibly made her snap while on the stand. I can understand why the DA doesn't want you up there but when I'm trying to break someone on the other side of the aisle I use whatever advantages I can. Seeing the face of someone who you feel betrayed you is a big mental screw job," Avery finished.

"I'd have liked to have been up there," Mallory said. She might not hold much bitterness in her heart, as she was too mature for that, but the things Anna had tried to do to Green during the time he was undercover was too much for Mallory to forget and let go of for quite some time.

"There isn't much for us to do, other than relay information that's already out there and what's already happened in the courtroom. Once the jury deliberates and comes back with their decision we'll do a few pieces on how the system finally worked for the people and how the bad guys got what they deserved," Courtney said.

"That is if we get a win. If we get a loss, I don't know how we'll report it," Mallory said.

"Let's not even put that into the air," Joseph said. He couldn't imagine Anna going free. All of the women nodded in agreement, but there was worry. So many things could go wrong in a jury trial.

"There rarely is any interest in a case after the perps head to prison. There will be a few days after the trial ends that receive a bit of airtime but that will be it. Of course, there are the book and movie deals that will surely come Anna's way, but tragedy sells. There's too much drama for there not to be publishers and movie studios salivating. My recommendation would be to get someone working with Damien and his family to ink all of those things and get them published and produced before Anna has the opportunity to direct the narrative. Even those from prison can spin an audience in whatever direction they want them to go," Avery told Joseph.

"That's smart thinking," Joseph said, although he didn't think Damien would go for it. "We're about to wrap things up on our end as well. I'm proud of how each of you have worked through this and what a great job you've done. Each of you have become family, and as all of you know, my biggest priority in life is to take care of family. It's been wonderful seeing you each circle around this and help ensure what happened to Damien will never happen to anyone ever again. Thank you so much."

"As much as I haven't enjoyed the reason we had to come together as a team, I *have* enjoyed the process. None of this would've been possible without all of us assisting the other. You never know, Joseph, you might now have a fearsome foursome on your hands who might just be able to take over the world," Courtney said with a laugh.

"Nothing would bring me more pleasure than to see you four rise to the top," Joseph said, meaning it. "That wraps up our meeting today." He smiled big as he pulled out a cigar and got more comfortable. "Now, I want to hear more about Courtney and Eyes."

That caused a burst of laughter from all of the women. "Of course you do. What would your life be like if you didn't get to meddle?" Avery bravely asked.

Joseph was absolutely delighted by her words. "It wouldn't be nearly as wonderful," Joseph admitted.

His life was good even when tragedy did strike. It was good because of who he chose to surround himself with — strong, beautiful, brave, diverse, and loyal friends. It was because of his relationships that he knew he'd weather any storm that blew his way.

CHAPTER FIFTEEN

Eyes smiled as he looked out over the lake he was fishing for trout in. It was a rare early evening; he'd spent the entire day alone, and he was happy, which might sound strange to some as that was the norm, wasn't it? Yes, he'd been content for most of his life, but true happiness was pretty allusive for a man who lived on adrenaline and witnessed the worst in humanity far more often than anyone should.

His pole dipped and he quickly lifted it to set the hook, but the little bugger got away and he laughed. It had been a while since he'd had any time to sit on a dock and fish. He wasn't surprised he had difficulty reeling one in. He didn't care though. He had a cooler full of beer next to him, and the world around him was nice and quiet.

Eyes was thinking about Courtney as he did most evenings. Their relationship couldn't in any way be described as typical. Their first date had been a disaster, and it seemed he'd been chasing her forever.

What was shocking to him was how much fun he'd had in his pursuits.

He really liked the woman. He enjoyed his time with her even when everything that could possibly go wrong did. He enjoyed the spark between them, enjoyed her witty sense of humor, and truly enjoyed how she made him feel about himself. She had a natural enthusiasm for life that he'd forgotten people could possess. He wanted to be around her a lot more — maybe forever.

As Eyes had that thought, he simply shrugged. He certainly wasn't going to admit to the guys that he might've caught the marriage flu he'd been so against, but it seemed he had. He was beginning to imagine his life with a wife at his side. He was beginning to feel that life would be better with a partner than without one.

Sure, there were amazing benefits to being single. A man could go fishing in the middle of the night if he wanted to without having to think about a partner. A man could spend long weekends with the boys in Hawaii. He could go to Vegas and flirt. He could even sleep with a slew of women every other night if he chose to.

Those thoughts had all seemed appealing to Eyes not that long ago. What he'd realized in the past year though, as he'd watched his team members fall in love, was that they didn't feel they'd lost something in giving up their bachelorhood. It was quite the opposite in fact. The men had found something in their partners they'd never thought possible. They'd found a friend, a companion, and a lover they knew and respected.

Sure, it had been fun to have a different warm body to explore several times a year, but those warm bodies hadn't looked so good in the light of day. He hadn't cared where they were going when they'd left his bed. He hadn't needed to take the time to find that special place on them that made them sigh in utter contentment or scream in true pleasure. He'd wanted his companions to have a good night, but it hadn't been his goal to make them never forget him. He'd been selfish, and that had been good enough for a very long time.

Eyes also had enjoyed not being accountable to anyone, had enjoyed doing whatever it was he wanted whenever he wanted. He'd never realized how lonely his life had been. He was well aware of that now. He wanted a partner, a friend, a lover, and a family. He didn't want to only be a star on a wall or a cold grave in the ground that no one cared enough to visit. He didn't want to simply exist anymore — he wanted to live and grow and be the kind of man who was loved and respected — he wanted to be like Joseph Anderson.

Eyes finished his final beer, packed up his fishing gear, and walked the half mile back to his SUV. He had an early morning date with Courtney the next day, and it took all he had to drive back to the lonely operations building instead of heading over to her house. He was sure she wouldn't mind a visit, but he wanted to show her that their relationship meant more to him than simply sex — though that was phenomenal with her. He wanted to show her that he wanted more. He was determined to give her a date that didn't end up in disaster with one of them face planting. He laughed as he walked inside the building that had been his home for about a year.

They'd had a great date at the movies until they'd been hit by a car. Then, they'd had no disaster on their fun center date with relatively no harm coming to either of them. But he wanted to give her more — he wanted to give her everything.

Eyes went to sleep relatively easily that night, another feat as he'd had a hard time sleeping more than a few hours at a time. Now, it seemed all he had to do was close his eyes and picture Courtney lying in his arms and he could fall asleep with a smile on his lips.

The morning sun streamed in through the high bulletproof glass of the operations center, waking Eyes from a dead sleep. He was lucky to be one of those rare people who woke up fully alert and ready for the day. On this particular morning he woke wearing the same smile he'd fallen asleep with.

It didn't take long for Eyes to go through his morning routine as he quickly showered, dressed, slammed down some food, then packed a bag for his date with Courtney. He was whistling as he walked out the door. The guys all had weekend plans so it was just him at the center and he was more than happy to leave it behind as he jumped into his vehicle. He couldn't wait for a morning kiss with the woman he was falling hard for. He refused to use the word *love* yet. When he spoke those words for the first time with a woman, he wanted her to be sure they were true.

He arrived at Courtney's place, and it seemed she was just as eager to see him as he was her. The door to her house flung open and she stepped onto her porch with a big smile, and dressed for adventure in athletic pants that showed every muscle in her sweet legs, and a top that had Eyes drooling to see what lay beneath. Of course, he knew, but he definitely wanted a reminder. He climbed from his SUV and met her on the walkway, immediately pulling her into his arms.

"You're early," she said, her sparkling eyes brighter than the sun shining down on them.

"I couldn't wait to see you," he told her.

She threw back her head and laughed. "I felt the same. It worries me a little," she admitted.

"I'm not worried at all," he told her.

Their faces were close and her smile faded as wonder shone in her expression. She lifted her hand and cupped his cheek, her thumb brushing against his lips.

"You're like a forbidden treat I've been told I can't have," she said, her fingers driving him crazy as they caressed his skin. "The more I try to tell myself not to have you, the more I crave your taste."

Eyes agreed with her statement. He wound his fingers in her hair and took that morning kiss he'd been thinking of since the second his eyes had opened. She sighed against his lips as he tasted strawberry on her tongue. Their bodies connected, and he was ready to take her back inside her house and show her exactly how much he'd missed her. Before he scrapped their day of adventure he reluctantly pulled back.

"You're stunning and consume all of my thoughts," he said, his voice a husky whisper.

"You make it difficult for me to report because all I can think about is you," she said with a chuckle.

"At least we're both in a drugged state," he said.

She laughed again at his words. "I've been in lust before, and I've had some serious crushes as well, but I don't think I've ever felt anything even close to how I feel when I'm with you."

Courtney's trust in him to admit her feelings made his heart grow a few sizes bigger. He felt like the Grinch on Christmas morning, hearing the Whos sing even though they'd lost everything. Was this what it felt like to fall in love? If it was, he was ready to sign on the dotted line right now.

"I don't have to think," Eyes told her. "I *know* I've never felt this way." He paused as he reluctantly pulled out of her arms and opened the passenger door for her to climb inside. "I promised you a day of adventure, and I'm determined to deliver."

She laughed as he shut her door. He jogged to his side and climbed in. Her scent surrounded him, and he knew he'd never want another woman sitting in her place. This had to be what love was all about.

"You told me to dress for adventure. I hope we make it through without anyone getting hurt," she said. "I've been klutzy my entire life which really sucks sometimes."

"I think it's very charming," he said. It was crazy but he didn't think there was anything about her he didn't find charming.

"Let's see if you're still saying that in five years," she told him with a laugh.

Eyes reached over and squeezed her hand as she launched into how her meeting had gone with the women who were all married or about to be married to his best friends in this world. As she spoke, he thought about her last sentence to him. He realized she hadn't noticed she'd said it.

If a woman would've told him they'd be together five years from that moment at any other time prior to meeting Courtney, Eyes would've instantly panicked and found a way to break their date. With Courtney, though, the thought of being with her in five years elated him. He couldn't imagine not being with her in the future. He might need to go ring shopping.

As he had that thought, he wondered if it was too soon. They'd barely dated. Eyes was quiet as they drove up to Poo Poo Point, which he'd picked because the name had cracked him up. It was where they needed to be for the date he had planned, but the name was an added bonus.

He went back to think about buying a ring. Was it too soon? Who made the rules on the proper time to propose? Who decided how long you had to know a person? He'd been told by the guys that when they knew, they knew, and there was no changing their minds. Did he know?

"We're hiking?" Courtney asked as they parked in the crowded lot at the trailhead to the mountain.

"Yes, and then we're flying," Eyes told her as he pulled out his pack that contained his paragliding equipment.

"Flying?" she asked. She looked a bit excited and a bit terrified.

"Yep, I've been paragliding for years, and I've done a lot of tandem jumping so I promise you're in safe hands."

"I've read a lot about paragliding, but I've never had a desire to do it," she said. Eyes found himself practically holding his breath as he waited to see if she'd trust him enough to do this. He wanted to soar above the ground with her. He wanted her to believe in him enough to literally put her life in his hands.

"What do you think?" he asked. If she didn't want to fly, they'd have a nice afternoon of walking and then a yummy picnic. It wouldn't be as great an afternoon, but anytime he was with her was amazing, so he'd take her as she was.

"I think with you I'll be fine," she said after a few more seconds. "I trust you, Eyes."

Those words crumbled the last of his walls. He looked at her and there was no longer the smallest hint of doubt inside of him. He was in love. How did a person know when they were in love? It was quite simple, he realized. It was when you knew the happiness of the person you were with meant more than your own joy. It also meant that your happiness was actually better because their pleasure in life was your own.

He almost told her right then and there that he loved her but he somehow managed to keep it in. Not because he wanted to hide it, but because he wanted to make her soar first.

They walked the steep trail to the top of Poo Poo Point, Courtney easily keeping pace with him through the forested switchbacks that were dotted with stone steps.

"This is stunning," she told him as they rounded another corner.

"I've been here a few times since moving to Seattle," he said. They had to squeeze to the side as a couple moved down the trail.

"I've never been, but I'm sure I'll come back," she said.

"Unless we're somewhere else," he told her. He knew he wouldn't stay in Seattle once this job was done. He'd come back and visit as he had many friends there now, but Eyes needed adventure and he needed to travel. He didn't want to make Seattle his home base. Courtney shocked him with her next words.

"Where will we be?" she asked.

Was she in the same place as him? Had she given up fighting whatever was happening between the two of them? Were they going to talk about it, or simply move onto the next phase in their relationship?

"I can see us paragliding all over the world. There's some stunning places in Africa I wouldn't mind trying," he said as they got closer to their launching point. The trail was only about a mile and a half on the south side of the mountain.

"I've been to many places in the world reporting fascinating stories, but I haven't been to Africa yet. I think we definitely need to go there," she said just as they broke into the clearing where several paragliders waited for their turn to leap off of the mountain.

It was a beautiful sunny morning, and they had a clear view of Mount Rainier, a breathtaking mountain to behold.

"Then I'll take you there," Eyes told her as he began getting their paraglider ready. A person jumped with a woman strapped to his front, and her laughter flew back at Eyes and Courtney.

"Wow, I've never seen jumpers so close," Courtney said as she watched the man and woman soar through the air. "It's fascinating to watch . . . and a bit scary," she admitted. "How high are we?"

"Don't look straight down at first. It's about eighteen hundred feet up, which sounds scary, but I've learned a lot about this and I've never had an injury," he assured her. "At least not in this activity." In reality Jon's body had been injured a lot with bullets and broken bones, but flying through the air was freeing, and he'd perfected landings so he didn't cause his body any further pain.

"I'm not scared of heights," she assured him. "It's just a bit scary to launch yourself off of a perfectly safe mountain." She laughed as she watched another person run off the edge of the cliff. A gust of warm air lifted them higher up and the man laughed as he gave a thumbs up to the people watching him.

"I'd say eighty percent of the people I've spoken to love to paraglide. The other twenty percent were terrified the entire time and said they'd never do it again. If you have a serious fear of heights I'd say it's probably not the most fun activity for you."

"It's a good thing I don't have a ton of fears," Courtney said. "Maybe though, that's because I'm a fear junkie. You have to be a bit crazy to go in for the best stories."

"I agree with you there. I worry sometimes that you put yourself at too much risk for some of yours stories," he told her.

She laughed at his words. "Are you the kettle or the pot?" she finally asked. He laughed with her.

"I know. I know. I'm a total hypocrite. I guess that means I care about you," he said. He was giving her a preview of his feelings.

She smiled big. "I guess I won't complain if you care enough to worry."

Damn! How had he been so lucky as to find this woman? She was his equal in so many ways. She was adventurous — and funny — and brave — and kind. She was exactly the sort of woman he hadn't even known he'd been searching for.

"What's the farthest you've flown on this?" she asked as he laid out his Shute.

"The longest flight has been from here actually," he told her. "Of all of the places in the world I've glided, I did a six-hour flight from here."

"Holy moly," she said. "We're not doing that today, are we? I don't think I could go that long without peeing my pants, which would be a bit embarrassing."

Eyes laughed hard at her words. "I don't think a woman's ever said that to me before, but I like it," he told her as he wiped the corners of his eyes. Damn, this woman made him smile a lot. "No, we're not going that long today. I want to give you a taste. If you love it, we'll go a bit farther each time. My six-hour flight landed me over a hundred miles away. It was glorious."

"I think I'll want to do that sometime after I haven't drunk a bunch of coffee," she said.

"That sounds like a deal. Now, come here and get strapped up. We're almost ready," he told her.

She didn't seem nearly as nervous, now that she'd had time to watch others successfully launch. He got her straps hooked up, and then they were on the launch site and ready to go.

"Just run with me when I say go, and within the blink of an eye we're going to be soaring," he said.

"Okay," she told him, her voice breathy, a touch of fear, and a whole lot of excitement ringing through loud and clear.

"Go!" Courtney didn't hesitate at his command.

They ran together and the sail and the wind did its job and within seconds they were launching off of the mountain, Courtney gasping as they sailed into the air, the trees and ground below them. Her laughter was music to his ears as he searched for pockets that would lift them, giving her a few fun thrills before he took them down to the ground.

It was several minutes before Courtney spoke; he knew to give her time to take it all in before he said anything. He wanted her to love this as much as he did. He wanted her to go with him a thousand times.

"Have you ever hit any trees?" she asked as their feet dangled a couple of hundred feet above the tree line.

"No, I haven't crashed into any trees," he told her. "However, if I had to crash I'd rather it happened in the trees where only my equipment would be damaged instead of my body." She sucked in a breath. "Don't worry, I wouldn't take you where I feared there was a possibility of that happening.

That's beginning pilots who don't study the weather and don't know enough. Yes, accidents can happen as they do all of the time in life, but those of us who have been through the most extreme circumstances know that luck is made not granted."

They flew out a bit farther before he began their descent. He was never ready for the flight to end, and with her in his arms he was even more reluctant for this ride to be over, but all good things eventually had to come to an end. Courtney laughed as a dozen birds circled them, then moved on.

"This entire experience is surreal. I don't know how else to describe it," she told him.

"I agree. There are times I feel like a feather being blown on a breeze, and other times I feel like an eagle soaring high in the sky. No matter how many times I do it, I can't get enough of it. Man wasn't gifted with wings, so we made our own."

"I used to have dreams of flying, but I grew up and realized they were just fantasies. I guess you've made one of my fantasies a reality," she said.

"I want to make all of your dreams a reality," he told her, meaning it. He took in a deep breath. "I love you, Courtney. I know it's quick, and I know it might not sound sincere, but I feel as if I'm going to burst if I don't get the words out." He did feel relief at having said those three little words he'd never said to a non-relative before.

She turned so her profile was clear to him. There was a beaming smile on her lips.

"It is too soon, but I love you too," she admitted. He leaned forward and brushed her cheek with his lips, glad he'd said it while they were soaring above the earth. He wasn't sure how love happened, he just knew Cupid had struck him hard.

"I've always been told if I want something I need to earn it," Eyes said. "I haven't earned you yet, but I will each and every day you don't give up on me."

She laughed. "Why don't we earn each other," she suggested.

"I think that's a damn fine idea," he said.

As much as Eyes loved soaring above the earth, he'd never wanted to land so badly. If he didn't pull Courtney into his arms and hold her tight while pressing his lips to hers, he just might shatter. He loved this woman and he wanted to shout it to the world.

They were getting closer and closer to the landing pad where a lot of people stood around as they waited for their own parties to land. "It's so odd to see cars, people, dogs, and life that we're normally side by side with down below us. I can imagine how God must feel looking down at his creations," Courtney said.

Eyes laughed again. "I'm sure He shakes his head in disappointment a lot," he told her.

"I disagree. I think He's very proud of the struggles we face and how we manage to pick ourselves up again," she told him.

"That's only one of the reasons I love you," Eyes told her. "You're the most positive person I've ever met. You truly are the beacon that draws people to safety in the middle of a storm."

"That might be the best compliment I've ever received," she told him.

"Being up here makes any problems I might think I have simply float away," she said. "This is purity at its finest."

"I couldn't agree more," Eyes told her.

"Thank you, Jon. Thank you for being you, and for helping me to be the best person I can be," she told him. He took one arm and squeezed it around her. He wanted her turned around, wanted to wrap his arms around her and pull her tight. She rarely used his real name, and he loved the sound of it coming from her lips.

"It's me who should be thanking you for helping me fly," he said. He meant that in so many more ways than actually flying in the clear blue sky.

"I think we help each other," she said. "Maybe that's what people have meant every time they've ever said *their other half*. I've always scoffed at that. I'm not laughing anymore because I'm starting to believe in yin and yang, starting to believe we truly do have another half of ourselves out there that we've been searching for without understanding something was ever missing."

Jon "Eyes" Eisenhart knew he was going to spend the rest of his life with this woman. He could wait, because he knew they had forever. Their feet touched the ground, and then he was pulling her into his arms. He'd get to do that for the rest of time and through all of eternity — he was sure of it.

He was more sure of that than anything in his entire life. He'd found the one woman in this world he refused to live without, and he couldn't be happier at his fall to the ground.

CHAPTER SIXTEEN

Mallory Black-Meeks picked up Jasmine at 0500, just as they'd agreed to a week prior, and Jasmine was on full tilt. In two weeks, Jasmine would start college, so this was one of the last times she'd be able to train with Mallory on a weekday due to her class load.

"Good morning," Jasmine said, practically bouncing in her seat.

"Good morning. You a little excited?" Mallory asked with a smile.

"Dang straight!" Jasmine smiled back.

"We'll see how excited you are at the end of the day. You might not want to hang out with me after we're done," Mallory said with a chuckle. She knew who, and what, the eldest granddaughter of Joseph Anderson was. She was exactly like Mallory had been at her age.

Jasmine had life by the horns and was full of wonder and interest, wanting to conquer the world in one bite and swallow it whole. Even knowing the world didn't, and wouldn't, work like that, she was going to try it anyway. Like Mallory, it wouldn't get her down when she didn't succeed. In fact, it would have the opposite effect — she'd try even harder and push herself that much more. Life experience would slow her down some but her love for adventure would never disappear like it does in so many people as they become stuck in their jobs and the comings and goings of their ordinary lives.

Mallory pulled away from the house, and the subtle light radiating from the dashboard lit up Jasmine's smile like a beacon on a stormy seashore. Mallory wasn't cynical, and she didn't hide her joy in seeing others happy, so when she noticed the cemented smile on her passenger's face, she couldn't help but bring up the corners of her own mouth as well. It was true that you became the best or worst of yourself by who you chose to surround yourself with.

This was the fourth meeting between the two women. The first three had been spent going over the mental aspects of the FBI. Mallory had brought training manuals, which Jasmine devoured like a starving bear sitting at a waterfall waiting for some salmon to jump directly into its mouth.

Once the boring stuff was finished, Mallory had requested Jasmine complete an assignment and present her findings to a group of family and friends. The eighteen-year-old had lost hours of sleep getting it done and the room of thirty people had been rightfully impressed when she'd been able to handle all of the questions that had come at her, many of which Mallory had provided prior to the start of Jasmine's presentation.

The last part of the assignment had been deciphering codes that had grown in complexity with each step. Usually those brain-teasing intellectual tests were reserved for people going into specific fields of study and rarely did individuals who tried them for the first time get past the fifth page. Jasmine had completed eight tests before getting stumped. Only after she'd accepted defeat did she get told there was *no* solution, except to turn it in and state there was no solution.

Jasmine loved the training Mallory was giving her, and as Jasmine had been told in previous meetings, most FBI work was mental. The physical interactions were rare and almost never seen in the field. On this particular day, the physical aspect of being an FBI agent was going to be put to the test.

"Do you recall what the instructors are looking for when you're at the Basic Field Training Center?" Mallory asked Jazzy. She was speaking about the twenty week FBI entrance training at Quantico, Virginia.

"Yes," Jasmine said, counting them off with a finger matching each reply. "Conscientiousness, Cooperation, Emotional maturity, Integrity, Initiative, and Judgment."

"Well done," Mallory replied. "And what are the physical requirements?"

"For me, it's as simple as eating pie. Push-ups, sit-ups, pull-ups, a three-hundred-meter sprint and a one-and-a-half-mile run. You know I can pass that portion of it any day of the week," Jasmine said with confidence. She wasn't being cocky, she just knew that the workouts she'd been doing with Smoke had her in the best shape of her life. Since she'd been working out with him her overall fitness had increased exponentially.

"Yes, I do, but can you do it soaking wet, with a full suit on, and completely geared up?" Mallory asked, looking at her young protégé from the corner of her eye.

"In a suit? Wet? What gear?" Jasmine asked.

"Well, it's easy to take a test when you're in workout gear. That isn't real life though. You'll never be chasing down a perp right after you've walked out of the gym." She paused and laughed. "Okay, *almost* never," Mallory corrected herself as she remembered taking down a guy who'd tried robbing the gym where she'd been taking a spin class.

"This morning though, I'm going to get you dressed and geared in what you'll wear on the job. After that you're going to dive into a pool and then your exam begins. There will be no rest period, there will be no time to take a bathroom break, and there won't be any time to stretch before the exercise begins. Understand?" Mallory asked.

"Completely. I can't wait to crush it," Jasmine replied. The smile she'd been wearing all morning was replaced with singular focus.

What neither of them expected was the dramatic temperature drop overtaking the Pacific Northwest the last few days. The lows were getting close to freezing and the ski resorts were already showing large layers of snow at the higher elevations. A low cloud cover was pushed out overnight and the clear sky allowed the cold air to move in faster.

When the duo arrived at the track where a large trough had been filled with water, Mallory gave pause. Was this too much for her trainee? Quickly though, Mallory realized that in the mental exercises one of the positions was in knowing when to give up because the solution wasn't available. Mallory was going to allow Jasmine to decide how the morning's events were going to take place. Jasmine didn't bat an eye after she came out of the vehicle dressed in her *run of the mill daily suit for women in the FBI.*

"Okay, ready," Jasmine said as she walked directly to the water, stepped in, submerged herself completely and then jumped back out.

"Push-ups. Go," Mallory barked. They needed to keep adrenaline at full capacity the entire day.

The FBI doesn't have a timeline on push-ups, but they do have a minimum requirement that must be completed, which is forty-five for women. Jasmine demolished the minimum by completing seventy-two.

"Three hundred meters. Go!" Mallory yelled while starting the timer on her watch.

As Jasmine ran hard, Mallory could see the spray of water from her shoes and pants shooting high in the air. As her speed increased on the straight stretch of the track it made the suit look like a blur. Fabric was being pushed and pulled at the same time. It wasn't easy running in wet clothes, especially those made of cotton and polyester, and tugging and twisting on a cold body.

In an extra hard push at the end, Jasmine crossed the finish line with a time of forty-four seconds. Mallory was astonished at the speed and agility of the young woman in these kind of conditions. She was doing better than Mallory had done in her beginning years of the FBI.

"Sit-ups. Go!" Mallory said not giving Jasmine time for a break. Criminals didn't pause for time-outs.

As soon as Jasmine was on the ground Mallory started her watch. Jasmine had to get thirty-two within one minute. She finished her required amount in thirty-seven seconds, then continued until her minute was up.

"You feeling okay?" Mallory asked as Jasmine slowly rolled to her side and used her arms to assist in rising to her feet.

"I'm good. Let's destroy this run," Jasmine said.

"Okay. Go," Mallory said and clicked the timer button.

Jasmine finished her fifth of six laps and the strain on her face confirmed that she was feeling the difference of completing these exercises in heavy, wet clothing. The strain on her muscles was real and the heat that had been sucked out of her body from the cold air was making it even more difficult. By the time she was on the last half of her last lap her speed had dropped dramatically and it was the first time Mallory had ever seen Jasmine struggle.

"Let's go!" Mallory yelled across the field in encouragement.

Jasmine gave her all, pushed with all she had to finish the timed run, and then fell to her knees after she crossed the finish line.

"Get up," Mallory commanded.

"Ugh, let me rest a second," Jasmine whined.

"Nope. You're not going to do this. The worst thing you can do right now is stop in your wet clothes, especially with this freezing air," Mallory informed the exhausted girl.

Mallory held out her hand, offering to help Jasmine up and the young woman took it begrudgingly. She wanted to lay there and regain her energy but there was no way Mallory was going to let that happen.

"You need to change into dry clothes. There's a towel in the trunk, and you can throw your wet clothes back there when you're done," Mallory said as she clicked the key fob for her trunk, popping it open.

"All good," Jasmine called out after she'd finished changing.

"Well done, Jazzy. How are you feeling? Was it as easy as you thought it was going to be?" Mallory asked as she put the car into gear and started driving.

"Piece of cake," Jasmine said with a smile, her lips still tinged with purple from being so cold.

"Oh really? I can turn us around and go back and have you start again," Mallory said, eyebrows raised and ready to do just that.

Jasmine couldn't hide her reaction, knowing her mentor would do such a thing, and decided against being a wise ass any further. "No need for that. Whatever we have planned next is fine."

The two of them started to laugh while enjoying the warmth of the car's heater. It only took a few minutes for Jasmine to get her core temperature regulated and back to a level where her teeth weren't trying to crush each other from involuntary shivering.

"Where are we headed next?" Jasmine asked as they made their way from the parking lot.

"I'm taking you in," Mallory said.

"Taking me in?" Jasmine asked.

"Yep. To work; I'm taking you to my office," Mallory said.

It took several moments for Jasmine to regain her composure. She wasn't sure if she was supposed to shout with joy, act stoic, profusely thank Mallory, or sit there acting as if she was going to just another ordinary place. Internally she was jumping out of her skin like she'd done the first time her parents had taken her to Disneyland. Both were fairytale lands in her eyes that she'd never thought she'd be able to see in person.

The drive went by quickly and as Mallory presented her identification at the gate, and it opened without incident, Jasmine knew she was actually entering hallowed grounds. There was no way she could suppress her smile as the car came to a stop and was powered down.

As soon as the two women stepped out of the car a large commotion roared toward them. Men and women came swarming out of the building, running to different vehicles, moving out of the parking lot as fast as possible.

"Matt! What's going on?" Mallory yelled at a man as he raced toward them.

"We have a bank heist, multiple gunmen and at least thirty hostages. On top of that there's a bomb threat for the buildings surrounding it. Grab your gear and ride with me," the man said.

Mallory ran to the car she'd arrived in, popped the trunk, and pulled out her bulletproof vest and a briefcase that had some obvious weight to it by the way her arm snapped down once it was free from the back of the car.

"Jazzy — listen carefully, you're going to ride with us and you won't ask any questions. Do you understand? Call your dad and have him ready to pick you up. I'll give you the location as soon as we're moving. After that, no calls, no texts, no social media," Mallory said in a stern tone.

"Yes, of course," Jasmine said. She didn't want her dad to pick her up. She wanted to see a real FBI takedown.

The two of them jogged to the awaiting car. Before their doors were fully shut Matt smashed down the accelerator and the car came to life. Black cars spilled from the parking lot, only inches from impaling each other. Jasmine didn't know what to think of the situation.

The cars raced down streets, then onto backroads, everything getting closer and tighter. The only thing the recent high school graduate could do was watch the cars in front of them and grimace each time they seemed to come dangerously close to hitting an object.

There was constant chatter on the handheld radios in the front, the codes and words not making sense to Jasmine. Then she heard commands to take the next right to create a flanking position and the car she was in was the car receiving that command. Matt turned the car hard and if it hadn't been for her seatbelt, Jasmine would've been squished face first into the opposite side window.

"This won't work, Matt. We can't leave her. She can't stay out here all alone. Call for another car," Mallory barked as the driver swerved, barely missing old boxes that littered the street.

"There aren't any other cars, Black," Matt said. Even though Mallory had married Green and taken his last name of Meeks, the transition to calling someone by a new name was a slow one.

"Damnit," Mallory thundered. Then she turned. "Jazzy, listen carefully. When we stop you will follow every single instruction I give you. Do you understand?" Jasmine nodded. "Put this on," Mallory said, then handed Jasmine the bulletproof vest she'd been wearing.

"Don't worry, Black, I've got another vest in the back," Matt said as he came to an abrupt stop.

The radio squawked again, telling Matt and Mallory to enter the door they were stationed at. They immediately followed instructions. They stepped into utter darkness. Not even a hint of light was visible.

"Jazzy, put your left hand on my right shoulder and don't take it off," whispered Mallory.

Jasmine did as instructed, and the two of them followed Matt. He had a small flashlight that provided only enough light to see fifteen to twenty feet in front of them. There was a small shuffling sound and when Matt directed his light to it, up a flight of stairs, there was a person running away at the top.

"FBI, Stop!" Matt yelled.

Then he started running after the person fleeing from them. Mallory followed suit and Jasmine was like a leech, stuck hard to Mallory's shoulder just as she'd been instructed to do.

The trio ran hard up the steps, over a catwalk area, and down steps, the person staying far enough out of range to not be in the light but not pulling away to be lost in the darkness. The chase continued across the open warehouse floor, back up another flight of stairs, then down again.

"We have a perp at our location. In pursuit, headed southeast inside building," Mallory yelled into the comm system.

There was no reply.

She tried again and there was no reply.

"I'm not getting anything, Matt. We need to pull back. This situation is bad, especially with Jasmine here," Mallory called to her colleague.

Matt stopped, breathing hard. Mallory was also short of breath while Jasmine was gasping for as much oxygen as she could consume. He did a quick sweep of the area they were in and saw an office door. Quickly making his way over to it, he found it was unlocked.

"You two go in here and wait. I'll go on," Matt said.

"No," Mallory said firmly.

"Jasmine, go inside, lock the door, and don't answer it until I return. Do you understand?" Mallory requested.

As Mallory was saying this she was walking Jasmine through the threshold of the door and inside a room that seemed to be even darker, if that was possible. Jasmine was starting to get freaked out and didn't want to stay alone in the room waiting for an indefinite amount of time while some lunatic was on the loose. Mallory gently nudged Jasmine forward another step.

"You'll be fine, Jasmine," Mallory said, then gently closed the door.

As soon as the handle clicked shut an explosion of light engulfed Jasmine. She immediately shielded her eyes. The noise she was hearing didn't make sense. It sounded like people cheering and clapping.

Then all of her senses reset. Her eyes dilated, her ears focused, and her body felt more under control. Standing before her were all of the special ops men, including Chad. They called out *surprise*, making her jump.

"What is this?" Jasmine asked, utterly confused.

"This is your sendoff party," Mallory said from behind Jasmine.

"What?" Jasmine asked again as she turned to her mentor.

"The guys and I wanted to have a send-off party for you. This summer has been a great one and I've been blessed to work with you. As you enter college and start taking on new challenges I hope everything we did together is a benefit to you," Mallory said with a shimmer of water pooling in her eyes.

Jasmine turned back to the men, Mallory now at her side, and beamed from ear to ear. As the two of them walked to the group, she looked at Mallory with a shaky smile. "I both love and can't stand you right now."

"I've felt the same many times in life. Did you really think I'd take you on a real FBI mission? My butt would've been fired, and your grandfather might've personally wrung my neck," Mallory said.

"It seemed pretty damn real to me," Jasmine said.

"That's because we're good," Smoke said, the first one to step forward. The other men were right behind him.

Jasmine gave each man a hug and thanked them for all they'd done for her over the past year. She told them her time with them had been the greatest experience she could've ever hoped for and she was glad they'd come into her life.

"Chad, you've dealt with my craziness for the better part of a year and I appreciate your patience with me. Even when you didn't want to have any. Thank you — I love you," Jasmine said as she gave one of her earliest heroes a hug and a kiss on his cheek.

"Smoke . . ." Jasmine had to catch her emotions as she looked up to the man who'd become more than just a mentor to her. He'd become someone she knew she could call on in any situation, at any time, and anywhere and he'd be there for her. He'd become family.

"Smoke, I'm at a loss for words right now. I'll never be able to thank you enough for what you've done for me. All of the time you've spent training me, all of the time you've given me guidance and advice, and all of the time you simply listened to me, which I know was a considerable amount of time, has meant the world to me. Thank you, Tyrell, I love you," Jasmine said as she wrapped her arms around him and silently let a tear fall.

"Love you too, kiddo," Smoke replied, returning the hug. She had a feeling he might be fighting a tear or two of his own. He might look tough as nails, but he was a big marshmallow.

"Now, let's party!" Mallory interrupted, knowing they'd all be crying soon if they kept up the mushy talk.

The food arrived, and Jasmine was starving after her adrenaline-fueled morning. As the team ate, Jasmine opened gifts from each of the people there, and they told her about the entire set-up and elaborate planning to get her to her party. She hadn't had a clue as to what they'd been up to. There were many stories shared and Sleep even kept most of his from becoming too raunchy. Everyone laughed and had a great time. As the end of their celebration was drawing near Jasmine stood up, held out her glass, and gave a toast.

"To each of you sitting with me, thank you. My life is better because you're in it. To those who hate us cause they ain't us, they can kiss my ass!"

The men and Mallory hooted and slapped their hands on the table vigorously in agreement with the sentiment of their unofficially adopted kid. It didn't matter how old Jasmine got: she'd always be a little girl in their eyes — but a badass one at that.

Jasmine couldn't wait to see what her future held.

CHAPTER SEVENTEEN

"Please, be seated," Judge Scott stated as she sat on her bench above the attorneys, the jurors, and the audience.

"Members of the jury, today you'll hear closing statements from the prosecution and defense. Both sides have been allotted fifteen minutes to present their closing arguments. When they finish you'll be taken back to your conference room and asked to deliberate on the case until a unanimous verdict is reached. There's no timeline for this, and I ask that each of you be earnest in having your voice heard. Discuss this case, and *only* this case. Outside interests have no weight in this and I know each of you will showcase the highest level of integrity. Sir, the time is now yours," Judge Scott finished, looking at the district attorney.

Since the failed kidnapping attempt of the defendant, along with the bomb scare, the courtroom had been absent of any outside individuals. Cameras were allowed to film but there were no operators behind them. If the station decided to focus on one individual, or on the entirety of the courtroom, they'd have to live with those results.

Each of the owners of the cameras were required to wait outside the doors, which caused considerable stress but if they wanted any footage at all they were left with no choice but to comply with the judge's orders. The common theme was having the camera focused on either Anna Miller, the jury, or the entire courtroom. Tension was high for everyone, both outside of the courtroom and inside it.

The district attorney slowly stood, only briefly looking at his notes before letting them slide smoothly back down to their resting place on the table he'd previously been sitting at. It was all for show. He'd gone through this dog and pony show too many times to count.

For the majority of his life, he'd worked at perfecting his mannerisms in the courtroom . . . who to look at first, who to make eye contact with, and who to never give a second of attention to, silently letting the jury know that person wasn't worth their time or attention. He'd perfected how to put the most effective inflection into his words to make his message clear and understandable to the men and women who held the decision of a win or loss in their hands.

As the only child in his family to not only go to college, but to graduate with a law degree from Harvard, he knew there was a specific way to talk to different people. Even decades later he always remembered what his late mother and father had taught him about how to treat people, and in moments like this he prayed they were nodding their heads in approval.

The DA started. "Good morning ladies and gentlemen. It's been a long two weeks, hasn't it?" He paused as if they'd actually answer. He looked them in the eyes as they smiled or nodded. Good. They were alert and paying attention.

"For all of us: you, Judge Scott, the defense team, Mr. Brohm, the bailiff, and Ms. Johnson over there on the stenograph, it's been mentally and physically challenging to be here. We all have not only been expected to stay focused on a lot of information that had to do with the case, but we've been shocked that a juror involved himself in an unscrupulous way. We've had to fear for our lives with a bomb scare, and we've had to endure hours of being kept in this room." He sighed as he paced in front of the jury box. He had their sympathy. They were all in it together.

"I can promise you that in my thirty plus years of working in a courtroom the kind of things that have happened the past week have never occurred before." He gave another dramatic pause. "And trust me, I've seen the worst of the worst of cases, but this has topped them all. It would be easy to make jokes about it, and it would also be easy for each of you to request to be pardoned from the trial after any of those events, but I'm ever thankful each of you has stayed. It shows the character of each one of you, and I'm proud of your service in all of this. Hold your heads high when you walk out of here as there are few on earth who possess the strength each of you has."

The DA slowly walked to the front of the jury box, ensuring he could make unquestionable eye contact. "There's been testimony from doctors, forensic data technicians, and an entire armada of men and women in the security world of the FBI. Each one of them has laid out the multitude of laws that Anna Miller has broken. Her signature, her face on date-stamped video, her personal *and* her forged accounts she thought she'd hidden from those who are a lot smarter than her." He stopped again as if it was a cut and dry case and there was no other decision for the jury other than a guilty verdict.

"All of this evidence has been verified without a chance of reasonable doubt creeping in. The sad thing about this case is that the financial aspect is just a tiny piece of the whole picture. The other, and to me the more insidious, is what she's done to her own brother."

He then did a small turn so there was no denying his focus was now at the defendant's table, and specifically on Anna Miller. "How many of you have siblings? How many of you have sons and daughters? I have two brothers and a sister and also three children. A son and two daughters. While every family is different, there's no denying the truth of siblings. I can honestly say that my brothers and I used to fight like cats and dogs. There'd be times that we'd get going so hard our mom would come in swinging a switch. Whoever was at the receiving end of that stick was the unlucky sibling of the moment. My own children have tested every single boundary their siblings have set and sometimes crossed it just to see their brother or sister get spun up. I'm sure each of you have similar stories. Some days my wife and I want to send all three of them to the moon on the outside of a rocket ship just to get a few minutes of peace and quiet."

A few chuckles from the jury box told him the connection had been made.

Then the DA put on his cool, calm, and sensitive voice. "Then there was the rest of the time. In all of the arguments, in all of the fighting and yelling and pure craziness, there was an understanding that we seriously loved each other. Yes, we could say and do some hurtful things but each of us knew that at the end of the day any disagreements stayed right there and we moved on. To actually wish harm upon those we've spent our lives with is incomprehensible to most of us. But here we are in this case. A sister, who the brother never knew, had been plotting evil outcomes for nearly forty years. It could've only been a sinister story, but the depths of her depravity was deeper than anything any of us could've ever imagined. Instead of using her intellect to better people, to enhance those around the community, she put all of her energy into creating one of the most complex spider webs known to man to destroy her own brother. It isn't only sad, it's morbidly grotesque."

He stopped to make sure his words fully sank in. He then turned his attention back to the jury as he slowly walked toward his table. "I'll leave you with this. When you look in the mirror at night, do you think you could do what Anna Miller has done? Do you think one of your siblings could do to you what she did to her own brother? Damien Whitfield has been a model citizen in this world, helping children, the poor, the community, and making this world an all-around better place. Damien, his wife, and his precious daughter have never asked for these atrocities to occur but here we are, trying our damnedest to send a lawful message to the entire community — that we won't tolerate hate and deceitful people who bend and break the laws at their whim. Laws the rest of us follow. These power-hungry elites believe they can get away with their illegal activity because of their position in life. They think the people they're supposed to represent are to serve them instead of the other way around." He was good at knowing when to pause and let things sink in. The jury was rapt as they followed each and every one of his movements in the courtroom.

"It's because of this, and because of the *overwhelming* evidence provided, that allows me to know each of you will join me in saying — Anna Miller is *guilty* on all charges." He slowly moved to his table and sat as if the conclusion was set and there was nothing for him to worry about. The tension his monologue had created was as thick as pea soup. The only noise heard in the courtroom was the faint humming of the furnace as it worked deep in the underbelly of the courthouse to heat all of the rooms.

The corporate news stations might not have been in the room, but they were live streaming and their fingers were working as fast as the prosecutor spoke. Once he finished his closing statement, hashtags were instantly created and went viral within minutes. The highest rated ones were #DefendDamien #LifeforSenatorAnna and #MillertheWannaBeKiller. Before long those tags were scrolling at the bottom of newsfeeds across the world. It was obvious where the heart of the people lay: in agreement with the prosecutor — Anna should be put away for a very, *very* long time for what she'd done to her brother *and* to the people she was supposed to have been representing.

Though the DA wanted to show confidence that the decision was already made, he truly loved his country and loved that in the great nation of the United States of America, the defendant always had the opportunity to be heard. He'd lost cases where he knew the defendant was guilty, but that was law and order and the right to be judged by a jury of your peers. Sometimes it didn't go the way he wanted, and it angered him, but the system couldn't be infringed upon.

That might rub some people the wrong way, especially when a case was as obvious as the one he'd just tried, but that was what separated those who cared about the sovereignty of the country and those who thought freedom was simply a suggestion instead of a universal right. He'd choose freedom every day over government rule, even if that meant the bad guys got away with murder once in a while. For the former senator, her only chance at freedom lay in the hands of twelve men and women and whether or not they'd bought her story over the facts presented to them.

Anna Miller's legal team had been brilliant, insightful, and charged so much money they rarely lost. They didn't take low profile cases, and someone had to have a small fortune to buy their representation.

Some people thought it was better to look like they were losing in the beginning only to have a triumphant victory at the end. Some liked to take the lead right up front. Anna's team of lawyers liked to look like winners from the start. The DA didn't think they'd achieved their goal in this case. He was well aware the defense attorneys made a point to win in whatever manner was needed, including walking the thin line between lawful and lawless, just as long as the end result was their client walking out of the courthouse with them.

Throughout the trial the team had done an excellent job of making sure each witness the DA put up seemed questionable in their information and testimony. Even the most educated and highest ranked members of specific industries didn't walk off the witness stand as untouchable and brightly polished as they'd appeared when they'd entered the courtroom.

Even when Damien gave his testimony that included a plethora of photographs submitted as evidence showing what he'd gone through the night he was attacked, Anna Miller's legal team was able to poke holes into what was presented via the prosecutor. They might not have been big holes, but even the smallest crack could potentially lead to a sinking ship over enough time. Her lawyers had worked hard at finding and exploiting cracks whenever possible.

Avery, Sleep's wife and former defense attorney extraordinaire, watched the closing arguments with intense interest. She didn't miss defending people, and she had no desire to be in the courtroom on that side of the aisle anymore, but she could remember the rush of being in that position.

"You know, this team representing Anna is great," Avery said over her shoulder to Sleep. Her husband simply nodded. They were all tensely paying attention to the television now.

For the next ten minutes practically every person in the Washington area was watching the closing remarks with rapt attention, straining to hear each word said to the jurors. This was history, this was life altering, it was a testament for a community, a city, and a country . . . and no one wanted to miss a single sentence. If there was anyone hoping for Anna Miller to be found *not guilty* you'd have had to search for a long time near and far to find them. Thankfully, at least for the moment, the defense team only had to worry about the decision the jurors would make.

"Jurors, we're now at the point where I instruct you of your duties and remind you of the charges set forth. In a moment I'll release you to deliberate your decision. Any and all questions, remarks, and inquiries regarding the law or this case will need to be written down and given to the bailiff. Please remember that this trial requires a unanimous decision for the defendant to be considered guilty. Juror number three is the foreperson and will be responsible for communication between you and the courtroom. When you've reached a verdict, the foreperson will notify the bailiff and then all of you will come back into the courtroom to hand me the verdict and then the foreperson will read it out loud. Do you have any questions regarding the process henceforth?" Judge Scott asked.

The jurors shook their heads in the negative and were subsequently sequestered to a conference room to begin their deliberation.

The lull in the action was the most difficult time for those awaiting a response, either in the positive or the negative, from the jurors. If the men and women responsible for the ruling found in favor of the prosecutor it was an instant ride to prison for Anna. If they ruled that Ms. Miller was not guilty then the state had spent a lot of time and resources on a trial that should've been a slam dunk. Each side had their own stress to live through for an indefinite amount of time.

"I believe the state did everything in our power to show the depravity of the defendant and I have no doubt the jury will agree with us that she's guilty," the DA said to a throng of reporters.

"We know without a shadow of a doubt that Senator Miller is not guilty of any of these crimes. I've never seen a larger amount of gross negligence in all of my years as an attorney and I *will* be suing the state of Washington for the disgraceful witch hunt they've put Senator Miller through for no other reason than to create a political game that she refused to play with them in," Anna Miller's legal representative all but shouted into the cameras.

He was great at selling hope and diverting attention from the actual issue that he, along with everyone else, knew how grotesquely illegal Anna had been dealing with money, politics, and personal safety. The platform was a good one for him to stand on and he put up the ultimate act of doing all he could to save his so-called innocent client, but it was all a façade.

Almost everyone in the courthouse, including both sides of the legal spectrum, had left the courthouse and were eating lunch when they received notification that the jurors had finished their deliberations and were ready to read the verdict. Both sides stopped conversations, quit eating, paid their bills, and all but ran to the courthouse.

They'd decided too fast. The prosecution team was worried. The Special Ops team was worried. Everyone watching on television was worried. There was a lot at stake if this woman took power again.

With everyone in their respective seats, the judge started the process.

The jury handed a note to the bailiff who handed it to the judge. She didn't show a single expression as she looked at it, making the viewers even more tense.

"Foreperson, the jury has come to a decision?" Judge Scott asked. Was there an edge to her voice?

"Yes, your honor," juror number three stated as she stood.

"Please read each charge and the verdict for it. Once you're finished please seat yourself. Go ahead ma'am," Judge Scott instructed.

"Your honor, the jury finds the defendant not guilty on all charges," the foreperson said calmly then sat down.

There was an extended pause of shock from the judge who finally showed her disappointment in the verdict, the DA and his team, and the defendant's table. The first sound was the faintest of laughs, and then an all-out cackle of laughter filled the courtroom. Anna Miller was almost leaned completely forward in her chair when Judge Scott hammered her gavel, demanding order in the court.

Judge Scott took a few moments to piece together her thoughts as she was shocked at the outcome as well as how quickly the jury had come back with their verdict. Was there something illegal going on? She damn well wanted to find out.

"Foreperson, to ensure I understand, the jury came to a *unanimous* decision on all counts?" Judge Scott asked.

"The jury did your honor."

"Thank you, you may be seated," Judge Scott stated.

"Ms. Miller, in all of my years of serving as a judge, and as an attorney before that, I cannot say that I've ever seen an outcome such as this. I refuse to speculate as to why the jurors found you not guilty, but they did and that's all that matters in the eyes of the law. Effective immediately I release you from the custody of the court. There are some papers you'll need to sign but you are free to go," Judge Scott said as she banged the gavel down and then walked from the courtroom shaking her head in disbelief.

While she was a fair and respected judge among her peers and throughout the legal community, rarely showing any emotional outpouring, this was too much for her to contain, and the last thing anyone heard after the chamber doors were closed was, *what in the hell was that?*

The bailiff opened the courtroom doors, allowing the media and all others waiting for entry to pour inside. Due to the live streaming from the news networks most of the people were just now getting notifications on their phones of the not guilty verdict and to say it was chaos was an understatement. There was a mad rush for the reporters to get their cameras and phones into the face of Anna Miller and ask questions.

The defense team kept the onslaught of individuals behind the barrier and told Anna to try to keep it as brief as possible and to prepare to make a public announcement at a set time, giving her maximum control over the questions and flow of information and what she wanted to say. She agreed with the strategy and with little more than a smile and saying how grateful she was for the jurors, she disappeared from everyone's sight out of the side doors.

Joseph Anderson and the team he'd assembled to stop the monsters from plaguing Seattle sat in stunned silence. They weren't sure what in the hell had just happened, but they'd damn sure find out.

CHAPTER EIGHTEEN

Courtney didn't want to be one of those women who were all googly eyed and simpering, but she found that's exactly what she was. She couldn't seem to do anything other than think about Eyes. She'd believed she'd been in love before — she'd been wrong. Never before had she felt anything like what she felt for Jon Eisenhart.

She was sitting at the local library going through old articles on their ancient computer as she chased down leads on the drug trafficking case she and the other women were diligently working on. There was a sudden shift in the air. She quietly laughed as she looked up . . . and then her breath was taken from her as she gazed at the tall, dark, and handsome man moving toward her.

In the span of two seconds, she'd just broken two clichés. It was ridiculous. The first being the shift in the air. She'd heard before where a person could tell that their partner was in the room because they literally felt static in the air, something that made their heart race and their senses tingle. She'd never believed that was a real feeling until this very moment.

The second cliché was worse. She'd just thought of Eyes as tall, dark, and handsome. How many times, and in how many ways had men in romance books, romantic comedies, and at every bar on every corner in every small American town been described by those three little words? She wasn't sure of the count, but there was no doubt it would be in the billions. She was a damn reporter, dang it. She could certainly do better than tall, dark, and handsome.

She smiled as Eyes came close, a smile on his lips, his eyes bright with promise. How about mysterious, dangerous, exciting, alluring . . . mine. He was hers, he was *all* hers. She could read it in his eyes, in his voice, in the way their hearts beat as one when he held her. She was the lucky woman who got to call him hers. She hoped that never ended.

"Hello beautiful," he said, grabbing a chair, flipping it around, and sitting down with his arms resting on the back of the chair. She might've drooled if she hadn't caught herself as his thick muscles flexed when he rested his chin on his arms. Dang, he made her feel like a teenager . . . and she liked it.

"I'm trying to get work done. How did you find me?" She held up a hand and laughed, stopping him from replying. "Brackish," she finished. He gave her a grin that took her breath away. It was terrifying how much this man got to her.

"How much work do you have to do?" he asked, giving her that lost puppy dog look that seemed to melt her from the inside out.

"It's unending," she told him.

"Do you want to take a break and get a drink?" he asked. He actually batted his eyes at her, his surprisingly long lashes only adding to his appeal.

"I could give you a few minutes," she said. She wouldn't be able to work now anyway, not when he was once again consuming her mind.

"Perfect, there's a great bar right around the corner. Then if you insist on coming back, I'll leave you be," he promised. She didn't want him to leave her alone.

Courtney packed up her bag, then stood and put her light jacket on. It was still warm in Seattle, and she wasn't ready to break out her fall clothes yet. The longer she held on, the longer the warmer season she reasoned, even if that wasn't exactly how it worked.

As soon as they hit the sidewalk Eyes placed Courtney's hand through his arm and guided her down the street, keeping her on the inside of the sidewalk. It was a protective gesture she loved. They chatted as he pointed out a few treacherous places in the cement, always on the lookout for danger. It didn't take them long to arrive at the small bar. He held open the door and she stepped inside.

They found a back table in the corner, the lighting dim, the chatter mild in the early evening. It wouldn't remain that way much longer. The waitress took their order and then they were all alone — well, as alone as they could be with strangers milling around them.

"I've been thinking about getting you into bed all day," Eyes said casually. Courtney was glad she hadn't been drinking right then or she might've spit out her drink at his words. Her stomach did a few flips as it was. She was spared from responding when the waiter brought their drinks and said her cheese-smothered French fries would be there soon.

"Do you think of anything else other than sex?" she finally asked.

Eyes laughed. "Surprisingly, I think of a lot of things when it comes to you. I'd be lying though if I said I didn't want to chain you to my bed." He wiggled his brows as he drank his beer and leaned back, completely at ease with himself and their situation.

"Maybe I'll be the one doing the chaining," Courtney said right as he took a drink. She made him cough at her words, making her feel a bit smug. She could dish it out with the best of them. She didn't want him to pigeonhole her, after-all. It was good to throw in a few curveballs once in a while.

"That'll never happen," Eyes assured her.

"We'll see," she said. Let him wonder if she was serious or not.

Their waitress dropped off the fries then left them alone again. Courtney picked one up and chewed on it.

"Do you believe in fate, Jon?" she asked. It was surprisingly easy for her to switch to calling him either Eyes or Jon. She noticed that when she was more serious she tended to call him by his given name. When she was utterly comfortable she called him Eyes.

"I didn't used to," he admitted.

"So you do now?" she pushed.

"I've seen these bad-ass men I respect and like all fall in love in the past year . . ." He paused and looked straight into her eyes. "And then I met you, and I'm happier than I've been in a very long time. If that's fate, I don't want to mess with it. If it's just a coincidence, I'll never know. I guess I don't mind believing in something more powerful than we can imagine being out there. It's better than emptiness being there."

"I agree. I like that attitude. If magic doesn't really exist, we'll never know so it's so much more beautiful to believe there are simply things out in the universe we can't explain. I really like to imagine I have a guardian angel walking with me especially with some of the places I end up in while searching out a story."

"I hope you have a dozen guardian angels with as many risks as you take," he said with a laugh. His drink was empty, and he signaled the waiter for refills as he helped eat her fries.

"Our entire lives are one big risk. We can either keep ourselves wrapped up in a bubble or we can truly live. I prefer the latter," she insisted.

"You know very well there isn't a big enough bubble out there to keep me safe," he said with a laugh.

"You've been injured in your line of work more than any person I've interviewed," she said. "It's truly a miracle you're still alive. That confirms my belief in guardian angels."

Eyes laughed. "I'd much prefer my guardians didn't have such a sense of humor. Maybe then, they'd actually guard me before bullets riddle my poor abused body."

"I think we're tested every day. Maybe all of your adventures have been tests. You're too extraordinary a man to have a simple test. You've been challenged with things that would break the average man, leaving him unable to rise again if he went through even half of what you have."

Eyes puffed out his chest a little. "You're stroking my ego," he said. Then he leaned in closer. "I have a few more places you can stroke if you like."

"You *do* have sex on the brain tonight." She leaned back, a wicked smile on her lips. "I might need to take care of that for you."

He inhaled a sharp breath and Courtney enjoyed her power over the man. She needed to enjoy it because she was sure the tables would be turning *very* soon. She might've shocked him a few times this evening, but he'd be giving it back really quick, and then he'd be the one making her gasp soon enough.

They didn't last long after that. Soon, both were done with flirting. Eyes rose then held out his arm to Courtney. She gladly took it. He pulled her to her feet, knocking her off balance. She easily fell into him, a giggle escaping her.

"Ah, I finally have you right where I've wanted you all night," he told her. Before she could respond his mouth was on hers in a kiss that not only took her breath away but made her more anxious to get him home.

There wasn't much talking as he loaded her into his vehicle and drove far above the speed limit in his haste to get her back to her place. She squirmed in her seat as he reached over and ran his hand up her thigh. She was nearly coming without a stitch of her clothes being removed.

His SUV screeched to a stop and he was out of the vehicle practically before it stopped moving. She'd just gotten her seatbelt off as he wrenched her door open and pulled her out and straight into his arms, kissing her again, making her knees wobble.

"Let's go inside," she demanded breathlessly. Each time they were together it felt like the first time.

They were both smiling and panting as they made their way up her path. She opened the door, and he kissed her one more time as soon as they stepped inside.

"Do you want a drink?" she asked, not needing one herself.

"Why don't we take a bath?" he suggested instead.

"I think that sounds heavenly," she said.

He took her hand and led her down the hallway, knowing exactly where her room was. The two of them had showered together and it had been heavenly, but she'd never taken a bath with a man. It wasn't the biggest tub by any means, but where there was a will there was a way.

"Bubbles or no bubbles?" he asked as he lifted a bottle of her peach scented soap.

"We definitely want bubbles," she said with a giggle. She was slightly nervous, which made zero sense. He'd already explored every square inch of her body . . . but he hadn't done it while it was covered with suds.

The water was running and the scent of fresh peaches and puffs of steam filled the small room. The heat, tantalizing smell, and low lighting made the butterflies in Courtney's stomach take flight.

"I could get used to you taking care of me," Courtney told him.

He turned and smiled at her. "I could get *very* used to taking care of you," Eyes replied. He stood as the water continued running. "For now, though, I'm going to strip you piece by piece."

Courtney didn't say a word, just smiled as she lifted her arms in the air. The low groan in Eyes's throat was all of the satisfaction she needed in order to be willingly compliant.

Eyes grabbed the hem of her shirt, then slowly peeled it over her head. Her knees went rubbery as he knelt before her and unzipped her pants, then slowly slid them over her hips and down her legs. She was grateful she was wearing her favorite matching red lace bra and panty set.

He leaned forward and placed a kiss on her trembling stomach while he whispered his fingers across her thighs and briefly brushed the silk of her panties. She groaned as he stood up. She needed far more touching than that. He turned her around, unhooked her bra then pulled the straps down her arms, not touching her aching nipples. With her back to him, he slid his thumbs into her panties and pushed them down her legs, leaving her completely nude and trembling.

He ran his hands over her skin slowly, smoothly, lingering on each inch. He stroked her arms and shoulders, then trailed down her back and around to her stomach and over her hips. He cupped her ass and squeezed.

"Do you like that?" he whispered in her ear, his hot breath making her shiver.

"I need more," she told him, her voice tight, her pleasure building. He knew how to pleasure her, and he loved taking his time. "I like touching you just as much," she said, trying to turn. He didn't let her. He gave her a little swat on the butt and told her to stand still.

She sighed and leaned back against him as his hands circled back around to her stomach and slid up and over her breasts, his palms rubbing against her taut nipples. He held one hand over her breast then slid the other one back down, his fingers tickling her right above her sweet spot.

"More," she demanded.

"Mmm, I love it when you get bossy," he told her.

"You're going to see me get *real* controlling if you leave me wanting like this," she said, her husky words not showing a bit of irritation.

His gravelly chuckle whispered across her neck as he used his foot to push her thighs apart, opening her up to him. His hand finally slid back around her then traced the slit of her ass up to her heat, finding her wet and ready for him. He slipped a finger inside of her and they both groaned together as he slowly pumped in and out.

He pulled his finger from her and slid it over her clit, making her jump in his arms as she drew closer to the orgasm he was rapidly building within her. He kept his rhythm slow and steady, making her breath grow more ragged as her stomach clenched.

With one more slide of his finger Courtney exploded in his arms. He had to hold her as her knees gave out from the intensity of her pleasure. He always made her soar. She wanted to do the same for him. When she was sure her legs would once again hold her, she turned in his arms, finding more pleasure in the slant of his eyes and the firmness of his lips. She kissed him, slow and soft, gently running the tip of her tongue along his bottom lip before sucking it into her mouth and gently biting down. He reached around her and squeezed her bottom as he pulled her against him.

"My turn," she said, pulling back from him. She unbuttoned his shirt and pushed it down his arms, taking a nice long look at his solid chest and tight abs. Then she stepped back and sat on the edge of the tub. "Yummy," she purred as she undid the button on his pants then slid the zipper down. It took a bit of effort to free him from his pants and underwear, but then he was in her hands and she ran her fingers over the smooth velvet of his thick hard skin, her thumb tracing his wet head.

Courtney leaned forward and took him in her mouth, moaning against him. He groaned as he grabbed her hair and held on. She sucked up and down on him, taking him deeper and deeper as she tasted his excitement on her tongue. She swirled her tongue and felt his stomach tremble as she moved faster and faster. His fingers tightened in her hair. She smoothed her hand up his thigh, then cupped his balls and lightly squeezed as her thumb traced the smooth skin.

"Let me take you," Eyes told her, trying to pull her head back. She gripped him tighter with her mouth and opened her throat taking him deep as she felt him pulse. "Courtney!" he yelled. She squeezed her throat as she wiggled her tongue.

Eyes let out a cry as he pulsed inside her mouth, his heat warming her. His fingers tightening as he pumped his pleasure over and over again. Courtney licked and sucked until he was spent. He slowly pulled from her mouth and leaned against her for a moment.

"I love you," he said, satisfaction filling his voice.

"I love you," she told him, looking up and smiling at this man she didn't want to ever live without from that day forward.

The tub was full and he leaned over and turned off the tap, then lifted her in his arms and stepped inside. The two of them snuggled together in the hot water, her back against his chest as he ran his hands over her skin, washing and igniting desire all over again.

When the water cooled, Eyes stood, then helped Courtney from the tub. He dried her off and led her to the bedroom; they climbed into her bed together where he pulled her into his arms. She was sleepy as she snuggled against him, happy exactly where she was.

"You're mine, Courtney," Eyes told her.

"And you're mine, Jon," she replied, her eyes shutting as she snuggled against his chest.

"Yes I am, more than you can imagine," Eyes told her.

Courtney let everything go and drifted off to sleep, a smile on her lips and her body completely satisfied. She was in love, and she couldn't imagine she'd ever feel differently. This was the beginning of the rest of her life. The days would get better and better from then on. She was sure of it.

CHAPTER NINETEEN

Joseph walked into the library he'd built for Katherine nearly fifty years earlier. It was her favorite place in their colossal house. If he ever wanted to find her, that's where he'd look. She was sitting in the corner in her favorite chair, reading her favorite book, Pride and Prejudice, the cover worn, the paper soft from the many, many times she'd turned the pages. It was a comforting sight, seeing her where she was happiest.

"Hello, Darling," Joseph said as he leaned in and kissed her cheek.

She jumped, then looked at him with wide eyes. "Who are you?" she gasped, her book dropping to her lap as she held a hand against her heart, fear in her eyes.

"Katherine, it's me, your husband," Joseph said, feeling his heart lodge in his throat.

"Who?" she gasped, scooting back in her chair.

He'd been warned she'd have moments she wouldn't remember him, but he hadn't realized how much it would hurt when that happened. He felt as if he'd been stabbed. He backed away from her, hating that he was causing her the remotest moment of fear.

"Katherine, Darling, I'm your husband, Joseph," he whispered, holding out his hand but not touching her.

"Joseph?" she questioned. The fear turned to confusion and then frustration, as if she was trying to solve a very difficult puzzle.

"It's okay, Darling, I've startled you," Joseph said. He took another step back, then moved over and sat in the chair he'd sat in many times before, enjoying the view of his wife getting lost in a book. He'd been content to watch emotions flash across her face many, many times in their long life together. He'd never imagined a day she wouldn't recognize him. He'd have to get used to that, he'd have to deal with it.

"Joseph," she said again, drawing out his name.

"Yes, your husband," he gently told her.

How would he get through this? How could the love of his life not know who he was? He had to remind himself that this wasn't about him, it was *only* about her. She was silent for several more moments. Time seemed to stop as he internally begged her to remember him. Her Alzheimer's was progressing too quickly. He hadn't had enough time to prepare for this.

"Of course you are," Katherine said, her smile returning. "Why are you telling me you're my husband?" She chuckled, and he realized she'd already forgotten she hadn't known who he was when he'd walked into the room. He took in a deep breath and told himself he'd be okay. She was still with him, and he'd remind her every hour of who he was if that's what it took.

"What are you doing, Joseph?" she asked him as she picked her book back up and then began flipping through the pages without looking at it, a habit she'd had since the day he'd met her.

"I was strolling through the house and thought I'd come and visit with my favorite person in this world," he told her.

"Ah, you always make me feel so special," Katherine said as she reached for him, her delicate fingers sliding into his giant palm. He gently squeezed her hand and had to fight back tears. She truly was his everything.

"I need you to know every single day how much you mean to me," Joseph said to her.

"Well, you did vow on our wedding day to tell me every single day you loved me," she said. "It feels like just yesterday we were married." She gazed up at the ceiling with a secret smile on her lips. "Isn't it funny how time seems to slow. I can't quite remember how many years it's been but at least twenty," she told him. He nearly laughed since it was over double that amount of time, but then he looked at her and realized she wasn't kidding. She truly believed it had only been about twenty years. He felt another pang to his heart. He didn't show it.

"I promised you when I married you that I'd always make you feel young," he told her instead.

"And you do, my wonderful husband," she said with a girlish giggle that made his bleeding heart soar.

Before Joseph could say something more, Katherine yawned. "I don't know why but I'm very tired all of the sudden. I should have more energy," she said as she set her book on the table next to her.

"Ah, we aren't spring chickens anymore. It's okay for us to take a nap now and then," he told her.

"I agree. The wonderful thing about being a stay-at-home mother is that we can nap when the children are at school," she said. He didn't try to correct her that they now had grandchildren who were in school. If she wanted to take twenty or thirty years from their lives, he was okay with that. He wouldn't mind another fifty with his beautiful wife. He wouldn't mind one little bit living their lives over again. He'd do it all the exact same way they'd done it the first time. There wasn't a single moment he'd change because it had all shaped them into what they were today.

He stood and held out his hand to help her up. She slowly stood then placed her hand in his elbow as he carefully walked through their huge house to their bedroom — the same room he'd shared with her for most of their lives, the same room their three boys had been conceived in, the same room he'd lain beside her going to sleep each night, knowing that the next day would be just as wonderful as the last as long as he had Katherine with him. There was no chance he'd be able to sleep in that room without her.

"Thank you for the walk," Katherine said as they stepped inside the huge double doors that led into their bedroom. She leaned up on her toes and gently kissed his lips. "Now, you run along so I can rest. I'll never get any sleep if you stay in here with me."

Joseph chuckled as he wrapped her in his arms and hugged her. He couldn't imagine a day he wouldn't be able to do that. He couldn't allow his mind to go there. It was far too painful to even imagine. He gave her one more kiss and reluctantly left his wife.

Joseph's lips were pinched as he fled down the hallway to his den, the place he'd always needed to come to when his world felt as if it was spinning out of control. He'd worked hard for his entire life, and this room had always been his safe haven.

He stepped into the room then went straight to his liquor cabinet where he poured himself a double shot of Scotch. He downed it far too quickly, making his throat burn. He finally took in a deep breath, then placed a piece of ice in his crystal glass and poured a second generous glass. This one he'd sip while smoking a cigar. He'd earned it.

Joseph didn't realize a tear was falling down his cheek until he sniffled. Once the floodgate opened he had to set down his glass and grip the bar. He shook as sobs ripped from him. Joseph couldn't remember the last time he'd cried so hard.

"Dad?"

Joseph froze at the sound of his oldest son, Lucas's voice. He wiped away his tears and took in a couple of more breaths before he turned.

"I didn't know you were coming over, son," Joseph said, trying to push away the pain that was nearly breaking him in half.

"What's wrong, Dad?" Lucas asked. Then his son looked as if he was going to cry. "Is Mom okay?" The final word came out in a whisper, his son's voice choked.

"Your mother is well," Joseph said. Then he remembered Amira's words, and he sighed as he grabbed another glass and poured his son his finest Scotch. "She didn't know who I was for about a minute," he told Lucas, his eyes filling again.

Lucas quickly covered the distance between them and threw his arms around his father. "I'm so sorry, Dad. I can't imagine how difficult this is for you. It hurts all of us to see Mom sick, but there's not a minute that goes by that any of us forget she's your wife, your entire world," Lucas told him.

Lucas stepped back and Joseph felt his knees shake. He dropped to the floor and the floodgate opened all over again as he cupped his head in his hands. Lucas dropped down beside him, placing his hand on Joseph's back.

"I'm so sorry," Lucas said over and over again. "I know the words aren't enough, but I truly am sorry."

They both went silent while Joseph gathered himself together again. He then took a deep breath and gave his son a wobbly smile as he climbed to his feet. It certainly was more difficult to do the older he got.

He and Lucas grabbed their glasses and moved closer to the fireplace and sat down. Joseph knew the tears were over. He also knew he'd needed to shed them. It wasn't going to help him get through the next few years if he held all of his emotions in at all times.

"I'll be okay, Lucas. I'm sorry you had to see that," Joseph said. Lucas started to speak and Joseph held up his hand. "I'm not sorry you were here. I needed you without realizing I did. I can make it through this, even if Katherine eventually forgets who I am for good. I can make it through because I have enough love for the both of us."

"Yes, you do," Lucas said. "I pray every single night that Amy and I will have the same epic love story as you and mom."

Joseph managed to smile the slightest bit. "You're off to a great start," he told his son.

"I think so because I've had two role models I've learned from."

Silence greeted those words for several heart beats. Joseph took in some deep breaths before he was able to speak again.

"I vowed to love your mother through the good times and the bad, and I'll always keep my promise. She's my entire world and I won't stop loving her even after my final breath in this body."

"I believe that," Lucas said. "A love like the one you and Mom share is rare. She's lucky to have you as you are to have her. I'm very grateful you're my parents."

"And we're both very grateful to have you, Mark, and Alex as sons," Joseph said.

Lucas grinned as he took a sip of his Scotch. "But I'm the favorite so you're really glad to have me," he said.

The words were just what Joseph needed to hear. He and Lucas laughed for a second, and then they sat back and spoke about work, the kids, and anything other than sickness and death. By the time Lucas left, Joseph felt better. He stood up and made his way to his bedroom. It was time to hold his wife. Amira had been right, he needed all of the love and support he could surround himself with.

When he opened his bedroom door and found his beautiful wife sleeping in their large bed with a secret smile resting on her lips, Joseph knew the world would be right again. He took off his shoes, then carefully climbed in beside her. It only took seconds for her to seek him out and snuggle into the safety of his arms — right where she belonged.

Katherine might forget Joseph, but she'd never forget their love when she was the most vulnerable, and he'd always be true to his words and love her in good times and bad. He closed his eyes and once again thanked God for giving him a love so strong and true.

CHAPTER TWENTY

Damien was still in shock at the realization that nothing in this world could truly be safe when someone as evil as Anna Miller was found not guilty. Even worse, he was sure money had exchanged hands . . . and most likely threats had been made. There was no way that jury had found her not guilty without being pushed into that decision.

The thing that was frightening to Damien was that she hadn't been seen since she'd given her press conference, expounding on how the justice system had worked perfectly and freed an innocent woman. She'd then gone on to announce to the press how she planned to get back into the political world again after taking a couple of weeks to recuperate from her traumatizing ordeal. She'd created her campaign ad right there by telling reporters she was going to fight for all of the innocent victims who ended up on the wrong side of the law because someone had it out for them.

Damien had decided he didn't care. He wasn't going to give Anna Miller another moment of his time. But that all changed in a heartbeat. There was one fear above all other fears for a parent — one trauma parents prayed would never come to their lives . . .

Damien received a message from his daughter's phone. She was staying the night at a friend's house, so he didn't think much of the text and didn't look at his phone right away, but when another message came through, he looked. His heart was suddenly ripped from his chest.

There was a photo of his only child . . . tied to a chair . . . with a message on her lap that simply read, *it's you or her.* The next message gave him very explicit instructions on what to do and when to do it.

Pack all of your cash and jewels and put them in a non-descript bag. If you try to place a tracking device in the bag it will end badly. Don't call the police. Don't attempt to circumvent any part of this. This phone will be destroyed so there's no need to try to track it. Answer any and all calls from this moment forward. The phones will be burners so don't bother trying to track location. Do you understand?

His only response was, *I understand.*

Damien rushed to his bedroom, grabbed his wife's cell phone, and dialed Joseph, explaining everything that had just happened.

"Obviously I can't confirm yet, but I'm sure it's Anna," Damien said.

"Okay. I'm calling Chad. We'll figure out what to do," Joseph replied.

After the brief call concluded Damien did all he could to keep his wife from exploding into a billion pieces. Her little girl was being held captive because of a psychotic maniac, and she felt as helpless as he did. In a moment of desperate frustration, she grabbed the television remote sitting on her nightstand and threw it across the room, embedding it in the wall. Neither she nor Damien said a word about the damage, letting fragmented pieces of drywall crumble into a pile of dust.

"Damien," he answered as the screen on his phone displayed an unknown number.

A person immediately spoke. No introductions were needed.

"Good boy. The minimum amount of cash had better be at least three hundred thousand. The jewelry needs to look like a pirate's treasure chest. I have no room for negotiations, Damien. Either you do as I say, or your daughter and I disappear . . . forever," the digital voice said.

"You're never going to get away with this, Anna," Damien barked into the receiver.

"Anna? Who's Anna?" the voice inquired.

"Stop the games. I know it's you, you piece of shit!" Damien was at the end of his emotional limit.

"Oh, do you mean *Anna Miller*? This isn't her. In fact, if you turn on the channel nine news, I believe she's speaking at an event right now," the voice calmly replied.

Damien took three large steps to the wall, ripped the remote from it, and smashed buttons until the television came to life. He found the local news and there was his *sister* dressed up and looking at ease in front of a crowd of reporters. His stomach sank, confusion ripping through him, and the capacity to figure out any next steps vanquished. Not realizing it, he dropped the phone, only his eyes working as they focused on the images on the screen in front of him.

"Damien . . . DAMIEN!" his wife called.

His cognitive abilities returned as he looked at his wife questioning what she wanted. She pushed her phone at him.

"It's Chad," was all she said.

"Hello," Damien forced out.

"We're on our way," Chad said.

"How soon?" Damien replied.

"Now." There was a pause and the lights suddenly went out in the house. Damien felt his heart thunder.

"Is that you?" Damien asked, hating the fear coursing through him. It wasn't fear for himself but for his wife and for his daughter.

"Yes, the men are securing the premises, making sure no one is watching your house," Chad told him. "I can hear them on the comms. So far so good. I don't think Anna has the balls to come back to your place. I'm sure she's assuming we've put security up." Damien heard him say copy to someone, followed by, "Okay, Damien, we're coming in. You can relax. Your place is secure."

Damien ended the call as his front door opened and Chad walked inside with the five special ops men flanking him. The last time they'd been to Damien's house, he'd been near death. This time it was his little girl who'd been taken. He'd give his life any day of the week to keep his daughter from going through the trauma she had to be currently enduring.

"Thanks for getting here so quickly," Damien told the men as he shook each of their hands.

"I know you and your wife are stressed beyond measure right now, but let's focus so we can get your daughter home. I want you to start at the beginning and tell me exactly what happened and the timeline of it down to the second," Eyes said, stepping up and taking charge.

Damien walked the men through the texts and the phone calls, and the image of Anna on the television screen. He just wasn't sure if she was a part of this or not. She had to be, but she couldn't be in two places at once.

"Give me both of your phones," Brackish demanded.

"They told me they're using burners, so there's no use trying to track them," Damien said with irritation.

"That's a myth. They're just as easily tracked as any other phone. Trust me, I'll get the location and then we'll get your daughter," Brackish said as he hooked both phones up to some technical gadgetry he'd brought with him.

Almost as soon as the connections were made Damien's phone rang and another unidentified number came across the screen.

"Damien," he answered.

"We must've been cut off when you saw Anna Miller giving her speech," the person said in that same robot voice.

"We were."

"Don't let that happen again. Now, where were we? Oh, yes, we were talking about you bringing cash and jewelry to me. In one hour you're going to be sent directions on where to go with that bag. You shouldn't test me if you care at all about your daughter. If you have anyone with you, you'll never see your daughter again. If you bring police, you'll never see your daughter again. Are you willing to risk your daughter's life? If not, do anything outside of what we ask you and you'll see how petty I can be," the person said and then promptly hung up.

"We're going to have you fully covered, Damien. I promise you they'll never know we're there, no matter where they send you, we'll be there," Eyes said.

"But what if they see you? I can't risk it," Damien said.

"Damien, I know this is difficult, but you need to trust me. I've made it my life's mission to save people and I'm damn good at my job. We're going to bring you *and* your daughter home," Eyes promised.

"That call came from a marina in Des Moines," Brackish said flatly.

"That's interesting," Eyes said.

"Water escape. Major balls on that one," Sleep said.

"Okay. This is the plan. It's likely they feel safe at that marina, and that's where the exchange is going to take place. Chad, drop Mrs. Whitman off at your house, then meet up with us. Damien, you're riding with us to the center. From there we gear up and get your daughter back," Eyes said to Damien as they started toward the front door.

As the team was pulling up to the command center, Damien's phone rang again. They gave instructions on where to meet, and like Eyes thought, it was going down at the marina. The kidnappers gave Damien forty-five minutes to get to the parking lot at the Des Moines Marina Pier.

"Okay. Listen guys, this is all happening fast. Brackish — you're here. Launch the entire armada into the sky. We're going to need as many eyes feeding us information as possible. Total number of bodies, positions, radius, all of it. You don't need me telling you what's needed — just know we need it all," Eyes said.

"On it," Brackish said and then went to his office. With each step he took he quickly reached out and hit power buttons. Monitors and machines came to life behind him as he reached his chair. Brackish was far more valuable right where he was than out in the field.

"Green, get your gear — long gun and whatever else you need. I won't be able to have a spotter for you, and, obviously, it's going to be black out there but we'll be able to laser them so you'll have a sight line. If you need anything else, grab it and work with Brackish on what the best vantage point will be. We don't know the exact location yet but you'll need to work all of that out," Eyes told Green, and Green was gone without a response.

"Sleep, Smoke, get your swim gear, and get on a boat. I don't care how you acquire it, but make it happen fast. We need you two on the water and near the mouth of that pier. Don't wait for us to get down there." He paused then looked at them with raised brows. "You two should be gone already," Eyes finished with a command that all of them knew well. His mental juices were firing on all cylinders; this was him at his best.

Eyes switched to speaking over the comms so the rest of the men could hear his plans. "Chad and I are going to get into position a few minutes before Damien arrives. Once Brackish has his drones confirm where the kidnappers are, which will be well in advance of our arrival, we'll go down a different dock and board a boat like it's our own."

"Copy," was repeated four times through the comms and the men did what they did best. They got into position exactly as planned with all of the gear necessary to complete their operation. A rag tag group of fools wasn't going to stop this team from saving the daughter of one of their own.

"Radio check," a voice came over the comms. It was Brackish and he was ready to start feeding information.

"Clear," Eyes said. There were several clicks from the other men acknowledging that they could hear.

Brackish was in his element and spoke quickly. "We have five bodies on a sixty foot white and blue yacht on the south dock at the end. Two perps are on the deck, one in the aft, and two bodies are showing below deck. There don't appear to be any additional contacts in the surrounding area. The drones haven't picked up any other souls or equipment. These fools have underestimated Damien, and therefore us."

By the time Damien arrived in the parking lot all of the team members were in place and ready for a green light. Green had located a building that overlooked the entire marina but had a broadside view of the yacht. Sleep and Smoke had acquired a low-slung, sleek black boat and they were outside of the marina entrance, getting the last part of their swim gear on. As soon as they finished they dropped into the water. Chad and Eyes made their way onto a boat three docks over from the yacht and readied themselves for a water entrance as well.

"Damien, stall for sixty seconds before exiting your vehicle," Eyes said over the comms.

"Okay," Damien replied.

The time allowed Sleep and Smoke to slip through the mouth of the harbor and get close to the yacht. Chad was tasked to slip between the boats and under the docks until he was below the dock the yacht was attached to. Eyes made his way to the back of the yacht, staying in the shadows and ensuring he wasn't seen.

"Damien — green light. I can hear everything you say and I'll guide you through this," Brackish said. He had a full view of the entire scene. He could see the heat signatures of all of the men in the water, and was surprised Green wasn't showing up on any of the infrared detection. That man was as good as it got in the hide and seek game.

Damien slowly walked forward. His heart thundered as he thought about his daughter, Samantha. If something happened to her he'd go to the ends of the earth to seek revenge. He moved onto the dock and his step hitched when he saw Anna Miller. Of course he'd known it was her, but to truly know made his emotions boil over. How could one human being be this evil?

He gripped the bag that held the money and jewels and clenched his jaw as he fought the urge to spring forward, leap onto the boat, and strangle her to death. He knew he'd be dead before he came anywhere near the woman, but it was almost worth it to relieve some of the stress he'd been under.

"Come aboard my sweet big brother, please come aboard," Anna yelled. The smile she wore was pure evil.

"Let my daughter go!" demanded Damien.

"Oh please. My niece is safe. She might need some ice for that lip. She does have quite the temper on her. I wonder who she got that from," Anna said over the banister of the yacht.

"Anna, take me, take this bag that has close to one million dollars in cash and jewels, and do what you said you'd do; let Samantha go. She has nothing to do with any of this or these damn games everyone has been playing," Damien pleaded.

As the two were talking a man covered from head to toe in black walked up next to Anna. Two other men at the aft of the yacht also appeared. All of their faces showed confidence. In their minds Damien was clearly outnumbered and they held the higher ground. They could take him out with a single bullet if they chose. From the expressions on the men's faces, Damien was sure they were hoping their leader, Anna Miller, requested just that.

Anna whispered something to the man next to her and he disappeared. The two men at the back of the boat gave a small nod in understanding and stayed right where they were.

"One of the bodies below has just pulled up the other body as the third person entered the room. I now know which one is Samantha," Brackish said through Damien's comms. "She's moving forward. Stay calm, and this will all work out."

Damien needed to hear the words more than he'd thought. His little girl was on her own two feet and moving closer to him. There was no doubt in his mind that he'd get her back. These special ops men surrounding him were the best of the best and they'd never allow something to happen to a teenager, not while there was still a breath inside of them.

Anna's team of goons didn't know about Sleep and Smoke lurking in the black water on the aft side of the boat. After receiving confirmation from Brackish, the two men silently swam to the side of the yacht and with no sound at all pulled themselves onto the side deck. No one heard or saw a thing.

"Swimmers, hold. They're almost to the top deck," Brackish whispered, speaking about Samantha and her captor.

The next moment Damien's daughter, in handcuffs with a gag pulled tight across her face, was pulled up next to Anna. Samantha looked over the rail, her frightened eyes connecting with her father's.

She nodded at him as if to tell him she was okay and she was brave enough to keep standing through this.

"Isn't this sweet?" Anna said with a cackle. "If you could see your face right now, Damien, you'd be laughing too. It's absolutely pathetic. It's the reason I don't get attached to anyone. If you have something to lose, then you're completely and fully controllable."

Anna turned and said something to the man in black next to her. The man pulled Damien's daughter tightly to his side.

"I've done what you want, Anna. Unhand my daughter and take your damn money," Damien said. He was sick of these monsters touching his little girl.

"You aren't the one in control, Damien. I'd suggest you keep your damn mouth shut before little Samantha here becomes fish food," Anna said as if she could care less either way. Damien knew beyond a shadow of a doubt that she didn't care. Both he and his daughter could be killed right then and there and she wouldn't even blink. The woman had no soul. He couldn't imagine what had happened in her life to make her into this person.

"Okay, Damien, now," Brackish said.

Damien moved to the edge of the dock and unzipped the bag. He'd had enough of Anna's games. He was more than glad to do as Brackish had instructed earlier. He was going to hold the open bag over the water. If they shot him the money and jewels would scatter. If they shot his daughter, he had nothing to live for anyway and again, the goods would scatter. Sure, it was retrievable, but not in minutes or even hours. It would take days to gather it all up, and some would be lost forever. Anna didn't have that kind of time. She'd lost everything with the trial and the seizure of her assets. It would take a lot of time to get even a percentage of it back. That's why she was extorting Damien right then.

"The cops will be here. You can't think I'm such a fool as to go one on one with you," Damien told her. "Release my daughter and bring her to my side or this goes to the bottom of the sea. I have nothing left to lose, Anna, so don't test me," Damien said.

"I'm the one who shouldn't be tested," Anna screamed. He could see the fury in her face. She didn't like the tables turning on her. "I will kill her," she finished as she grabbed Samantha, making his daughter cry out as Anna yanked her hair.

"We told you this would be the reaction, Damien. Anna's forehead is in my sights. If anyone even twitches they'll all be dead before your daughter can be injured. We need to get Samantha off of that boat. Anna needs the money in that bag. *You* have the power," Brackish assured Damien through the comms.

Damien reached into the bag and pulled out a diamond and ruby necklace worth over a hundred thousand dollars. He let the sparkling showpiece dangle over the murky water.

"Last chance, Anna," Damien said. "My fingers are getting really, *really* tired." He trembled his hand as if he was going to lose the jewels. He didn't give a shit about the jewelry, his money, or any possession he owned. All he cared about was his daughter.

"Fine," Anna snapped. She pushed Samantha at the man who'd brought her from below deck. "She's coming to you now. I want you to take three steps back from the water."

"There's no a chance of that happening, Anna. If I move, you shoot both of us," Damien said.

"What makes you think I won't shoot you both after I have the bag?" Anna snapped. She truly was losing her cool.

"My daughter will reach the top of the docks and be gone before I move from this place. I don't care what happens to me then," Damien said. An angry growl rushed from Anna. "What's the matter, dear sister? You don't get to kill us both? I don't know how you became what you are, but it shouldn't be easy for you to kill your own niece, even if you didn't see her grow up."

"I don't give a shit about her, and I certainly don't care two cents about you," Anna told him.

His daughter was pulled off of the boat. Damien looked at her with fear and love. "It will be okay, sweetie. Just get out of here," he told her.

"No, daddy. I'm not leaving you," she sobbed.

"Do it now!" he yelled. He couldn't ever remember yelling at his daughter before. He was terrified though, and while he had utter confidence in the men who were all around him, he didn't want a stray bullet finding his precious daughter.

Samantha sobbed as the man pushed her away toward the exit, then stood between her and Damien as Samantha walked toward the top of the docks. She was almost there.

"Now!" Anna screamed.

The man suddenly leapt toward Damien, while another man jumped off of the boat and began chasing after Samantha. Damien dropped the bag, the loaded suitcase spilling into the water just before the thug could secure it. Anna's scream echoed through the boat docks as the man's fists connected with Damien's jaw.

Before the pain could even register, Damien heard Eyes as he said, *go time*. Smoke and Sleep stood just as Brackish cut all of the lights in the marina, plunging them into total darkness. The yacht was plugged into power via the marina but after only a couple of seconds the onboard generator would kick on. Still, it was enough of a diversion that there was no way the two men at the back of the yacht had any chance of seeing what was about to happen to them.

Chad grabbed Samantha, flung her over his shoulder, and told her she was safe as he quickly ran to safety. She sobbed as she gripped his back, thanking him, and begging him to save her father. He assured her there were five very capable men who were helping her father. She stopped struggling at those words.

The lights flashed back on and Anna looked down at Damien who was now standing alone.

"Where's Paul?" Anna asked as her eyes frantically searched the docks.

"He must've fallen in," Damien said with a shrug. His daughter was safe. He no longer cared what happened. "What are you going to do now, Anna? What's your end game to all of this?"

"You shouldn't have done that, Damien," she said. She was furious, but her mask was slowly easing back into place. She might've lost the money, but she always had a backup plan. She didn't know the meaning of the word *lose*.

"Well, Damien, I guess the plan is for you to die," Anna said, her forked tongue dancing around her snake-like mouth. "I'll come for your daughter again, and you've seen that when I set my mind on something I don't ever give up. So just know in your final thoughts that I'm going to go after your wife and daughter, torture them, then send them to hell where you can see them again."

"She won't get the chance," Brackish said in Damien's ear. "Samantha's secure, sitting back with a Pepsi and a donut, and driving Chad crazy as she keeps demanding he go help in your rescue."

"I'm glad to be driven crazy," Chad said. "But hurry it up, Damien. I forgot how much teenage girls can whine when they don't get their way." There was an umph at the end of his words. Samantha had obviously smacked him.

"Anna," Damien said, smiling at this sister he hadn't known he'd had too long ago. "Before you kill me, can you please, for the love of all that's holy, tell me how you got a not guilty verdict from a randomly appointed jury?"

Anna laughed. She felt in control again. "Peons, all of you are absolute peons. Did it ever occur to you that maybe, just maybe, my influence and clout reaches every corner of this country? All but two of those jurors were professionals. And even if the two *thought* I was guilty, there are *very* few people who have the balls to stand up to an entire group and tell them they're wrong. The DA had no clue what the shell game was, but we played it to perfection. If it wasn't for that judge being one of those *letter of the law* types, I would've been out on bail and you'd be dead already."

"Well, I'm glad she hasn't been corrupted by insidious creatures like you," Damien said in a casual voice he knew was ticking Anna off.

"You know, Damien, I can't wait to get out of here. I think I'll kill you now," Anna said as she reached into her jacket and placed her hand on the butt of her gun. She pulled the gun out, a silencer at the end of the muzzle, and began lifting it to point at Damien.

"Damien, on three you need to drop. Don't try to catch yourself, and whatever you do, don't move once you're down," Eyes said into the comms.

"One, two, three . . ." Eyes let out and then there were two shots fired. One was at close range, only a few yards away. The other was from a much bigger caliber weapon and carried a boom that bounced around the boats, the echo not fading for some time.

The shot from the big gun did its job to perfection. The smaller one that hit Anna wasn't a fatal shot. While she did lose control over the weapon she'd been holding, she was moving quickly away from the railing.

Anna found her gun and turned toward Damien to finish what she'd started but the man who was her brother by DNA rushed up the plank of the boat and straight at her and a struggle ensued on who'd be able to maintain enough strength and balance to take control of the gun. The two of them rose to their feet, slowly spinning and pushing at each other as they drew dangerously closer to the railing.

"You're going to die, you bastard," Anna said through clenched teeth, blood starting to seep from her mouth.

"Not today, and definitely *not* by you," Damien replied and then saw his move.

Since the shooting Anna had been favoring her right side and when Damien saw this he quickly reacted. He spun her so her right side was closest to the rail, then he trapped her right leg on the ground while lifting up on her torso. The balance was unequal, and her fight or flight reaction changed in an instant as their momentum started pushing them over the rail.

Damien stopped thinking about the consequences of harming someone and continued his movement, lifting her higher and pushing harder. Just as he got Anna over the rail a shot went off, hitting him directly in the chest. Anna went over the rail, and as she fell twenty feet down he could see her smiling at getting the last laugh, shooting him before she dropped.

The impact her torso made as it hit the side of the boat while her legs slapped the deck of the yacht was almost grotesque. For a moment she looked at Damien above her, smiling at fulfilling the promise to her mother that she'd destroy the offspring of the man who'd traumatized them so much. The last thing Anna's earthly eyes saw was Damien pulling off his shirt to expose a bulletproof vest which had worked flawlessly in stopping the round that was meant to kill him. Anna Miller died in agony. Both physically and mentally. Her reign of terror on Damien and his family was over.

Damien stared down at the lifeless form of Anna Miller. She'd died with a smug grin on her lips. Even in her final moments she hadn't relented, hadn't had a moment of mercy or regret. He couldn't move for several moments, not believing this whole thing was over so quickly.

"Damien," Brackish said through the comms.

Damien didn't respond. He was quickly going into shock.

The special ops men exited the water, then slowly approached Damien knowing he was unpredictable in his shock. Sleep put his hand on Damien's arm. "It's over, Damien. Let's get you to your daughter."

Those words finally snapped Damien out of his shock. "Yes please. I need to hold my daughter."

They made their way up the ramp and when Damien reached the top, Samantha came flying out of nowhere and launched herself into her father's arms.

"Daddy, I was so scared I wouldn't see you again," she sobbed as she buried her head against his neck.

"It's okay, baby girl, it's okay," he assured her, wondering if everything truly was okay.

"I know it is. I knew you'd come. I was just so afraid you wouldn't walk away," she sobbed.

"I'd never voluntarily leave you or your mother," he assured her.

"Let's go home," she begged.

"Yes, that's exactly what we'll do," he said. He kept Samantha wrapped tightly at his side as they walked to Chad's vehicle. He climbed in the backseat with his daughter unwilling to let her go.

It was over. It was truly over. The bad guys were all gone now. No one was coming for Damien or his family. He told himself that the entire drive to where his wife was pacing as she waited for her family to be reunited again.

While Damien was getting reunited with his family Brackish called Sheriff McCormack about some bad men who needed to be picked up who just so happened to be tied up with a nice little bow on top for him. Brackish told the sheriff there was video evidence of exactly what had occurred minus the presence of five special ops men, of course. When McCormack asked what had happened, the men did what they did best when it came to the law, they played dumb. How it had happened, or what had happened, was unknown.

Anna Miller's legacy would never be what she'd hoped for, and for all intents and purposes the exact opposite. She'd died alone and weak just as how she'd lived her entire life. She wouldn't leave behind a legacy, she'd just leave the world — and the world was a better place without her in it. The world was a better place all together because of a team of five men who never gave up.

CHAPTER TWENTY-ONE

Courtney was getting married. It was odd because, looking at herself in the mirror, she wasn't sure what she was feeling. She knew she should be feeling something, but for once in her life she wasn't sure what emotions were coursing through her.

She glanced at her perfect hairdo and expertly done makeup and saw herself, but it was as if she was looking at a stranger. Who was the girl looking back at her? Had this happened too quickly? Was she on the verge of a panic attack? Her breathing grew more accelerated.

"Don't worry. I had a bit of a panic attack myself," Erin said with a laugh. "It's perfectly normal. You're in love with this man and the only regret you'll have is if you try to run."

The words were exactly what she'd needed to hear. Erin placed the veil on Courtney's head, and as the delicate lace whispered down the sides of her face, she finally felt like a bride.

"You're stunning," Erin told her.

"Here, here to that," Amira said as she held up her mimosa and smiled.

Mallory stepped up to her with a little black box. "Here's your something borrowed."

Courtney took the box and opened it to find a stunning pair of teardrop diamond earrings. They were gorgeous.

"Oh, I don't know if I want to wear these. What if I lose one?" Courtney asked. She'd never owned a piece of jewelry like the sparkling gems resting in the box.

"You won't lose them, and they're perfect for a perfect bride," Mallory said.

"Let me help," Avery said as she pulled the earrings from the box and handed one to Courtney who placed it in her ear. It took only a second to have both of them in and boy did they sparkle.

"They are a perfect match," Amira said.

"And this is from all of us for your something new," Avery said as she held out another box, this one a little bigger.

Courtney opened it and inside was a stunning diamond bracelet.

"You guys shouldn't have done this," Courtney gasped. "It's too much."

"We're a team now. We're crime fighters and all of us have taken the plunge into marriage with incredibly amazing men. We *had* to do this," Amira said.

"We *are* pretty amazing aren't we?" Courtney said with a laugh as Avery attached the delicate bracelet to Courtney's wrist.

"Dang straight we are. We're successful, beautiful, and confident. We might've had a few bumps in the road in our lives, but we've never let that hold us back. We have every reason to be proud of who we are," Erin said.

"I'll toast to that," Amira said as she once again held up her glass. All of the women took a sip of their mimosas as they chuckled.

"Don't forget the something blue," Mallory said as she pulled out a sexy garter belt with a thin blue ribbon woven into it.

"Oh yes, Jon will have a fun time removing that from your leg . . . with his teeth."

"I want to do my honeymoon night over and over again. We always have great sex, but that night it was magical," Erin said with a sigh.

"I've decided I want to get married every five years. I think it's smart to remind ourselves of how much we love our husbands. The world has a way of interrupting my marital bliss, so that means I have to work that much harder to show my husband how much I love him," Erin said.

"I think that's a brilliant idea," Amira said. "You could get married in new places all around the world and *always* be on your honeymoon."

"That's exactly what I was thinking," Erin said. "I think marriages fall apart for stupid reasons a lot of the time. If you fell in love in the first place, there has to be a reason. We just have to search for those reasons sometimes when life wants to kick us in the teeth."

"How have we gotten so lucky?" Courtney asked. "Just a second ago I was panicking, and now I feel like the luckiest woman alive."

"We got lucky because we were open to it," Avery said. "I didn't know I wanted marriage and babies until I met Carl, but now I can't imagine my life without him."

"Yeah, Sleep is one of the good ones," Courtney said. "He and Jon have been friends a very long time."

"I think the bond these five men share will last a lifetime," Amira said.

"Oh, we almost forgot your something old," Erin said as she pulled out a bag. "Jon left this for you earlier. I think he was trying to get a peek. It seems he doesn't like this twenty-four-hours of not seeing his bride." That produced more giggles.

Courtney opened the bag and found a delicate hair clip that seemed to have real jewels in it. It was gold with red and clear stones.

"Oh, it's real," Amira said. "He told us it belonged to his great-grandmother who wore it on her wedding day. Those are rubies and diamonds."

"It's the most beautiful thing I've ever been given," Courtney said as Erin took the clip and placed it in Courtney's hair. The sun streaming in through the window hit the clip and rainbows shot from it.

"Hey, the bracelet is so much cooler," Avery said.

"Yes, it is," Courtney agreed. She was so damn happy she couldn't contain herself. Her momentary panic had been for nothing.

"Are you ready?" Amira asked.

"Yes, I can't wait to marry the man I love," Courtney told her.

"Good, because you are beautiful, definitely blushing, and you're going to knock your man's socks off," Erin said.

The women were going to walk down the aisle with her. She didn't have her father to lead her down the path so she wanted to be surrounded by her best friends. That's what they were now, truly best friends. They'd bonded through circumstances that most people never even imagine existed in the world. They might go their separate ways, but they'd always come back together — Courtney was sure of that.

The music began and Courtney stepped through the double doors at the back of Joseph Anderson's huge mansion. She'd wanted to marry Jon quickly once they'd decided that's what they were going to do.

She smiled as she thought of Joseph. If a person wanted to marry fast he was the man to turn to. He'd had the entire wedding set within a week, generously offering his backyard. It was absolutely perfect.

Her friends surrounded her in their teal dresses as they made their way down the aisle. Though there were a couple of hundred people there, the only person Courtney saw was Jon. He was absolutely breathtaking in his fitted tux, a smile on his lips and a sheen in his eyes as they gazed at one another.

When she reached him, he took her hand as her friends went on either side of them to stand with their husbands, who Courtney was sure looked just as handsome in their tuxes as her man did. She couldn't testify to that as she had eyes for only one man right now.

She barely heard their vows as they promised to love one another, and then the preacher pronounced them husband and wife. Eyes swept Courtney up in a hug, dipped her back, and kissed her like it was the first time . . . and it was, it was the first time they were kissing as husband and wife. It was absolutely beautiful.

They went straight from their kiss into an epic reception. Joseph had hired a live band that started right up, beginning with *Another One Bites the Dust* as they made their way back down the aisle, making everyone laugh. Yes, another one had bitten the dust and he was now a married man.

They were swarmed with friends as soon as they cleared the rose-strewn path and Courtney found herself dragged away from her new husband. She couldn't wait for their honeymoon where they'd have two solid weeks without interruption — no criminals, no friends, no work . . . just lots of sex, love, and laughter.

"What has that look on your face?" Avery asked as she stepped up next to her.

"I'm just thinking about how happy I am to be a married woman," Courtney easily replied.

Avery laughed. "Yes, I still feel the same way. You'll find it strange at first when people refer to Jon as your husband. I thought it would come naturally but it took a bit. However, in saying that, it always gives my heart an extra thump when I realize again and again that he's mine forever."

"I never would've imagined a year ago that I'd be married to the sexy soldier I'd interviewed years ago who'd intrigued me so much. I thought he was cocky and had too big of an ego," Courtney said. "I was right, and I think that's what I love about him the most."

"Confidence is something these men have in spades," Avery agreed.

"That's for sure. But I wouldn't want it any other way," Courtney told her.

"Amen," Amira said as she moved up next to them.

"I've gone from my career being the most important thing in my life, to it being second best. I want to be a great wife, a mother someday soon, and a friend. My career is great and I want it to grow, but it's not everything. Family is truly what matters at the end of the day," Courtney said.

"I agree fully," Amira said.

"I'll drink to that my lovely bride," Eyes said as he walked right up and pulled Courtney into his arms. "This party is wonderful, but I want to get you all to myself. Want to run away now?"

"Yes, please," she said with a giggle.

"Oh no. You two have to wait just like each one of us had to," Avery said with a laugh. "Come on, let's go cut some cake. I need some sugary carbs."

Courtney and Eyes groaned, but they followed along. On the one hand Courtney wanted to run away with her husband, but on the other she appreciated all of the traditional moments of their wedding reception. She could look back at the picture in ten years and think about how happy she'd been on her first wedding day. She was going to marry this man over and over again, so she'd have many more times she'd get to add to her memories when times might seem rough.

Hours passed and Courtney found herself in her husband's arms on the dance floor. Her cheeks hurt from smiling so much that day, and it was all worth it. She was tired, but she was happy, very, *very* happy.

"How are you holding up?" Eyes asked.

"Very well. There's something I want to talk to you about, though," she said.

His smiled dimmed as he reached up and cupped her cheek.

"You can talk to me about anything," he assured her.

She couldn't believe she was going to say what she was about to say. She felt as if she'd burst though if she didn't get it out, and soon.

"I want to have a baby. I thought I wanted to wait. I know we should take time together, but all I keep thinking about is a beautiful little blond-haired boy with your eyes and laugh. I can't think of anything else."

Jon looked stunned, just as she'd been expecting. But then he shocked her when his lips turned up wide and he gazed at her with so much love she wondered how anyone survived not ever getting to feel how she was feeling now.

"We're leaving. It's time to start the honeymoon and make a baby," he said.

She didn't get a chance to answer him before he turned. "Thank you everyone. We appreciate all you've done. Now, we're out of here."

There were a few protests and then a lot of laughter as Eyes picked up Courtney, fluffy dress and all, then flung her over his shoulder and ran from the reception. She smacked his ass a few times, but she was laughing as much as the crowd was.

Courtney was happy. She was very, very happy, and nothing was going to stand in the way of that ever again. She'd still report, she'd still have a life outside of her marriage, but she was going to live like there was no tomorrow each and every day, because life was a gift and she wanted to unwrap it every single day.

EPILOGUE

Joseph leaned back in his chair and listened to the chaos all around him. The room was filled with alpha men and women who all insisted on being heard. Normally, Joseph was right there in the mix with them, but this time he found it was much more fun to listen in than to be a part of the conversation.

"What are you doing here in the corner all alone?" his brother George asked as he sat in the chair next to Joseph.

"I think he's pouting," Richard, his other brother, said as he sat in the chair on the other side of Joseph.

"What would I be pouting about?" Joseph asked.

"Your newest project is neatly wrapped up. The bad guys are all in jail, the good guys have a victory, and your team of warriors is disbanding," Richard said.

Joseph chuckled. "I might be a little bummed it's all wrapped up," Joseph said.

"You know they'll stay if you give them another project," George said. "You got them all married, but I'm sure you can find another crime to solve."

"I thought about that," Joseph said. "But I want to see what they're going to do on their own. I think each of the five men is a force to be reckoned with, and it will be great to sit back and watch. We've formed a bond, and nothing will break that now."

"Well, with Smoke and Mallory taking Jasmine under their huge wings, you'll see quite a bit of them," Chad said as he took a seat next to the Anderson brothers.

Joseph smiled. "Jasmine will do great things in life," Joseph said. "She couldn't have better mentors."

"Do you worry that she's so excited about this criminal world?" George asked.

Joseph nodded. "I always worry, but I want all of those I love to follow their dreams."

"Yeah, and it helps alleviate the worry when you have her followed twenty-four-seven," Richard said with a laugh.

"Yes, that certainly helps," Joseph said, not in the least ashamed. He'd do anything for his favorite grandchild, though he wouldn't admit that she was the favorite — at least not out loud.

Richard was about to say something else when Smoke made a comment.

"Wait," Joseph said, holding up his hand. "I want to hear this."

"Me too," George said.

"It's too bad we don't have popcorn for the show," Richard said.

The three men pulled out cigars and they had no guilt whatsoever about listening to conversations by these warrior men . . .

Eyes, Sleep, Brackish, Green, and Smoke narrowed their circle. The party was at its peak all around them, but they might as well have been in their own little bubble. They didn't need privacy for their conversation, they were just happy to be where they were and to share the news with one another.

"Has everyone figured out what comes next?" Eyes asked.

Smoke laughed. "The team leader wants to know our plans," he said. "Once a leader *always* a leader."

"Damn straight," Eyes said. "I'll miss not working with you guys on a daily basis."

"Me too. I'm sort of shocked by how much I'll miss it," Brackish said.

"Yeah, I've had the world at my fingertips for a very long time now, but this will go down in history as my favorite time," Green told the guys. "Not only have I loved working with you guys, but I've had a lot of fun doing it."

"I won the Super Bowl and now I'm going to Disneyland," Smoke yelled as he jumped up and threw his arm in the air.

Chuckles erupted all around the room as people shook their heads. Leave it to Smoke to make a spectacle of himself.

"What are you really doing, Smoke?" Eyes asked.

Smoke sat back down. "I'm going to travel," he said with a big grin. "I'm taking my absolutely stunning wife to all the corners of the world for a year long trip where she gets to help other doctors treat Alzheimer's patients, and we're going to do a lot of swimming, fishing, and love making. We'll have to come back for a few days every couple of months so she can keep an eye on her patients here who she loves, but we want to see the world."

"You wouldn't want to come back so often to check on your favorite student, would you?" Sleep asked with a laugh.

"I'm thinking Jazzy might have to come spend her breaks from college with us and get some training," Smoke said, knowing exactly who Sleep was talking about.

"I don't think you'll have to twist her arm to do that," Brackish said.

"No, the squirt and I are tight," Smoke said.

"Yeah, it's been pretty amazing to see that little girl shine," Green said. "I think someday she's going to be able to kick our asses."

"I wouldn't have it any other way," Smoke said.

"What about you, Green? What's next for the man who's done it all?" Eyes asked.

Green put both of his hands in his pockets, looked down at the ground, and kicked the floor a couple of times, trying to put his thoughts into a sensible array. "We'll probably stay in the area for a few months. The FBI asked Mallory to withdraw her resignation until after the trial, which she did, and just as all of that crap came to a *thud* they found an interesting new case to work on."

"What is it?" Eyes asked.

"Can't say quite yet, and she still hasn't accepted, but if she does we'll probably stay in the area. You guys know I'm an Oregon boy, and I'll never give up my hunting, but I have to admit this area has grown on me. If any of you ever tell anyone I said that I swear you'll never say—"

"GREEN LOVES WASHINGTON MORE THAN OREGON!" Sleep yelled to the crowd.

Green and Sleep instantly started wrestling, calling each other terrible names that only two friends could get away with.

Smoke separated the two, gave a bit of a shoulder roll, flexing in front of both of them while saying, "Don't make me put the two of you in a timeout."

"Your big brother won't always be here to save you, Green," Sleep shot out while looking over their huge team member's shoulders.

"Does that mean you're staying in the area? If so, I change my mind, I'm leaving tonight," Green said, giving a feigned kick toward Sleep behind Smoke's back.

"Of course we're staying. Avery has a great thing going and I can work from here. Eyes already approved it and if the money men back in San Fran don't like it, we'll just open our own company. Until that part gets figured out, I'm going to learn how to hunt and show off how much better I am at it than Green," Sleep said with a laugh.

"Sleep, the only thing you've been better at than any of us is running your mouth," Brackish piped in, all the men laughing in unison at his timing.

"No one asked you, Nerd-Alert 5000. Don't you have some screen to go geek out in front of?" Sleep replied. The two men had sparred verbally the entire time they'd been together, and they loved it.

Sleep found he was closer to Brackish than everyone else on the team except for Eyes. Though they were completely different, the two really clicked with one another. Maybe it was because when Brackish wanted to, he could be just as cutting and outlandish with his words, and few men stacked up as well as Sleep in that realm.

"I do and that's why you're actually sticking around, knowing I'm the only one who can actually turn on a computer for you. Erin and I just bought some land and are building a house on it. With the contract for developing the security for Mr.

Anderson's house, along with many of the Anderson buildings, I'll be busy for a long time. And Erin's pregnant again, so I might as well put down roots and raise a family," Brackish finished with a massive smile.

The men crowded him, slapping his back, shaking his hand, and congratulating him multiple times over.

Then they all paused, recognizing the moment for what it was and silently acknowledging the importance of each of the team members. Each of them took a step back before Eyes lifted his drink.

"We were asked to perform a mission, and we completed it well. We were asked to change a city for the better and transform it we did. We were asked to do this in silence and to be unseen by that city we were fixing, and we were. I'm standing before you, brothers, to let you know you are seen, and your work is beyond reproach. There are no awards, no medals, but I raise this glass to each of you now and tell you that no better men could have come together than this team. Thank you for allowing me to join you in the fight against an insidious monster. Moreover, thank you for allowing me to become a friend; a brother," Eyes finished and in unison all of the men clinked their respective drinks together.

Each of them knew they could go on and on about how great this time together was, but they let their leader's words be the final accolade before they moved on to laughter and life decisions. It was the perfect way to end this chapter of their lives.

"It looks as if those boys are going to change the world," George said as he looked at Joseph.

"There's no doubt in my mind," Joseph assured his brothers.

"For many, they already have. Seattle's as clean, beautiful, and safe as it's ever been," Chad said.

"I'm going to miss seeing them so often," Richard said. "Plus, I feel overall safer with them here."

Joseph laughed. "I know what you mean.

Suddenly the door was flung open, making everyone turn and look at the tornado that had whipped into the room. All five of the special ops men had rose to their feet before the door had hit the wall. Their bodies instantly tensed, but as soon as they saw who it was, they relaxed and smiled.

"Now what has my beautiful granddaughter smiling so big?" Joseph asked as Jasmine stopped in the center of the room. She turned and gave her grandfather a beaming smile, then she met Smoke's eyes and jumped into the air.

"I'm in!" she shouted.

"You're in where?" Smoke asked. Brackish was always monitoring Smoke's favorite student so he had a good guess of what she was about to present.

Jasmine held up a piece of paper that nobody could read.

"I've officially been accepted for an FBI Internship program!"

Thunderous applause erupted as Jasmine was circled by her family and friends. The next chapter of her life was coming — and it was coming in a *big* way. Smoke would be right there at her side.

After Jasmine made her rounds, thanking each person for helping her, supporting her and being a great friend or family member through all of the years, she finished the rounds standing in front of her grandfather.

"Hi gramps," Jasmine said before the two embraced in a hug that squeezed the air from both of their lungs.

"Jazzy, you've grown up in the blink of an eye. From the day you were born and I was holding you in the hospital, to this very moment, time has gone by faster than I could've ever imagined." He paused as he got all choked up. "I wouldn't change a single moment."

He then pulled away, resolve in his voice to not crack under the weight of the emotion he was feeling. The rest of the party fell away, and all of the noise dimmed as the two of them stood face to face knowing this was a moment when one of those monumental transitions happened.

"I'll miss you, gramps," Jasmine said.

"No matter where you are kiddo, I'll always be there for you. I know you have zero doubts about that, but I'm saying it anyway — never look back and proudly go conquer the world. No one, and nothing, can stop you from realizing your dreams. Work hard, study hard, and play hard. Fall deeply in love and have a wedding that is talked about for generations to come. You'll be a phenomenal wife, an amazing mother and just like it is now, everyone in your life will be better for knowing you. Now, go have fun," Joseph said as he gave her another quick hug and turned her toward the crowd of kids dancing and enjoying the party.

As Jasmine walked away Joseph said, no louder than a whisper to his two brothers; "With Jazzy begins a new generation of Andersons who will have a need for their grandfather to help continue with the circle of life. I wonder who will be man enough to take her hand in marriage."

"I'm sure you'll find him," George said with a chuckle.

"There's no doubt in my mind," Joseph said.

The three brothers raised their fine glasses of Scotch and made a toast. Their story would continue on, and no one and nothing in this world would stop it.

IT BEGINS

If you enjoyed this story, then you can catch up on all of the characters you're going to see in and out of the series in the books listed below. Any of these series can be read alone, but it's also a lot of fun to read them in somewhat of an order. Each family has their own unique dynamic, and Joseph is the key character who pulls them all together. His meddling knows no bounds.

Also a side note from me . . . The Andersons originally began as a three-book series when I started my writing career. I fell in love with Joseph and the Anderson dynamic. I went on to write other series, but I kept bringing Joseph along, wanting to take him with me to all of the worlds I was creating. So in came his twin brother George, who just happens to be named after one of my favorite uncles. He lived in Cordova, AK, where I spent a summer when I was sixteen, which is why I sent my couple there in *The Blackmail*. I loved that town. He moved to Anchorage, and I can't wait to go there again and do some fishing, which I've become addicted to.

At the end of book seven of the Andersons, I thought it was finished once again. Then a fan sent me an email saying they'd had a dream that Joseph and George were staring at a newspaper and saw a man who looked just like them. I was in love with the idea of a stolen baby plot. So in came Richard, who is another favorite uncle of mine. Richard, their triplet, was stolen at birth. Back when Katherine had her babies, fathers weren't often in the delivery room, and the doctor figured she already had two babies and wouldn't miss a third. So in came five more kids for Joseph and George to play cupid with.

At the end of that story, Joseph went on to meddle in the lives of his friends' children, so his legacy has continued to grow. I left openings in many of my books because I can never truly say those magical words *the end*. A new branch of Andersons are found in my Montlake series, *Anderson Billionaires*.

I storyboarded ideas with friends, and this newest spin-off happened: *Anderson Black Ops*. This series is so much fun because I'm co-writing it. I have a friend who knows the world of black ops, so he's giving me strong outlines and chapters for these new men we've created in this fun new world. We have a lot of ideas for where this will all lead.

I'm getting a lot of emails asking about the order to read my books. I've created so many stories at this point even I'm a little lost on the order, but I'm going to list it as best I can by staying in the right timeframe. The newest, of course, are easiest to keep track of, but since I bring in so many other series in the middle of writing these books, it does get a bit confusing.

So here we go. And as always, I love feedback from you. After all, I can't do this job, can't write these fantastic stories, and can't live in my dream world without your support. You make the magic happen. You give me a voice to put on paper, and you make my dreams come true. If the order is at all messed up, then please let me know and we'll adjust.

I work with a fantastic team, and we're constantly changing and fixing things. It's amazing how easily we can fix things in this digital world we now have. Before the world of epublishing, if there was a mistake, it couldn't get fixed until the next set of books were printed. Now, it's just a few hits on the keyboard, and voilà, we're good to go again.

Thank you so much for your support. I hope you are well, are enjoying these stories, and are making magic happen in this crazy world we've found ourselves in in the parallel universe some call 2020.

Read Order for The Anderson Empire

The Andersons
1. Wins The Game
2. The Dance
3. The Fall
4. The Proposal
5. The Blackmail
6. The Runaway
7. The Final Stand
8. The Unexpected Treasure
9. The Hidden Treasure
10. The Holiday Treasure
11. The Priceless Treasure
12. The Ultimate Treasure

Now, you can read the Tycoon Series, which Joseph's in, but only one of the books is truly relevant to the continuation of the Anderson's stories. I'll list all of the Tycoon books here, but highlight Damien's story, which will come up later on in a twist for *The Billionaire* Andersons listed below.

The Titans
Book One: The Tycoon's Revenge
Book Two: The Tycoon's Vacation
Book Three: The Tycoon's Proposal
13. Book Four: The Tycoon's Secret
Book Five: The lost Tycoon
Book Six: Rescue me

And here we go again, with another insert. So, Joseph next appears in my Heroes Series. We have a visit from *Dr. Spence Whitman* in this book you've just read, which is in this series. You can read this series next to know Spence's story, but you won't be lost if you don't. So I'll list the entire series here, and again highlight the story that has Spence in it, adding it to the list. All of these books can stand alone, but I do bring my characters in and out of most of my series because I can't let them go. So if you read *Her Hometown Hero*, it's a complete story, but the brothers will all be throughout it.

Heroes Series
Pre-Book: Safe in his arms (in an Anthology called *Baby it's Cold Outside*)
Book One: Her Unexpected Hero
Book Two: Who I am with you
14. Book Three: Her Hometown Hero
Book Four: Following Her
Book Five: Her Forever Hero

And now, we come to Sherman, who will play a big role in this series. Sherman's another of those characters I seriously love! When I came up with Bobbi, Avery's mother, I knew right then and there, she was going to be a match for Sherman. By the way, Bobbi is named after my best friend's mother, who I absolutely adore! She mirrors some of her character traits too, and we'll be seeing a lot more of her. In real life she's married to Hal, who happens to be a fantastic man.

After I wrote the Bobbi character, I was telling the real Bobbi what she's saying and doing, and I might've made her blush. Hal's okay with it though. If he's gonna lose his wife, at least it's to Sherman, who happens to be a pretty great guy. We just spent a long weekend at their house in Northern Cali, and had a refreshing, fantastic time. But I was also putting them under the microscope for my upcoming stories. I use real life in my books all of the time because family events are definitely story worthy. So, Bobbi, beware because I'm gonna have fun with this character.

I list the Billionaire Aviators next, but don't number them because you don't have to read these to read all the rest, but if you want to get to know Sherman, then I'd dive on in. This series was one of my fav to write, because I love the characters, love the journey, and I was really growing in my writing at this point, getting a little more courageous with what I was doing within my fantasy worlds.

Billionaire Aviators
Book One: Turbulent Intentions
Book Two: Turbulent Desires
Book Three: Turbulent Waters
Book Four: Turbulent Intrigue

Joseph and other Andersons appear in my Undercover Billionaire world, where I started adding more suspense into my writing. Some of these characters will pop in and out of this world as well, because, like I said, I love to bring these characters into each world. So you can read this series, but again, won't be lost if you don't, so I won't number them.

On a side note. *Owen* is my *favorite* book I've ever written. I lost my dad in 2018, and it nearly killed me. I write men like Joseph, George, Sherman, and more because I'm a daddy's girl, through and through. He raised me with so much more love than I can even begin to explain, and he also taught me how to be independent and strong. He's the reason I'm an author, the reason I'm so strong, and the reason I still cry because I miss him so much.

He LOVED UFO stories, and when all of the news broke that they were releasing the government files on UFOs, my heart was breaking again, because he would've been so excited and absolutely glued to the internet. I know he's up in Heaven laughing because he has all of the answers now, but I sure would love him to be here with me so we could talk and wonder, and laugh . . . and so his arms could be wrapped around me.

My heroine loses her dad in Owen, which I'd begun writing before I lost my dad. I had to stop, and when I came back to the book, I cried my way through a lot of it. A lot of the lines she uses when she's talking about her father were things I asked and said. I was so lost for a long time after losing him. Writing Owen helped me heal. My heart will never be truly full again, but my dad loved me, and I love him, and I know he'd kick my butt if I didn't live my life with love, laughter, and triumph. He raised me to be a powerful woman, and I won't dishonor him by being anything less than that. So I'm gonna highlight Owen, not because it's needed for the Andersons, but because it's needed for my soul. ☺

Undercover Billionaires
Book One: Kian
Book Two: Arden
Book Three: Owen
Book Four: Declan

Now it gets a bit more confusing as I'm finishing out my Montlake series at the same time as we're writing *The Anderson Black Ops* series, so you get to go back and forth a bit if you want to stay exactly in the timeline. We're finally making it to the end . . . for now. But I guess I'll have to stay on top of this because I have no doubt that the Anderson world will continue to grow and grow and grow, even as I take time to visit other worlds in between. Thank you again for all you do. I hope you fall in love with these characters over and over again, just as I do each time I dive back into the Anderson Universe.

The Billionaire Andersons
15. Book One: Finn
16. Book Two: Noah

Anderson Black Ops
17. Book One: Shadows

The Billionaire Andersons
18. Book Three: Brandon

Anderson Black Ops

19. Book Two: Rising

The Billionaire Andersons
20. Book Four Hudson
21. Book Five: Crew

Anderson Black Ops
22. Book Three: Barriers
23. Book Four: Shattered
24. Book Five: Reborn

The Story Continues with this new series With Jasmine Anderson now working in Miami for the FBI

Truth In Lies
25. One Too Many
26. Two Secrets Kept

Made in the USA
Columbia, SC
16 January 2025